# Crowns We Save
Jessica Jude

# Contents


Author's Note      VI

1. "Unstoppable" - Sia      1

2. "Forever or the End" - Skillet      7

3. "Danza Kuduro" - Don Omar + Lucenzo      13

4. "Crown" - Camila Cabello + Grey      22

5. "Girl on Fire" - Alicia Keys      31

6. "I Love It" - Icona Pop + Charli XCX      38

7. "Warriors" - Imagine Dragons      44

8. "Breath of Life" - Florence + the Machine      50

9. "Seven Nation Army" - The White Stripes      58

10. "Castle" - Halsey      65

11. "Bring Me to Life" - Evanescence      73

12. "Don't You Worry Child" - Swedish House Mafia      81

13. "I Found" - Amber Run      90

14. "Unbreakable" - Jamie Scott      97

15. "Roar" - Katy Perry      105

16. "Castles Crumbling" - Taylor Swift ft. Hayley Williams    115

17. "Royalty" - Egzod + Maestro Chives    123

18. "Rise" - Katy Perry    135

19. "Stay" - Rihanna + Mikky Ekko    143

20. "Almost Lover" - A Fine Frenzy    153

21. "right where you left me" - Taylor Swift    161

22. "Paper Crown" - Alec Benjamin    168

23. "I Can Do It With a Broken Heart" - Taylor Swift    175

24. "Confident" - Demi Lovato    182

25. "Small Bump" - Ed Sheeran    187

26. "Kiss Me Like You Do (Movie Version)" - Ellie Goulding    196

27. "Little More (Royalty)" - Chris Brown    208

28. "Adore You" - Harry Styles    219

29. "The Lucky One" - Taylor Swift    226

30. "Waiting for Love" - Avicii    234

31. "Skinny Love" - Birdy    242

32. "Turning Tables" - Adele    246

33. "Let It Go" - James Bay    251

34. "The Scientist" - Coldplay    256

35. "Burn" - Ellie Goulding    265

36. "Euphoria" - Loreen    271

Also by Jessica Jude    277

# Author's Note

WESBOURNE IS A FICTIONAL island country set in the middle of the Atlantic Ocean between North America and Europe. While the country is a fantasy concocted in the playground of my mind, all of my books are contemporary and take place in the modern world.

The following book contains mature content and potential triggers, including: sexual abuse of child (off-page), miscarriage, infertility, pressure to have children, substance abuse and overdose (off-page), rape (off-page), verbal / emotional abuse, language, and explicit sexual content (chapters 26, 35). It is not intended for readers under 18.

Each chapter is named after a song that fits its vibe. Access the entire playlist on Spotify by going to https://jessicajude.com/crowns-playlist

And finally, I am not responsible for any damages inflicted upon books or reading devices by the consumption of this book.

xoxo Jess

# 1

# "Unstoppable" - Sia

"**W**HEN ARE YOU GOING to have a baby?"

The woman's voice isn't unkind, but it's loud enough to carry over the crowds gathered on the other side of the steel barricades. My heart skips a beat, like a stone flung over a lake.

I swallow, but it only accentuates how dry my throat feels. I glance around for someone, anyone, to help deflect the heat from the hundreds of eyes staring at me, waiting for my answer, but there is no one.

Henry isn't here, which has become the norm these days. I can't remember the last time we attended an event together that wasn't a formal gala or state dinner. Walkabouts are more effective if we split up and cover more ground, but I miss the days when we'd do them together, walking hand in hand like the blissful newlyweds we were.

A group of teenagers flutter their small flags, eager for me to look in their direction. I happily comply and grant them a smile. I feel uncomfortable moving on before answering the rude woman, but my feet are desperate to drag me down the line and away from the probing questions.

In the past two years, I've gone from "the girl who stole the crown" to "our beloved queen." Thanks in part to my mother's plan to put me within reach of the entire country and in part to the palace's brilliant press secretary, my image has come full circle. I am now Wesbourne's cherished sovereign.

Mum's reminder to "keep it that way" flits through my mind like she's chirping right into my ear. Too many wrong moves on my part and I could end up ostracized again. Not only that, but with all the anti-monarchy talk a while back, it could mean the downfall of not only the monarchy, but of Wesbourne herself.

When I took my oath nearly three years ago, I vowed to give everything for the good of this country. That includes saving her from self-destruction.

Before I've formulated an answer to the woman's question, another voice from the crowd calls out, "You only have a few more years to produce an heir!"

I don't need a mirror to know my face is flaming. *I'm twenty-nine*, I want to retort.

I could do without the parasocial relationships my people have with me. Just because the media dishes out as much information about my personal life as they can get their hands on, does not mean we are intimate friends.

These people don't know those details are carefully hand-fed to the press for exactly that reason.

They are speaking not out of disrespect, but from a place of love and care, like a nosy grandmother might. And as Rosalind is always quick to remind me, they weren't all taught the appropriate times to hold their tongues.

I force my smile a little wider. No need to let anyone know how these inquiries affect me. *Take everything in stride*, Preston's voice chants in my head.

I take a deep breath. It's time to address their questions and move down the line. "A baby will come in time," I say. I put as much conviction into it as I can. *Sell it*, I remind myself. That's the important part. Everything else will fall into place.

"Not without Prince Henry," someone shouts from the back.

I sense a presence near my arm and don't need to look to know that Davies has taken a step closer. Whether he senses a threat or just knows I need the extra strength, it's good to have someone I trust nearby.

"Let's keep moving," he says. His low voice has talked me through many situations just like this one.

I head further down the barricades. The cheering grows louder as the people begin waving their flags and signs. I accept a lovely bouquet of spring blooms from a young woman with two children at her side. She looks no older than I am.

Two years ago, I wouldn't have been able to do this, with the threat of assassination so real. It's only been possible to do walkabouts for the past year. Unused to seeing their monarch up close and personal, many people take time off work for these events to catch a glimpse of me walking down their street.

I don't have the time or stamina to shake hands with every person who came out, no matter how much I wish to thank them for coming to see me. The best I can do is give my attention to a few selected by my team and smile and wave at the rest.

One of my staff members steps forward and motions to an older man from the crowd. He grins at his good fortune as I step toward him. I hold out a gloved hand, which he kindly accepts. "Hello," I say. "How do you do?"

"Just fine, Your Majesty," he says, grin still in place.

We exchange a few more pleasantries. I'm about to keep moving when another voice, this one much younger than the others, calls out, "Your Majesty!"

I turn. A little boy is sticking his hand through the barricade, clutching a small bouquet of daisies. I grin and excuse myself from the gentleman.

The boy's mother is holding him back from charging his way through. "I'm so sorry," she says. A flush of pink tints both her cheeks.

"Don't be. It's fine." I squat down next to the little guy. Rosalind will lose her biscuits when she watches the news coverage, but it's things like these that endear me to the public, not the quality of my pantyhose or the perfection of my hairstyle.

I am careful to keep my dress from shifting to expose anything that shouldn't be exposed—not an easy feat given I'm squatting down on asphalt, trying not to touch the ground with anything but the soles of my shoes. Fortunately, it's tea-length with a looser skirt, so I have some extra fabric to work with. I make sure it's draped over the fronts of my legs as I'm eye-level with the little boy.

I'm not great at telling children's ages. I'm not great at anything regarding children, but that's when winging it comes into play. I would put him firmly between the ages of two and five. See? Not too bad.

I hold out my hand, and he shakes it with rigor. "I'm Queen Celia," I say. "And who might you be?"

He mumbles something unintelligible, shyness suddenly taking over.

I am out of my element here, but I have to do something. "Are those for me?" I say, pointing to the flowers still clutched in his chubby fist.

He nods and thrusts them at me.

I carefully disentangle the stems from his sweaty palm, then make a big show of taking a whiff. "They smell divine. Did you pick them yourself?"

He nods again, chewing on his thumbnail as he gives me a careful grin. In spite of his bashfulness, he's absolutely adorable. His eyes are a startling deep chocolate color, almost black. Thick brown curls hang from beneath the little cap he's wearing. His skin has a beautiful olive tone I envy.

But it's his smile that tugs at my heart. There's something about him, about the way his lips curve up that reminds me of someone. Someone I once knew or someone I met only in passing.

"It was a pleasure to meet you, young man," I say as I stand up again. "Thank you for the flowers."

He doesn't remove his thumb from his mouth, but he continues gracing me with that endearing grin.

His mother's smile is slightly abashed. "Thank you," she says. "He's been waiting for this day for a long time." She's young, blonde, and looks like she just left a modeling shoot, not like she's mum to a toddler.

I sense Davies at my elbow. Time to move on. "Pleased to meet you both," I say, then allow him to lead me to the next spot they've selected for me to stop at.

Less than ten minutes later, I'm ushered into the back of the limo. In the space of a half hour, I've spoken to thirty-six citizens and made the day of hundreds more.

"Was the media able to get coverage of the little boy?" I ask once I'm seated.

Maisie looks up from the tablet perched on her six-months-pregnant belly. "The angle was a little tricky, but I think they should have been able to get most of it."

"Maybe that should be corrected next time?" I suggest.

She darts a look at Garrett, our location coordinator. "I'm on it," he says.

"Preston?" I say, turning to the palace press secretary.

"Our crews got lots of good footage."

"With the little boy?"

"Of the whole thing," he says. "But yes, of that too."

"Good. That will be the highlight, correct?"

He nods, then gestures to the computer in his lap. "I'm already uploading the footage. The package will be out to all of the stations in"—he checks his watch—"no more than two hours."

"Okay." I allow myself to relax into the cushioned seat.

It was a successful walkabout, but that little boy was the jackpot of my day. Footage like that is sure to cement me in the minds of my people as a queen who cares about all her subjects, no matter how young or old.

It takes finesse to partner with the press, and fortunately, I have the best team in the business for that. The collaboration may be unlikely—usually celebrities try to hide from the media—but we've found a way to spin the attention in the best possible way.

By ensuring members of the press get the best seats in the house, so to speak, we are simply doing our job. They are the eyes of the world's viewers, and by giving them premium content, we are directly influencing how the world sees the royal family. It's a terrific arrangement.

The best part? By keeping the royal family in the good graces of her people, we ensure that Wesbourne need never consider doing away with her monarchy and crumbling her already shaky foundation.

# 2

# "Forever or the End" - Skillet

THE LIGHTS BLINK ON when I flip the switch, illuminating the white closet with its rows of gleaming cabinetry and glass, all bright and reflective surfaces. Even my shoes are hidden from view behind ornately carved doors.

I walk over to the drawers containing my jewelry and unlock the one holding my gemstone earrings. When I slide it out, glittering stones wink at me as they catch the light from the chandelier overhead. I remove the studs I'm wearing and nestle them into the empty spot Daphne pulled them from this morning.

A creak in the floorboards makes me stiffen. The scent of pine wafts through the room. I don't turn as he comes closer.

"I didn't know you were up here already," Henry says quietly.

I slide both my feet out of the heels I've been wearing all day and walk to the wall holding my shoe collection. Four hundred and seventy-six pairs, the last time anyone counted, and who knows how many have been added since.

"I'm tired," I say as I put the Bottega Veneta mules into their spot on the shelf and close the doors.

He doesn't respond right away. His gaze tickles the back of my neck, but rather than facing him, I work on the clasp of my necklace. It's stuck, but it's also 150 years old, so I have to be gentle.

Warm fingers meet mine, and I swallow the involuntary gasp that rises in me. He undoes the clasp and releases the ruby necklace into my hands. I take it, doing my best to avoid touching him.

His hands remain on my shoulders, squeezing the tension from them. "You're tight."

I remain silent as he kneads the knots from my muscles.

"How are you holding up?" His voice is soft.

"I'm fine."

"I saw the news."

I carefully lay the necklace back into the appropriate drawer. "It was a good turnout. The crowds were livelier than usual, but in a good way. I think the media got some good shots. Preston seemed satisfied." Now *this* I can talk about.

"It must have been hard."

I finally turn and meet his eyes. "What was?"

"The questions."

I drop my gaze to the rings on my fingers, then tug them off one by one. My throat hurts when I swallow. "They got that too?"

"Yeah." His voice is a brush of pine needles against my skin. "And the little boy. You were great with him. You held your composure perfectly."

"He was a sweet kid," I say, turning my back so Henry can undo the zipper on my dress.

He tugs it down, then slides his hands around my waist. His touch is hot, a branding iron searing my bare skin. His fingers linger over the small *H* I have tattooed near my hip bone as though he can feel it. I'm afraid his hands will wander, that he has plans for us tonight, but he simply rests them on my stomach, one on top of the other, and pulls me back until I'm resting against his solid chest.

His warmth seeps through the open back of my dress. I want to sink into it so badly. He's a tower of strength during the roughest of storms, both comforter and protector.

"It will happen for us," he whispers into my hair. "I promise."

I only nod in agreement. I don't trust my voice right now.

We stay like this for a few moments, caught in the silence of grief and guilt. He slackens his hold enough to caress my stomach. It's like the touch of a feather, all gentle warmth and strong tenderness.

"We could always get another dog," he says.

We've been down this road. Tundra is getting older, and it's starting to show. He no longer has the boundless energy he did when he first came to me. Henry thinks we should get him a companion so that when he crosses the rainbow bridge, it won't be quite as difficult for us, but it feels like a betrayal.

"I'm not ready for another dog."

"Okay," he murmurs into my hair. His tone matches his hands—soft and tentative. He waits a few beats.

*Don't say it.*

"Have you considered slowing down?"

I do my best to stop them, but my muscles stiffen anyway. I try coaxing them to relax. This is only a conversation. "You know I can't do that."

His fingers trace circles around my belly button, over and over. I shiver.

"We could hire another assistant. There's room in the budget for it."

"This is my *job*, Henry."

The muscles in his arms contract ever so slightly, a small hint of movement. "I know. But we both know stress can hinder—"

I spin out of his arms and face him. "I can't hand my duties off to someone else so I can put my feet up and hope I get pregnant!"

And like that, the fuse reaches the gunpowder, and the sweet scene we were acting out explodes into a million tiny pieces.

There is a distinct set to Henry's jaw that wasn't there minutes ago. "Delegating some of your duties to someone else would be in everybody's best interest."

I yank the dress from my shoulders and let it pool onto the floor. He doesn't let his eyes wander from mine. I guess there's nothing down there he hasn't seen a thousand times before.

"I *like* my job," I say. "You may have despised the idea of ruling Wesbourne your entire life, but this is the perfect fit for me."

"I never said it wasn't. I just think if you cut back a little—"

"I can't afford to cut back. Think of everything that would fall through the cracks."

He reaches for me, but I step away. "Victoria and Elizabeth had thirteen children between them, and they both did fantastic jobs as queen," he says as if it's the answer to everything.

I undo my bra and toss it aside. "Things are different now. Queen Elizabeth had something like four hundred engagements a year. I have over *eight hundred*."

"Most of those were added by you."

I open the drawer holding my pajamas and pull out a T-shirt and flannel pants. No need for anything sexy tonight. "And they've been successful in winning over the people. You saw the news coverage." I turn back to him. "They adore me, Henry."

He loosens his tie and pulls it out of his collar. "Of course they do. And they would adore you just as much if you cut back to raise a family."

"Maybe the universe doesn't want me to be a mum."

A sigh accompanies his tie as he flings it onto a nearby ottoman. "You know that's not true. You're great with kids."

"You've never seen me with kids."

He laughs as if I've said something ridiculous, rather than the truth. "Sure I have. I saw you with that little boy today. I saw you after Beatrice was born. You'll be a smashing mum."

"Then I'm sure it will happen when it's supposed to." I tug the T-shirt over my head.

He snags a handful of fabric and pulls me toward him. "Maybe that's tonight."

I slip my arms into the sleeves as he slides his hands over my jawline. "I'm not ovulating." I try to scoot backward and put some distance between us.

"Baby, I don't care about that. I miss you."

My muscles refuse to relax no matter how much I berate them. "I'm not in the mood tonight. Sorry."

"Okay." He drops his hands.

I instantly feel regret pooling in my stomach. How did we get here?

"Maybe tomorrow night?"

"Sure." He runs his fingers through his hair in that gesture I used to love. "I'm going to get ready for bed." He turns away from me and starts unbuttoning his shirt.

I should be putting on my pajama pants, but I can't help but watch as he slips it off, revealing that muscled back I used to relish running my hands over. It would be such a little thing to approach him and touch him, but it would need to bridge the huge chasm between us, one that's so big I have no idea how to reach the other side.

Henry starts to turn around, and I quickly drop my gaze to the rug, tracing the design with my toe.

"Babe, do you want to talk to anyone about it?"

"About what?" I say, looking up without thinking.

"The infertility? I'm willing to go get tested."

"I'm not ready for that yet."

"It's been over a year." The sadness in his voice matches that in his eyes.

"I know, but admitting it to someone else makes it feel so much more real." I choke the last words out.

He gathers me into his arms, into that solid wall of muscle he calls a chest. I breathe in his scent the way I hardly ever do anymore, all piney and masculine. He rubs his hands over my back in long, soothing strokes, imparting his strength to me. "I'm sorry. I shouldn't have brought it up. I wasn't thinking."

"It's okay," I mumble, snaking my arms around his waist. "I just get emotional about it sometimes."

"I know," he says, still rubbing my back. "Perfectly understandable."

We stand here for a few more minutes, each lost in our own fantasies of the future. Finally, he releases me.

I slip on my pajama bottoms while he strips off his dress pants. After putting on the shorts he sleeps in, he heads out of the closet we share. I'm carefully folding my dress over the ottoman for Daphne to take care of tomorrow when a chime sounds from my phone. It's still in my bag on the table near the door, but I know without looking at it that it's my ten o'clock alarm.

I silence it, then fish out the small round compact from the inner pocket of my handbag. I double-check the date—day twenty-five—then pop one of the small pink pills out of the foil. I swallow it without water, a trick I mastered a long time ago.

I snap the compact shut again and stick it back into the purse, where Henry will never find it.

# 3

# "Danza Kuduro" - Don Omar + Lucenzo

I'VE JUST FINISHED MY weekly audience with the prime minister when my phone rings. My lips lift in a smile when Adelaide's name appears on the screen.

"Hello, my lovely girl," she says when I answer.

"How are you?" I say. "How is Peter?"

"We're terrific. Well, I am. Peter is a twat."

I chuckle in surprise. "He seemed perfectly normal when I met him."

Adelaide and Peter have been dating—or what she calls "knocking boots"—for a few years. Neither of them have any plans of marriage, which she claims is the antidote to fighting.

"That's because when you met him he wasn't planning a fishing trip with his 'buddies,'" she says. "Bloody Americans."

I laugh again. "I'm assuming said fishing trip is interfering with your plans?"

"Of course it is. I need to practice my salsa dancing."

I gaze out the window that overlooks the peony garden. The gardener is plucking dead blooms from the plants. "Surely he won't be gone long enough for it to have any ill effects?"

Adelaide tuts. "He's planning to be gone for two whole weeks."

"Two weeks? You'll have forgotten how by then," I tease.

"No, I won't."

"See? That's the attitude."

"That's why I'm calling."

I close my eyes. "Here we go."

Her tone carries a definite note of smugness. "You're going to help me practice."

"Absolutely not."

"Why not?"

"Because I don't have time. What do you think I do all day, sit around?"

"Do you really want to know?"

I pause. "If you think I have time for salsa dancing, then no, I don't want to know."

"Then I'll keep my thoughts to myself. As long as you agree to help me."

"I don't know the first thing about salsa. I still think of it as food."

A loud *pfft* comes through the phone. "You can ballroom dance with the best of them. Salsa isn't much different," Adelaide says. After a few beats, she adds, "Less formality, more sensuality."

"You're not exactly selling me on the whole idea."

"You'll love it. I've already talked to Maisie. She said you're free between one and two. I'll see you then." She hangs up before I can protest.

I'm going to wring Maisie's neck. That one blissful hour was going to be spent taking a much-needed and long-awaited nap. I haven't taken a nap in *months*, and now I'll be whirling around the dance floor with a seventy-five-year-old woman who thinks she's still twenty-five.

When Maisie ushers Adelaide into my office that afternoon, I cut them each a look. They both pretend not to notice.

"Ready?" I ask Adelaide. "The ballroom is empty."

"Oh, let's not use the ballroom," she says. "I've seen it dozens of times before."

I cock a brow, catching Maisie's look of amusement over Adelaide's shoulder. "My office is hardly conducive to dancing." I glance around at the richly paneled walls and thick carpeting. "Of any kind."

Adelaide waves her hand like I'm being ridiculous. "Not in here, poppet. Let's use the Green Drawing Room."

"Okay," I say, dragging the word out. "May I ask why?" They should've made her queen. She was born for the position.

"Because I've been dying to see it ever since it was featured in *Traditional Homes*."

"It's open," Maisie adds.

I know when I've been defeated, so Adelaide and I head to the Green Drawing Room. As promised, it is empty when we arrive. It boasts light green silk tabinet on the walls, thick ornamental plasterwork around all the doors and windows, and several large chandeliers hanging from the ceiling. The center of the space is clear of furniture and covered in a dark green rug with a low pile. I have to admit, it is the perfect room for dancing.

Adelaide digs a Bluetooth speaker from her handbag, setting both it and her phone on the mantle. Latin music fills the air within seconds. That setup would have taken me five minutes. This woman is going to outlive me.

"Ready for this?" she asks, walking toward me with her hands extended.

"Not in a million years," I mutter.

"Okay, first things first. I'll be the leader. You will follow."

"Obviously."

Adelaide narrows her eyes. "Now the trick is timing. We'll follow an eight-beat pattern, okay? Your steps are the inverse of mine, so back, center, back—beat four is a pause—then front, center, front, and another pause. Got it?"

"Not even close."

"Just follow me."

I close my eyes to prepare for the disaster that is sure to come. She cocks her arm to reach my waist, and I rest my hand on her shoulder. We extend our joined hands to the side.

"Now mirror my movements," she says.

The concept should be simple.

The concept is *anything* but simple.

Within thirty seconds it's like I'm part of a traveling circus. Specifically, the part they keep hidden behind the curtain.

Adelaide sighs and drops both hands. "You're supposed to be following me."

"I tried! I had no idea where you were going."

"You're not supposed to," she says. "That's the point. You *follow*."

"I'm not much of a follower."

She looks at me over the top of her reading glasses. "You don't say."

I sink into one of the silk-covered chairs dating back to the eighteenth century, courtesy of the king of Spain.

Adelaide stares at me from across the room, hands on her hips. "Get up," she snaps. "You are not giving up."

I get back on my feet. God, the woman is relentless.

She grabs my hands again and puts them into position. "Now, remember, I am leading. You are following. Quit trying to figure out what I'm going to do. Just focus on your steps."

Something clicks for me this time, and we manage to get a good rhythm going. The music pulses through the room—which I bet has never heard Latin before—and before I know it, I'm smiling.

"Ahh," Adelaide says, catching it before it disappears. "The real reason I came."

"What are you talking about?" I lose count of my steps and go left at the same time she's going right.

"You haven't been happy," she says, getting us back on track.

"How would you know that?"

"I've got two eyes. Now spin." She twirls me in a circle before bringing us back to the same beat. "And your husband called me."

My feet shudder to a stop. "Henry called you? About me?"

"Calm down, poppet. He said you've been down lately and wondered if I might be able to help."

I let out an exasperated sigh and turn to the French doors leading into the garden. "I'm perfectly fine."

"That might convince the media, but you can't think it's going to fool those of us who know you well."

"Okay, you want the truth?" I turn around to face her. "I haven't been happy in a long time."

"And why do you think that is?" She studies me as if she already knows the answer and is just waiting for me to figure it out.

I lift my hands in frustration and drop them back to my sides again. "I don't have a bloody clue."

"I think you do," she says. The song changes, and she grabs my hands and pulls me back into a dance. "I love this song. Don't have a clue what they're singing, but I love it."

We dance a few more rounds of beats, but I know better than to think Adelaide's going to drop the topic. "You still love him, don't you?" she asks.

"Henry? Of course I love him."

"So things are good between you?"

I frown at my feet. I don't even know how to answer such a simple question.

Things are good. For the most part. We still make each other laugh, occasionally anyway. My heart still kicks up ten notches when he strolls into a room, unaware of the fact that he's stopped my entire world on its axis. We still have sex, at least when I'm supposed to be ovulating. Other than that, it's pretty hit or miss. Certainly none of the stuff from when we were first together.

Sure, he's annoyed with me about how much I work, but that kind of comes with the territory, doesn't it? If the roles were reversed, I'm sure I'd parrot those same words back to him.

And then there's the baby thing, or the lack thereof. But aside from keeping that teensy little secret from him—for now—and the way he keeps stressing about it, we're good. Great, even.

"Yes," I finally say. "Things are good."

This time it's Adelaide who stops the dancing. "Celia Eleanor, that was the biggest, most bald-faced lie you've ever told me."

Something inside of me cracks at her chastisement. "What do you want me to say? That we're like two strangers living in the same house?"

"If that's the truth."

"It's close." My voice comes out the size of a mouse.

"What is going on? You two were so in love."

"We are," I say, the words tumbling out on top of each other. "Things are just . . . *hard* right now."

"I imagine they're not easy for any couple in your situation. Care to tell me what's going on?"

In for an inch, in for a mile, right? I tuck a loose strand of hair behind my ear. "He wants a baby."

Her arms are crossed, she nods for me to continue.

"And I don't. At least not right now."

"That'll do it every time." She presses her lips into a firm line. "Do you fight about this a lot?"

"Not exactly. He's under the impression that we are struggling with infertility." I wince as the words echo back to me.

Adelaide says nothing, doesn't even move for what seems an eternity. When she finally does, it's to march over to the speaker to stop the music. The room is flooded with a silence that feels louder than those Latin beats were.

"You realize that is a bloody stupid idea, and it will, with 100 percent certainty, backfire, right?" Adelaide says, her eyes flashing with anger and disappointment.

"It has occurred to me, yes, but I fully intend to—"

"Celia, listen to me." She steps closer. "I've always pegged you as bright. But what you're doing right now is playing with fire. And people who play with fire—"

"Get burned. I know."

"—wet the bed. Or at least that's what I was always told. Regardless, this will not turn out well. For either of you."

"What was I supposed to do?" I ask. "He wants a baby, and he wouldn't take no for an answer."

"That doesn't sound like Henry."

I close my eyes and take a deep breath. "He didn't pressure me exactly, but I knew it was what he wanted, and—"

"And you couldn't handle the thought of him thinking any less of you."

When you put it like that, I sound like a vain bitch. "I just don't understand the rush."

"Then you should tell him that instead of lying to him," Adelaide says.

"It's just for a little while, just until I'm ready."

She cocks a brow at me. "Keep deluding yourself like this, and things will not end well, I promise you."

"I know Henry. He won't suspect."

"You're manipulating him."

"It's my body. That makes it my decision."

"Just be careful, Celia. Controlling others is what weak people think power looks like."

After that, things between Adelaide and me feel too much like cardboard, and while that kind of stiffness might work for ballroom dancing, it does not fly in salsa. She gathers her things, and I walk her to the private exit.

We're in the west gallery when Preston finds us. "There you are," he says, jogging to catch up.

We both turn and stop to wait for him. Preston is just over six foot, with a shock of thick, dark hair that he continually has to push out of his eyes. He is also devastatingly handsome, a fact I suspect he is more than a little aware of.

"So sorry to interrupt." He nods to Adelaide, then turns his attention to me, a boyish grin spreading across his face. "But I knew you would want to know right away."

"Preston," I say. "This is Dame Adelaide Mansfield. Adelaide, meet our press secretary, Preston Ansley." They exchange nods, neither one impressed by the other.

"I just got confirmation on the documentary. They want to start filming the night of the ball," Preston says.

We've been subtly pushing for a documentary about the royal family for over a year. When one was done on the British royals back in 1969, it was watched by thirty-eight million people the night it aired. It did more for that country than an entire year's worth of walkabouts.

And now Wesbourne is going to get her own.

"That's incredible news," I say. "I want all the details."

"I'll wait for you in your office." He winks and heads back down the hall.

I'm still grinning when I turn back toward Adelaide. Her glare immediately melts the smile off my face.

"What? What did I do?" I swipe at my mouth, afraid I've managed to smear chocolate all over it without even eating any.

"Did I just witness *flirting*?" She spits the word out as though it tastes like rubbish.

"Who? Me? *Him*?" I shake my head, unable to get anything more out.

"What is going on with you and that young man?"

I blink at her, words a foreign substance to me now. "What are you talking about? Me and Preston? Nothing. I swear to you. Nothing at all."

"He is obviously infatuated with you."

Shock ripples through me. A fire alarm would be a welcome diversion right now. "Apparently not that obviously," I mutter.

"You're blind as a bat. He was practically salivating all over these fine rugs." She gestures to the floor. "And didn't even have the decency to bow to his queen," she adds, shaking her head in disgust.

"We keep things low-key around here. You didn't bow to me either," I say as we head toward the door again.

"We're friends. He's a staff member."

I roll my eyes. "He's also not in love with me."

When we reach the exit, Adelaide grabs my hands in her own. "Please think about what I said earlier. I would hate for you to sabotage your marriage before it's even had a chance to start."

# 4

# "Crown" - Camila Cabello + Grey

WHEN I WAS FIRST crowned, I used to look forward to big events. There was something about the air of anticipation back then. These days, things are a little different.

I hold still as Daphne ties the stays at the back of my dress. It will take some assistance getting through doorways in this thing. The gown is enormous. My stylist thinks if they can't spot me from across the room, I've become invisible.

The outer layer is dove-gray tulle that has been hand-embroidered with gold silk in a beautiful foliage pattern. The bodice dips down into a sweetheart neckline while still remaining modest. It's one of the more exquisite creations I've worn, and that's saying something.

Daphne drapes a diamond-and-onyx necklace around my neck, but before she can fasten it, Henry joins us in the dressing room.

A jolt zips through my stomach. He looks incredible in his tuxedo and white tie, his hair freshly cut and styled, with just a hint of stubble further emphasizing his jawline. In a word, he looks devastating.

"I'll get it," he tells Daphne.

She nods and squeezes my shoulders before leaving us alone. It's something I try to avoid these days if I can help it.

Henry removes the gemstone-encrusted necklace and places it on the dressing table in front of me. "I got you something."

He holds out a box the color of cotton candy. Inside is a delicate gold chain holding a small flawless diamond. On either side of it is a tiny pendant, one in the shape of an H and one a C. The chain is so fine it looks invisible.

He slips it from the box and drapes it over my collarbones, then clasps it in the back. I touch the simple stone. It's a much better match for my dress than the heavy piece lying on the table.

My skin prickles where he touches it. I find his reflection in the mirror, but he's still fiddling with the necklace and doesn't look up. I'm hit with the sudden memory of our first ball together as a married couple, the second time around.

My dress was big then too—let's be honest, they're always big for these things—and he didn't see me until we were walking down the staircase together. He stumbled on a step when he caught sight of me.

Once I was close enough, he yanked me toward him and whispered, "I'm already planning ways to get you out of that thing."

The words, his scent, the brush of his voice on my neck all gave me goosebumps. We entered the ballroom soon after, and I lost sight of him in the large sea of people dancing and mingling.

He found me within half an hour, though, his hands on my waist from behind and that intoxicating voice in my ear. "Come with me."

I followed him out like we were two kids sneaking behind the school for a smoke, my nerves a tangled mess. What if people noticed we were gone? What if they got suspicious? What was he planning to *do* to me in the middle of a ball?

He led me into a small room down the corridor, rarely used but elaborately furnished all the same.

"What are we doing?" I whispered.

He sealed his lips over mine, and I forgot all my concerns. Kissing Henry is like that—all-consuming, a hotbed of passion and ecstasy. Within seconds, he was fumbling for the zipper at the back of my dress.

"What are you doing?" I said again, laughter in my voice. "Someone will catch us."

"Let them," he growled. "I need you, baby."

Those words, combined with the desperation in his eyes, never cease to make me weak at the knees. I surrendered to him, but the zipper got stuck partway down.

"I can't get this damn thing," he said. After struggling for a few more minutes, he gave up, and we both began to laugh. I laughed so hard tears ran down my face, and he had to help me wipe away the mascara under my eyes.

I'm startled out of my memory when Henry brushes his fingertips over my collarbone. "You look beautiful," he says. "As always."

I meet his eyes in the mirror. "Thank you."

How did we get to this place? From lovers to strangers, as though we simply lost touch with each other over the years. But how do you explain falling out of touch with the person lying next to you in bed?

He helps me to my feet but doesn't drop my hands once I'm standing. Instead, he tugs me closer to him, as close as the dress will allow.

My heart catches in my throat as he leans in, cupping my face in that way I used to love and pressing his mouth over mine. He tastes of spearmint, and the familiar flavor sends my body into a frenzy. It knows what to do in this situation, even if my heart doesn't.

The kiss is sweet, nothing like the passionate one I was just remembering. His soft lips moves over mine like an embrace, like he's comforting me in the only way he knows how.

Tears well up behind my closed eyes. There's something about the feel of his mouth and the way I'd recognize his scent anywhere. The way he's so gentle with me, like he doesn't want to hurt me any more than he already has.

The realization is so simple, so clear.

I miss him.

He pulls back, and I open my eyes to find him smiling down at me. I give him a shaky one in return, and the words are there, dangling on the tip of my tongue.

*I haven't been honest with you.*

*I don't want a baby. Not yet.*

*I do love you, even though I've pushed you away.*

I open my mouth, and there's a flicker across his brow, like a shadow crossing a window. "I—"

The trilling of my phone from the dressing table chases anything else I might have been able to say out of the room.

"It's Preston," I say, and answer it.

"You haven't forgotten about the documentary, right? The camera crews have arrived and are setting up in the east gallery right now."

"I remember. We'll be down soon."

After I disconnect the call, I turn to Henry, who is waiting to escort me downstairs. "They gave the green light on the documentary. Filming begins tonight." I reach up to adjust his collar.

He looks less enthusiastic than he should. "Is that the one Preston's been subtly-not-subtly hinting about for ages?"

"This is going to be huge for the family once it's streaming," I say. "People will get the behind-the-scenes view they've always wanted."

He closes his eyes and pinches the bridge of his nose. "If you say so."

The ballroom is stuffed with people, like the streets of the city during the King Frederick's Day parade, making navigation in a dress the size of mine all the more difficult. Light gleams from the chandeliers and the sconces on the walls, illuminating the damp faces of the people around me and increasing the heat in the room.

I could take a seat on my throne at the head of the room, but I'd rather mingle with the crowd. Besides, I'm currently stuck in a conversation with several cabinet ministers about the advantages of changing the current parliamentary process of introducing new members. Should they be formally introduced at a Parliament session or should a party be given each year in honor of the new members?

While my face is currently expressing what I hope is a modicum of interest, my eyes are scanning the room. As if there's a neon arrow above each of their heads, the members of the royal family stand out to me from each of their respective locations.

Rosalind is talking to the prime minister, likely berating him for a recent political debate that he had nothing to do with. Henry's mother, Olivia, is dancing with a naval captain who appears to have her captivated, but she has the unique ability to make anybody feel like the most important person in the room.

Beatrice is not on the dance floor as I'd expected, but sitting in a chair near the wall, sipping punch. Her face is drained of color despite layers of makeup. She smiles at the men swarming her, but even from here it looks weak.

Henry is exactly where I expect to find him: at the center of a gaggle of women of all ages, with a predominant skew toward those in their twenties. He throws his head back and laughs, which causes a ripple effect in the group, each of them seeking to emulate his actions.

One of the blondes places her hand on his arm. I imagine her nasal voice saying, "Oh stop it, you funny thing." She says something to him quietly, causing him to laugh again. Once he has composed himself enough to respond, they titter around like Lydia Bennett and her militia officers.

I stiffen my jaw and return my gaze to the men and women I'm supposed to be listening to. I murmur a quiet assent to whatever they're saying, but at the sound of that familiar laugh, I look up again, and Henry's gaze catches mine. There's a stilling of the universe as we stare at each other, mirth lingering in the corners of his eyes.

While I'm still trapped by that magnetic gaze, he says something to the women, and they part the Red Sea for him. I watch his approach, unable to look away, and when he stops behind the group I'm speaking with, I catch my breath.

"I'm so sorry," I say. "If you'll excuse me."

They all bow their heads and make room for me to slip past them, although there's not much slipping to be done in a dress this big. Henry leads me from the room, and once the doors close behind us, the sounds are immediately deadened, leaving only a still silence in the gallery outside.

He opens another door and holds it for me to enter. I step inside and recognize the same room we slipped away to two years ago. My cheeks heat. This is what he pulled me away for?

He shuts the door behind him with a click. The only light in here is coming from the moon, streaming in through the windows on the far wall. I'm suddenly nervous to be alone with my own husband.

I turn to face him. The moonlight accentuates that jawline, and I fight the urge to trace it with my fingertips. "What are we here for?" I say, my voice coming out sharper than I intend.

"What do you mean? You're the one that wanted to leave."

"You interrupted *my* conversation."

"Yeah, because you were giving me the let's-get-out-of-here look."

"That's what you thought?" I laugh. "Try I'm-going-to-snip-your-bollocks."

He takes a step closer and squints down at me. "That sounds decidedly less pleasant."

"Trust me, it's not intended to be pleasant."

"You want to tell me what I did now, or am I to stand here and guess?"

"Do you need me to spell it out for you?"

There's a flicker in his eyes as his jaw hardens. "Apparently."

I shake my head and half turn away. "Unbelievable."

"Come on, Celia. Get it off your mind. I'd rather you let it all out now than let it build up steam for the rest of the night."

I shoot him a glare. "I shouldn't have to. We've had this conversation often enough. Since you can't put two and two together, I'll tell you, but only because I need to get back to my guests."

Henry spreads his hands in front of him, as though saying, *Go ahead then.*

"You were flirting, you asshole. *Again.*"

His mouth pulls down at the corners, in sync with his eyebrows. "I wasn't."

"You were!"

"I swear to you, I wasn't."

"Oh my god. Are you actually going to stand there and defend yourself? I *saw* you."

"I don't know what you think you saw, but it wasn't flirting," he says.

"Let's go ask all those women *their* opinions, shall we?"

His mouth drops open, but he clamps it shut again. He thrusts his fingers into his perfectly styled hair out of habit, mussing the whole look. "You thought I was flirting with them?"

"I thought we'd covered this." I cross my arms.

"I was being *friendly*," he says.

"There's friendly, and then there's flirting. You must not know the difference."

"What? Because I was laughing? I was trying to be nice. God." He turns away and walks to the window.

"Do you have any idea what your brand of *friendly* looks like to everyone else?" I say to his retreating back.

He stands motionless, looking out at the moonlit gardens surrounding the palace. I think he's not going to answer me, that this conversation will end the way most of them do, with one of us storming off and the other not able to find the words to apologize.

But then he says quietly, "If you cared half as much about this marriage as you do about what people *think* about this marriage, we'd both be a lot happier."

It's as if someone has dropped a bowling ball into my stomach. The weight of it hits, and I reach for the mantle to keep myself from swaying.

"Is that what you think?" My words are barely above a whisper.

He turns around slowly, those broad shoulders filling out his jacket as though it's been painted on him. "Yeah. It is."

I lift my chin. "Is that why you told Adelaide to talk to me? Because you're unhappy?"

"No." The moonlight behind him leaves his face in shadow. I can't read his expression, but I can imagine it well enough. "I asked for her help because I don't know how to make you happy anymore."

The pain in my chest feels like stepping into a hot bath with cold feet. "I'm happy," I say.

"Good. I'm glad." He nods, but even a stranger on the street could see that we're both lying.

Henry walks to the door and opens it. For a second, I think he's going to hold it for me, but then he steps through it and leaves me alone in the room.

I blink before the tears can fall. I can't go back into the ballroom with red eyes or streaks in my makeup, especially not with the film crews here. I take a deep breath, doing my best to push his words away.

Because, while he may be right in saying that I'm more concerned with people's perceptions than with reality, the truth is, their perceptions matter a whole lot. If we don't retain their support, this country will crumble in a heap of dust as it pulls itself apart once more.

And just because I saved her once, doesn't mean I'll be able to do it a second time.

# 5

# "Girl on Fire" - Alicia Keys

NOT EVERYONE IS AS lucky as I am in the mother-in-law department. Henry's mum is warm, nurturing, and always smiling. I used to envy him when we were kids, because there is something about Olivia that draws you to her like apple pie on a windowsill.

She's a modern-day Jackie O, and while she may have lost her title and crown to me, she holds herself more like a queen than I could ever hope to. Her outfits are impeccably styled regardless of the occasion. She won't touch a drop of wine, let alone anything stronger, and is convinced she gets tipsy after a bowl of French onion soup, no matter how many times Henry and I have assured her the alcohol is cooked out of it.

She greets me with three cheek kisses—the only person I know who does three—and motions to the settee in the living room.

If the rest of the palace can be described as intimidating, overbearing, and lavish, Olivia's apartment is the exact opposite. Pale linen curtains frame the windows, the furniture is all sea blues and greens, and it always smells of lavender. Coming here every Wednesday afternoon is like visiting the spa, only much more relaxing, because spas typically aren't relaxing for people who abhor sweating and being touched.

Olivia handles about a dozen royal engagements a week. While she's technically not a royal anymore, Wesbourne adores her and demands her presence at enough events that it only made sense to include her in our household at the palace. With her husband locked away for another twenty-three years, I think she welcomes the diversion.

I've heard that William will be petitioning for release on good behavior, but I can't imagine him staying out of trouble long enough for that to happen.

"How's your sister, dear?" Olivia asks as she pours two cups of tea. "She told me at the ball the other night that she wasn't feeling the best."

Bea did look a little peaked, but it didn't occur to me to check on her afterward. Unlike Olivia, who has already spent years of her life in service of the people of Wesbourne, Beatrice is still earning her keep as a member of the royal family. She handles roughly 10 percent of our engagements. Compared to my 55 percent and Henry's 30, it's not much, but given the way she complains about it, you'd think she was being asked to scrub the toilets instead of attend charity functions and cut ribbons.

"I'm sure she's fine." I take the cup and saucer Olivia holds out.

"Henry tells me you're visiting Budapest in a few months," she says, taking the chair across from the sofa. She's wearing a soft-pink skirt suit with white trim, her blonde hair perfectly coiffed into a loose chignon. She's Barbie at fifty-five.

"That's right. The prime minister invited us for a state visit."

"Be sure to visit Margaret Island if you get the chance. It's simply stunning in the summertime."

I take a sip of tea. "I'll see if they can add it to our itinerary. You went when Henry was young, didn't you?"

She nods and sets her cup down. "I have pictures around here somewhere."

I hide my smile. She knows exactly where that album is. Olivia keeps mementos of everything. I'm confident there must be a room in the palace just for hanging all the bouquets she's received over the years.

Sure enough, she walks over to the bookcase and pulls a clothbound book from a shelf without even looking. "Here it is," she says with a smile, already flipping it open. She sits beside me on the sofa and lays it across both our laps.

She turns a few pages until she finds the one she's looking for. "There." She points to a photo of young Henry lying on his stomach, stirring a pool of water with a stick. "He wanted to jump in so badly—it was terribly hot that day—but we convinced him to make do with the stick."

She laughs at the memory, and my heart feels refreshed. Olivia laughing is like rain on a stifling day.

"May I?" I ask, motioning to the book.

"Of course," she says.

We flip back to the beginning, where Henry's baby pictures take up several spreads. He was adorable, and I don't say that in the way that everyone oohs and aahs over babies in general, nor am I biased because he's my husband. He was beautiful. He could easily have won the modeling auditions for baby Zara and Baby Gap if he hadn't already been busy being a prince.

In that round face and exuberant smile, I spy hints of the man I know, and of course I remember what he looked like when he was a few years older than in these pictures. His eyes haven't changed. They're still that deep, dark ocean of unspoken words.

"I didn't realize you took so many photos," I tell Olivia.

"I wanted to be a photographer," she says, "but my parents decided that wasn't a viable option, so off to Oxford I went."

I flip to the next spread. There are pictures of Henry's first birthday and a lock of hair taped to the page. Olivia strokes it gently. "From his first haircut," she says. "I could hardly bring myself to let them do it."

He had a smash cake decorated like a race car. "He liked cars even back then?"

She chuckles. "There wasn't much he didn't like. He's never met a challenge he couldn't conquer."

I smile at the memory that pops into my head. Henry and I were in a little rowboat on the small pond near the Sunken Garden. We were wrestling in that awkward way preteens do when they haven't yet figured out that they are probably too old for that kind of thing. In the process, my necklace broke and fell into the water.

Henry felt so bad he jumped in immediately, despite my protests. It took ten minutes of alternating between searching the murky pond and bobbing back up for air before he finally came up one last time, holding the pendant over his head like a trophy.

It was a cheap thing, but I wore it every day for the rest of the year.

I turn the page to a set of photos from Henry's toddler years. There are little captions under each one in careful, handwritten script.

*First steps.*

*Learning to open doors.*

*Favorite meal.*

That last one accompanies a picture of a child that resembles Henry, but it's hard to say for sure because his face is completely plastered with spaghetti sauce.

*First public event.*

*Fishing with Daddy.*

I rub my thumb over the photo of Henry and William, both facing the pond, fishing poles in hand. Henry's pose so perfectly mirrors his father's that it would be humorous if it didn't make my stomach churn.

"He wasn't always like that, you know," Olivia says, looking at the picture. "William, I mean. He wasn't always so . . . cold."

This is so different from everything I know him to be that I immediately chalk it up to her being a delusional wife, wanting to see the best in the man she's been married to for thirty years.

"The man I fell in love with was charming and thoughtful. He was aloof, yes, and he didn't often let me in, but the times he did, it was like seeing a whole other person. Like seeing the sun during an eclipse." Olivia gets a wistful look in her eyes as she stares out the window. "He used to fly all the way to Paris to get these macarons I loved, just because I once said they were the best I'd ever tasted."

"What happened?" I ask, not sure I actually want to know. The two of us don't usually have conversations this deep, and venturing into these waters has me slightly terrified she'll reveal something I would be better off not knowing.

She hesitates, then glances at me like she's not sure she wants to say it either. "The job changed him," she says. "When his father died . . . William thought he had a few more years of being somewhat ordinary. But when he became king so quickly, it was like it flipped a switch inside of him."

The lump in my stomach grows larger. Hearing that William once had a heart, that his job changed him—the job I now hold—does nothing to make me feel better.

"Did Henry ever tell you about . . ." I can't bring myself to finish the sentence. Because no matter how good William may have been at times, there is nothing—*nothing*—that can excuse what he did to his son.

Olivia's brow crumples as she turns back to the album in her lap. "A few years ago. After the arrest." A tear falls onto the page protector, and she brushes it away with the back of her hand. Her gaze finds mine again. "I want you to know I had no idea when it was happening. If I had—" Her voice breaks, and she reaches for the handkerchief she keeps tucked up her sleeve.

I rub her back in what I hope is a soothing gesture. I'm not good with tears, my own or anyone else's. I turn the thick page, hoping a distraction might help.

The next one is full of more candid shots of Henry. A few of them feature Olivia or William, but most are of him playing in the dirt of the herb garden, taking a bath in a huge porcelain tub with soap suds everywhere, including on his head, and making cookies in an apron roughly five sizes too big for him, flour covering both cheeks.

A laugh spills from my lips. "Was he ever clean?"

"Not if he could help it." There's a smile in Olivia's voice, and I consider myself successful.

There's something about these photos. Not only did his mother do a wonderful job capturing Henry's exact essence in each one, but it triggers a memory of something. Something I can't quite put my finger on. By the time I was three and Henry was five, we were the best of friends, but I have no recollection of him at this age, so it's odd that something feels familiar about them. Maybe I've flipped through this album before and forgotten.

I brush my fingers over his smooth baby face as Henry smiles at the camera in that lopsided "bloody hell, you caught me" look. I miss those grins. I miss the teasing way his eyes light up when he's up to no good but knows he'll get away with it anyway because I'm absolutely powerless when it comes to him.

"Your turn will come," Olivia says. "I know it will." She places her hand over mine on the album.

I knit my brows together as I try to figure out what she's referring to. Then I drop my gaze back to the page. "I—"

"I struggled too, after Henry was born. Did he tell you that?"

I shake my head and keep my eyes focused on the pictures in front of me.

"We tried for years. I had several miscarriages, even a late-term one. But nothing ever stuck." There is so much sadness in her voice, and I kick myself for making her sad twice in half an hour.

"We did a few treatments, but there weren't all of the options there are today." She pats my hand again. "That's why I know it will work for the two of you."

I clear my throat of the emotion welling up there, not for the reason she thinks but legitimate all the same. "Thank you."

I turn the page again, revealing shots from Henry's third birthday. There are a few of him at public events, wearing those adorable little shorts and knee socks.

"This was after William's coronation," Olivia says.

I can't shake the feeling of déjà vu. "Do you have any of these framed somewhere?"

She considers this, her dainty brow puckered in thought. "I don't think so. Just of his christening with the whole family, of course."

I've seen that one a thousand times. The portrait hangs in the west gallery among the other paintings of the royal family over the years. But there is nothing recognizable about a baby swaddled in white cloths.

I shake my head. "Something seems familiar about them. It's weird seeing Henry so small."

We continue browsing, and my gaze snags on one photo in particular. It was taken at a parade, Henry sitting regally in the open carriage between his parents. Olivia didn't take that one, which might be why it stands out.

I'm about to move to the next page when something clicks into place. Maybe it's the crowd behind them. Maybe it's the dark hair falling into his face. Maybe it's those eyes that have no bottom. Regardless, I know why these pictures feel so familiar.

The little boy in the crowd last week, the one who gave me the tiny bouquet of daisies and melted my heart right out of my chest—he's the spitting image of three-year-old Henry.

# 6

# "I Love It" - Icona Pop + Charli XCX

THE BEST WAY TO cope with finding out your husband may potentially have a love child? Work. Always work. Since I saw those old photos of Henry, I've gotten less than eight hours of sleep. In two days.

The other key to successfully dealing with such a situation? Put it as far from your mind as you can. You're Svalbard, it's Antarctica.

Every time my brain wants to pull me in the direction that would lead to analyzing what it might mean, I yank it back to the present with excuses, reasoning, and threats if I have to. I refuse to allow it to be true, and therefore it isn't.

Maisie steps into my office after a brisk knock on the door. I glance at the clock. How is it only nine? I've been sitting here for four hours already.

She sets the green box on my desk and takes a seat. "This week's letters are ready to go."

We discuss my upcoming schedule, any press mentions of the royal family that have been made since yesterday, and how the documentary is progressing. She gives me instructions on a few of the forms in the box, then leaves me to it.

I have no idea how I'll survive her sixteen-week maternity leave.

I open the box, which has held important documents for Wesbourne monarchs for over a century. Someone on staff makes sure it's always polished and that the hinges on the lid don't squeak. That familiar cedar scent wafts out, still there after all these years. As promised, Maisie put the stack of letters on top of the other papers in the box. She collects them throughout the week, then sorts through them and sets aside the ones she thinks I'll be interested in, either for responses or entertainment purposes.

I've been staring at reports and proposals for hours, and my brain is begging for a break, so I pull the first one out of its pale green envelope.

*Madam the Queen,*

*My name is Elizabeth Gable. I hope this letter finds you well.*

*I am writing about a matter of some sensitivity. Four years ago, I became pregnant. I gave birth to the sweetest little boy, and we are both doing very well. I never had any intention of contacting the father, as I did not think he would be interested in knowing he had a son.*

*However, recent events have made me reconsider this stance. My son is struggling with attachment issues, and I believe the influence of his father could be of some help in this case, not to mention the importance of having two parents whenever possible.*

*I sincerely hope you do not think me forward in coming to you with this. When you visited Hampshire Street on the 11th, you became real to me. I felt like you might be the kind of person who would understand and maybe even sympathize with my situation. You were so sweet with Axel that I suddenly had hope that we might be able to form some kind of plan together.*

*This brings me to the purpose of this letter. Please know that if you choose not to respond, I will not take any further action. I do not intend to cause you alarm, but I believe you should know that your husband is the father of my son.*

*It happened many years ago. Axel is now three years old. We are happy together and ask nothing of you but the chance for him to get to know his father and perhaps have him, and you, if you so desire, in our lives.*

*Yours sincerely,*

*Elizabeth Gable*

Something falls out of the envelope and into my lap. I let out a reflexive gasp. It's a photo of little Axel smiling at the camera. There's a tiny gap between his teeth, just like Henry's.

My chest feels like it's going to explode. I toss the letter and photo on the desk and stand up. What in the bloody hell is happening?

I walk to the window, but the bright sunlight on the gardens does not help. A giant ball of nausea is tossing and turning in my stomach like a ship in a storm.

My throat is suddenly parched. I reach for the water tumbler on my desk, but I miscalculate the distance, and the whole thing spills across my keyboard. "Bloody hell," I mutter, tossing some tissues onto the mess.

The muscles in my jaw are strung so tight I get an instant migraine. I use my thumb and index finger to massage them while my other hand reaches for my phone.

"My office. Now," I tell Preston when he answers.

He's here less than two minutes later. I hand him the letter and photo and turn back to the window, biting my nails as he reads. One of the gardeners is trimming the hedges in the Parterre Garden. The *snip, snip, snip* of his shears is comforting, as if reminding my heart of the rate it should be at, so much slower than the one it's currently keeping.

Preston clears his throat behind me, and I turn to face him. He tries to hand the letter back, but I shake my head.

"I don't want it."

Laying it on the desk, he takes a step closer. He towers over me, even though I'm in heels. "What do you want to do about it?"

My arms are clutched around my middle like a kid on her first day at a new school. I drop them and clear the cobwebs and any emotion from my voice. "What do you think I should do?"

He draws his brows together and picks the letter up again, scanning it. "Is it credible?"

I shrug, mainly to loosen my shoulders. "How should I know?"

He studies me. His eyes make him appear to always be smiling, even when he's not, as though he's in on some joke the rest of the room isn't. It's not helpful at the moment.

"I imagine this isn't the first time a letter like this has been sent to the palace?" he says.

"There have been a few in the past couple of years." My voice is finding its strength again.

I know the wheels in his head are spinning. This is what Preston does—he takes bad news and spins it for good, like the little man in *Rumpelstiltskin* who spun straw into gold. His job is dependent on keeping the royal family looking as spotless as possible.

"You have two options," he says, hands perched on his narrow hips. "Either respond to this woman or don't. If you choose to respond, you can either thank her and tell her you'll give it some thought—at which point you will promptly forget about it—or you can meet with her to find out what she wants."

I shake my hands to rid them of the numbness creeping over me. "I don't want to meet with her."

"Then don't. It says here she won't take any further action if you choose not to engage."

"Do you think that's the right choice?"

"She's not threatening to go to the press with it. If you want to hush this up, she's giving you the option to do so."

"You're right." I brush my fingers over my clammy forehead. "This woman clearly saw an opportunity and took it. We don't have proof that she's telling the truth, and if word of this got out . . ."

Preston lets out a barking laugh. "Then that would be a different story altogether."

The royal family's policy when it comes to requests and outlandish claims is simple: no comment. By not denying or affirming anything, we allow these rumors to die out as quickly as they started. But that doesn't mean it wouldn't cause a media circus if something like this were to get leaked.

"You don't think she'll change her mind and go to the press, do you?" I say.

"It's unlikely. Like you said, she saw an opportunity and decided to take it. She has zero proof that Prince Henry is the father of her child. Even the photo isn't hard evidence. You'd be surprised at what you can do with AI these days."

I nod in agreement while my head chants *Liar!* Maybe no one else on my team stood close enough to the boy to mark the striking similarities between him and Henry, but I did. And that is no AI-generated image. I also know my husband. I'm less familiar with his checkered past, but I know enough to be fairly certain the chances that this woman is telling the truth are about sixty to one.

"Would you feel better talking to him about it?" Preston asks.

"Who?"

He waits a few beats, then says slowly, "Prince Henry?"

"No." I shake my head so hard my hairpins loosen. "No, definitely not."

Adelaide's words choose that moment to float back, warning me that nothing good will come from keeping things from him. Under normal circumstances she's right. But this is *Henry* we're talking about.

The man has no regard for his image whatsoever. He spent ten years living like a party king, ruining his own reputation just to keep me away from him in an effort to protect me.

He fixates on things like a germaphobe with a hand-washing compulsion. If he knew he had a child, that would be the only thing he could focus on. It would overwhelm every other part of his life.

I would lose him for good.

Even though I'm fairly certain this lady is telling the truth and that Henry has a child out there, I'm 110 percent positive of something else: Henry can never, ever find out about it.

# 7

# "Warriors" - Imagine Dragons

T HE ROYAL FAMILY IS eating breakfast in the Chinese Dining
Room. Sunlight streams in through the sheer curtains covering
the French doors that lead to the terrace, spilling across the red and gold
furnishings that decorate the space.

I consider Olivia's comment about Beatrice, but my sister looks much
better than she did at the ball. The color has returned to her cheeks, and
she's immersed in something on her phone while popping a blueberry
into her mouth every few seconds.

Rosalind and Olivia are discussing a Parisian designer who made a
splash a few days ago. Apparently, mixing more than two floral patterns
is frowned upon. I wouldn't know.

Henry sits at the other end of the table, as distracted by his phone as
Bea is hers, although he still manages to shovel bites of omelet into his
mouth at an alarming rate.

"Oh my god," Bea says from my left. "Did you guys read this?"

"Beatrice," our mother warns. "No tabloids at the table."

"Mum, this is the *Sun*. You know I don't read the tabloids anymore."

Rosalind's face reflects my own thoughts: *What, since yesterday?*

"What is it, dear?" Olivia asks with a smile.

Henry is still glued to his device, oblivious to the scene my sister is trying to create.

"The *Sun* just released an article a few minutes ago," Bea says. "It's about"—her eyes cut to me—"us. Well, some of us."

That's when I feel it—a trickle of apprehension running down my spine. If the news was good, she would have just summarized it and we would all be finishing our meal by now. But her pause means it's anything but.

"I doubt it's appropriate conversation for the breakfast table, Beatrice," Mum admonishes again.

But Bea isn't listening. Her golden head is bowed over her screen as she reads. I'm tempted to pull out my own phone to look for myself, but some of us still have manners.

"Oh my god," she says again. She looks up at me. "Have you seen this?" Before I can respond, she begins reading straight from the article. "'She claims the resemblance between her son and the prince consort is not simply a case of doppelgängers—'"

I shake my head for Bea to stop, but she isn't looking at me. I try kicking her leg, but she's too far away.

"'—but that her child is the result of a dalliance she had with the prince herself,'" she finishes.

Oh god.

Have you ever worked so hard on something, then made one mistake and watched the entire thing crumble?

I'm reminded of the time Henry and I stacked dominoes on end around the entire palace library. It took us fifteen sets to fill the whole room. We were nearly to the end when my foot caught on a chair leg and I tripped, knocking over a single domino and setting off the whole thing before either of us was prepared to enjoy it.

The heads around the table mimic those dominoes as they take turns lifting to look at Bea. First is Rosalind, whose furrowed brow rarely makes an appearance but has decided this occasion is worth the wrinkles. Next is Olivia, who wears her confusion well. She's always believed in Henry's goodness, no matter what the tabloids would have her believe. She is followed by Henry, who has heard enough to drag his eyes up from his screen and join the rest of us in the room.

Their gazes are all locked on Bea, but when she tears her eyes away from her phone, they don't land on Henry, as one might expect. Instead, she looks directly at me, and everyone else follows suit. I don't know what they can read on my face, but considering it feels frozen in place, I'm assuming it's not good.

"There's more," Bea says around a wince. "She says when she approached the palace several weeks ago with her claims, she was promptly ignored, despite the evidence she provided."

It's impossible to slow my heart rate. My mind is already racing to find a way out of this mess. I should never have let it get to this point. Elizabeth Gable said she wouldn't take things further, but apparently that was a lie. And now we're going to have a media circus on our hands. I can almost hear the crowds chanting at the gates already.

The first thing to do is call Preston. He'll be able to come up with a plan for dealing with this. I pull my phone from my bag and am just about to dial when Henry speaks for the first time.

"Is this true?" he says, looking me dead in the eye.

"Which part?"

"You know damn well which part."

I set my phone down. "I'm afraid I don't have a record of all of the women you slept with before we were married."

Discomfort fingers its way through the room. I picture even the Chinese figures on the painted panels coloring in secondhand embarrassment. Olivia dabs at her lips with her white napkin, her cheeks a dainty pink. My mother is busy rearranging her place setting, as if the end of the meal is the appropriate time to do so.

Bea's focus alternates between me, Henry, and the article on her phone, awareness of the Pandora's box she just opened finally setting in.

"That's not what I'm asking." Henry's voice is as hard as the gold plating on my knife.

Olivia pushes back her chair and stands. "I have a car waiting, so I should be on my way." She whispers something into Henry's ear and presses a kiss to the top of his head as she walks past him.

Mum clears her throat, a private signal that means I'm supposed to look at her. I do so out of habit, and she subtly shakes her head. "At least wait until the staff are out of the room," she hisses, then rises from the table as well.

After they've both gone, Bea swings her gaze between me and Henry again. "If I leave, are you two going to kill each other?"

I wait several beats until the tension in the air is so thick it would take an ice pick to break through. I toy with my fork. "Not immediately."

She sighs and pushes back her chair. "I don't want to get caught in the middle any more than they did. But listen to me." She leans over the table so that she has both of our attention. "I love you both, and if either of you hurt the other, you'll have me to answer to." With that, she leaves the room.

I don't relish the idea of sticking around to listen to Henry's thoughts on the subject at hand, so I stand up, calling Preston as I do.

"Sit down," Henry growls from the other end of the table.

My eyes flash to meet his, and the warning lining his face makes my stomach flip. I glance at the footman standing at the door, his features a perfect mask of indifference.

"I have calls to make," I say.

"Celia, *sit.*"

I hang up before Preston can answer, then take a seat, glancing once more at the footman. He nods and closes the door behind him. "What?" I say, returning my attention to Henry.

"Tell me the truth."

"You know we get weird claims all the time," I say. "We handled it the same way we always do."

"Was there evidence?" His tone is calm, but anger bristles beneath the surface.

"Nothing that would hold up in a family court, trust me."

He fiddles with his fork, turning it back and forth, flicking it between his fingers. "Why didn't you tell me?"

"If I told you about every inane request or claim that comes through the correspondence office, we'd be stuck here all week."

"How many of them involve me?" he says.

I consider how to respond. If I tell him the truth, he'll ask why I didn't give this one more consideration. If I lie, he'll ask why he's only now hearing about it. "We have staff members to handle these things," I say instead. "Neither of us needs to worry about it."

"So you weren't about to call the press secretary for an emergency meeting on how to 'handle' this latest scandal?" He leans back in his chair, watching me carefully.

I narrow my eyes a fraction. "I acted in the best interest of the royal family."

"In a real marriage, these are the kinds of decisions a couple makes together."

"In a real marriage, love children don't pop out of the wainscot."

Henry's jaw flexes, and I curse myself for noticing. "So you think it's real? This claim?"

"Absolutely not," I say, even though I'm terrified it is.

"Well, real or not, I intend to be a part of the decision-making process for how to proceed." He pushes back from the table. "You can tell

Preston to expect me in that meeting, too." With that, he disappears out the door.

I try to identify the emotion seizing my body right now. It's like I'm standing on top of the highest pinnacle of the castle, looking down.

No matter which direction I turn, my only option is falling.

# 8

# "Breath of Life" - Florence
# + the Machine

T HE CORRIDORS BUSTLE WITH activity as I head to my office.
Preston has agreed to meet Henry and me there in five minutes.
The argument with my husband has thrown me off my game, and I
nearly walk into one of the cleaning staff, who is attempting to assemble
a ladder to reach the upper cornices on the wall.

"I'm so sorry, Your Majesty," she says while trying to bob a curtsy and
hold a long feather duster at the same time.

"Please," I say. "The fault is all mine."

God, how could I have let Henry get under my skin like that? I've
become so good at keeping him at a distance over the past year. We may
feel like strangers these days, but we are terrific at waltzing around each
other and all of our issues. It's a shame to let that go.

When he proposed two and a half years ago, I thought my heart
couldn't possibly hold any more joy than it did in that moment. I loved
him so much I thought I would die from it. My feelings had grown so
much bigger and more complex than when I innocently professed my
love to him at fifteen.

It had endured multiple betrayals and countless arguments. There were times I didn't think I could stand being around him for another minute, but as soon as he was gone, I missed him. I was as desperate for him as a junkie is for another hit.

I don't feel that way anymore. I still love him, sure, but it's cooled with time. We go our separate ways in the morning, but I always know I'll see him again that evening, and that he'll throw his dirty socks on the floor in the corner of the bedroom even though we have wicker laundry hampers for them, and that he'll pour himself a glass of whiskey without asking if I want anything, then proceed to drink it in bed while scrolling on his phone like I'm not even in the room.

Everyone says that happens in all marriages, but I thought ours would be the exception. Naive little me thought we'd keep the romance alive for more than a year, considering how driven we were in our need for each other. But even the sex has cooled to something we do when my fake ovulation chart says it's time.

My body still responds to him in the same way, getting all hot and bothered by the sight of him in his workout clothes or those glasses that are sex-on-a-desk enticing. But to cross the invisible lines we've drawn and confess how I feel would be like climbing a snow-covered mountain I'm not willing to try scaling.

So we'll continue arguing over breakfast for the next fifty years, or until one of us gets tired enough to say we're done.

Of course, if Bea hadn't decided to share that article with the table, that confrontation would never have happened, and Henry probably would be none the wiser. My little sister needs to learn when to keep her mouth shut.

As if conjured by my thoughts, she pops out of an alcove in the corridor ahead of me. She must have been leaning against the wall, waiting for me. Her face is flushed, and her mascara, normally so flawless, is in smudged steaks on her cheekbones. Her blonde waves hang limply around her shoulders as though she's been running her hands through it.

"Bea? What's wrong?" I ask, concern obliterating my previous train of thought.

"Can I talk to you?" Her voice sounds as broken as the rest of her looks.

"Sure. I'm on my way to a meeting, but come to my office in an hour, okay?"

She shakes her head and wipes her nose with the balled-up tissue in her hand. "Can we do it right now? I really need to talk to you."

I take a bracing breath and glance down at my watch. Preston and Henry will be expecting me any minute. "Bea, I need to go. Can't it wait?"

Tears spring to her already wet eyes. "Please?" she says. "I don't know what to do, Celia, and I'm so scared."

Bea is a master at manipulation. Even as a child, she found ways to control others' emotions by threatening to harm herself or refusing to eat until we gave her whatever it was she wanted. She's a modern-day Scarlett O'Hara with her sob stories and her tears. But something in her face tells me this isn't a "boyfriend won't text me back" issue.

The last time I put Bea off when she needed me, she ended up in Henry's arms. Despite how conflicted my feelings for him are at the moment, I will do whatever is necessary to keep that from happening again.

"Fine." I yank open the closest door and nod toward it. "In here. But I only have a second."

Bea slips through the door, and I pull it shut behind her.

I wasn't sure which room this was, but now that I'm inside, I recognize it as the 1901 Room, named so for the visit from US President McKinley three months before his assassination in 1901. Large oil paintings cover the walls, commemorating important people from the past, both Wesbournians as well as ones of other nationalities. My favorite is of

Wesbourne's Princess Elizabeth, painted when she was seven years old. She should have been crowned queen upon the death of her father, but as everyone knows by now, she was bypassed for what turned out to be her half-brother.

I turn my attention to Bea, who is knotting her fingers together in front of her and biting her lip so hard I'm afraid she'll draw blood.

"Bea, what is it?" A small trace of exasperation slips past my shields and into my voice.

She releases her lip, and it springs back, plump and glistening again. "Please don't get mad."

"I won't," I say. "What's going on?"

"Before I tell you, I want you to know that I never meant for it to happen. It was an accident."

My heart freezes in my chest, coming to a screeching halt like tires on asphalt. There is something in her voice, a warning maybe, that whatever she's going to say is the last thing on earth I want to hear.

I know I shouldn't jump to conclusions. I know I shouldn't write the narrative ahead of time. I know I shouldn't assume I have the facts. But knowing that doesn't stop me from filling in all the blanks she's leaving open.

There has always been this writhing black ball of *something* between us, something that gets in the way of us having a genuinely honest relationship with each other. Something that rears its ugly head every now and then to remind us that it is in control, no matter how badly we'd like to think that we are.

It stirs in the pit of my stomach, creating a vortex of nausea and dizziness. As it comes to life inside me, there is one word that keeps repeating in my head, dropping itself into all of the spaces Bea hasn't filled in.

*Henry, Henry, Henry.*

No. Please, god, no. I cannot bear to hear that my sister is sleeping with my husband after all this time. I thought we'd put this behind us.

But what else could those tear-saturated lashes and blotchy face point to? There is only one thing in the world that we both know would bring me to my knees.

I beg all of the superpowers of the universe I don't believe in to fly through time, into the past, and rewrite history, so that when I wake from this awful nightmare, Bea will tell me she's seeing someone Mum won't approve of, or has decided to move to Australia, or—

"I'm pregnant."

The room spins around us, a whirlwind of color and art and opulence. Bea is still standing in front of me, but instead of the scarlet *A* I mentally pinned to her breast, she's wearing the scared look of a twenty-two-year-old who has just found out she's going to be a single mum.

"You're *what*?" I say when I can't find any other words.

"I'm so scared," she says, reaching for my hands and grasping them in her cold ones. "Tell me what to do."

My mind is still trying to get off the merry-go-round that is my fury at finding out Bea and Henry are having an affair. "I—I don't know."

"Please, Celia. You have to help me."

"I will." I nod, hoping it will help clear my head. "Of course I will. Who is the father?"

Bea hasn't dated anyone publicly for several years. In fact, I don't think she's seen anyone seriously since Rhett Cole broke her heart the last time.

Her brows pull together, shaving ten years off her face, and she draws her lip into her mouth again. Before she can answer, the door opens and a maid walks in. When she sees us, she startles, then quickly curtsies. "I'm so sorry. I didn't realize the room was occupied."

"We'll only be a minute," I say.

She backs out, closing the door behind her.

I turn back to Bea, but the cloudiness has disappeared from her eyes. "Tell me quickly before it happens again. Who's the father?"

She shakes her head, still biting her lip, but resolve has settled in her eyes. "I can't."

I frown. "Why not?"

"I just can't."

"Can't, or don't want to?"

"Either. Both." She shrugs her dainty shoulders, making her loose dress shimmer. "How is that important?"

"Does he know?"

She shakes her head again, blonde waves floating with the motion.

"Are you going to tell him?"

A green pallor steals over her normally creamy skin. "Do I need to?"

"Don't you *want* to?"

The reality of what she's telling me sinks in. My sister, Princess Royal, is pregnant out of wedlock and not in a relationship with the father, at least not a public one. There will not be a quick hush-up wedding or a nationwide jubilation over the new royal baby. This is not a celebration. This is a nightmare.

Her hands start fidgeting again, tying themselves into knots. "I don't think that would be a good idea."

Whoever this bastard is needs to pay.

"You weren't . . . *hurt*, were you?"

She quickly shakes her head once more. "No, nothing like that."

"Okay." That's a relief at least. "Can't you give me a clue? He should have some responsibility in this as well."

"Please," she says. "I'll take full responsibility. I would rather no one found out. About us."

A prickling sensation crawls through my veins. "Bea, why—"

My phone rings from my handbag, and I pull it out. Henry's name flashes on the screen. He's probably wondering why I'm not at the meeting I called. I send it to voicemail and stick the phone back in my bag.

When I look up, Bea is still standing there, hopelessly begging for help, keeping secrets to protect someone. Who is important enough for her to go to these lengths to protect?

My bag vibrates with another call. I roll my eyes and reach in to silence it when it hits me.

*No.*

My stomach lurches with another wave of nausea, and I clamp my hand over my mouth. I remind myself to breathe. In, out, in, out.

Bea is starting to look concerned for me now. I drop my hand and inhale deeply through my nose, stealing myself for what I have to do. "Bea, I need to know," I say.

I'm ready for it. I've braced myself against the news she's going to deliver, feet planted on this floor, ready for something—anything—to take me on.

"I told you. I can't." There are tears in her voice, mirroring the ones hanging from her eyelashes.

I do not have the strength to go against her on this. If she wants to take this secret to her grave, fine. In fact, good. "You know what?" I say. "That's fine. I don't want to know."

It's true. I don't think I can handle the truth, no matter how hard I dig my heels into the carpet. Nothing can prepare me for the eviscerating knowledge that has the ability to tear my world clean down the middle.

I think about all the time Henry and Bea have been spending together. I was happy—*happy*—that they were becoming friends rather than potential lovers. I'm a delusional fool.

"You—you don't?" she asks. We both know that I am completely intolerable when kept in the dark.

I shake my head. "No. We'll take care of this ourselves."

My mind is already working out the possible options. The biggest priority will be keeping this from the press. Those bloody vultures would take the story and use it to bring our family down, and the whole monarchy with it.

Hope glimmers in Bea's eyes for the first time. "I knew I could trust you to help."

"I need to go." I'm already fifteen minutes late. "But we'll talk about this soon. You have options, Bea. And you're not alone."

*And you'll never be alone again—not if I have anything to say about it.*

# 9

# "Seven Nation Army" -
# The White Stripes

WHEN I WALK INTO my office several minutes later, I find Henry and Preston already there, as comfortable as two male cats in heat.

Henry pushes away from the desk. "There you are," he says. "I tried calling you."

I look at him, and all I can see is Bea's tear-stained face. I'm rewriting everything I've witnessed between them during the year since she moved into the palace as a full-time royal. The way they ganged up on me when I said I couldn't stand Tom Hanks. The way they always split a muffin at tea, her with the crumbly top and him with the "stodgy" bottom he dunks in his cup. The way he always waits for her to walk through the door after me, instead of walking behind me himself the way he's supposed to.

"Sorry. I got detained." I consider dropping Bea's name to gauge his reaction, but if he's been fooling me for all of these years, I have no reason to think anything would change now.

Preston clears his throat from the other side of the room, where he's apparently sequestered himself to get as far from Henry as possible. "I'm going to assume you'd like to discuss the story the *Sun* broke this morning."

I shoot one more look at Henry. His hands are perched on his hips in that "let's get this sorted" stance. I move around him to sit behind my desk, blocking out the memory of him stretching me across it, a smoky fire burning in his eyes as he whispered "I've been visualizing this for months."

"That's correct," I say, ignoring the way my pulse races when Henry turns and props his hands on the desk, veins and muscles clamoring for center stage. "The paper said she wanted to remain anonymous, but is it safe to assume this is the same woman?"

I spent sixty seconds scanning the article after leaving the breakfast table this morning, just long enough to get the general gist of what we're dealing with and make me want to hurl my phone across the room.

"You're saying *he* knew about it?" Henry jerks his thumb over his shoulder to indicate Preston and sends me a glare that makes me catch my breath.

"Henry, this isn't the time for theatrics," I say in a hushed voice.

"I'll show you theatrics," he says in the same low tone.

Images of him over me instantly fill my mind.

Preston takes a few steps closer to the desk, but he's still giving Henry a wide berth. What the hell happened before I got here?

"I would say there's a 99 percent chance we're dealing with the same perpetrator," Preston says to me.

Henry scoffs and pushes away from the desk, angling his body toward Preston. "*Perpetrator*? Did someone try to break into the palace and steal a painting?"

Red climbs up Preston's neck, but he squares his shoulders. "Until we know what this woman wants, it's best to assume she is a threat."

"Preston's right," I say. "Why wait so long to come forward if this isn't an act of sabotage?"

"And if it's not?" Henry says. "What if she's telling the truth?"

The steel tip of a knife inches its way past my bra, just far enough to puncture the skin over my breastbone, as I consider his hypothesis. If I'm not careful, the blade will slide right on in, slicing through my heart as though it's made of butter.

"Maybe you could tell us that," I say, standing so we're closer to eye level. "Did you sleep with her?"

His nostrils flare, a horse preparing for battle. "How should I know? No one has given me any information."

I keep my eyes glued to him, afraid of what he'll do if I look away, and not wanting to face the fact that I couldn't look away if I tried.

"Preston?" I say. "What was her name?"

There's a rustling of papers as he shuffles through the stack in his hands. "Uh, Elizabeth Gable. That's all we have. Well, that and the picture of the kid."

Henry whirls on Preston. "There's a *picture*?"

*Fuck.*

I round the desk as quickly as I can, my goal to obtain the pages in Preston's hands. Henry reaches him before I do and snatches up the entire stack without exerting the least bit of effort. Like a maniac, I try to grab it before he can see anything revealing, but he pushes me off like I'm an annoying fly trying to ruin his picnic. He lets the stack fall onto the desk, his fingers clutching the small photograph that accompanied Elizabeth's letter.

It feels like someone has stuffed me full of corn dogs and cotton candy, then strapped me onto a Tilt-a-Whirl and turned it on top speed.

Henry stares at the photo, his face completely unreadable.

I know what it means when he runs his fingers through his hair, when he shoves his hands into his pockets, when his lips draw into a half smile. I know that gold flecks in his eyes equal happiness, and that their black depths only grow when he's drunk with lust. I know that he can't hold still under any circumstance, and that the only time he stops eating is when he's sleeping.

I know that he sleeps in the weirdest positions known to mankind: with his head tilted back at a ninety-degree angle, or his legs hanging off the side of the bed, or on his back with his knees bent. I know that the only food he doesn't like is the palace's hollandaise sauce, but he doesn't have the heart to let the kitchen staff know.

I've seen him drunk off his ass on our honeymoon, when he said that in another life he'd be a mechanic working in a small-town garage, where people liked him for who he was and not for his name. I've seen him cry his heart out in grief over his grandmother's passing and in relief as his father was finally put behind bars. I've seen him blissed out on love, promising to buy me a private island if I just said the word.

Watching him now, though, I am completely blocked from everything going on in that magnificent head of his. I can't read his thoughts or his expressions. I can't identify his tells or his fidgety movements.

I've never seen him stare at a picture of his child before.

The air has been robbed of its oxygen by the time he lifts his gaze from it. I'm not sure what I hope to find in his eyes, but I do know that barely suppressed anger is not it.

"I cannot believe you would keep this from me," he says. Although his voice is quiet, there is a thread of hurt and indignation wound tightly through it.

"I was trying to protect you," I say.

"By keeping my son from me?"

"We don't *know* that he's your son."

"Did you even look at the bloody picture? He looks just like me, C."

"It seemed best to keep it under wraps until we could confirm—"

"Except you weren't going to confirm anything, were you? You were going to pretend the whole thing never happened. Just sweep it under the rug the way you do every—"

"Henry, stop it!" I shout. I don't mean to raise my voice, but my blood pressure is incapable of remaining at normal levels around him. Taking a breath, I try for an even tone. "Let's just figure out what we're going to do."

Preston clears his throat. "Good idea."

Henry shoots me a final glare before turning the full force of his anger-laced eyes on our press secretary. "Just what do you suggest? You're the pro, after all." The level of mockery in his voice could detonate a bomb.

If Preston is insulted by this, he does a great job of hiding it—yet another reason he's a great fit for the job. Between Bea's and Henry's escapades, the royal family would be sunk without his expert handling of the media and our image.

"The easiest way to get to the bottom of what she wants is just to ask," Preston says.

"How would we—"

"Sounds goo—"

Henry and I both break off to exchange glares. If I didn't trust Preston with my life, and more importantly, my secrets, I'd try harder to mask the animosity between us right now.

"We could invite her to the palace"—Preston holds up his hand when I open my mouth to interrupt—"for a *private* meeting. To find out if she's willing to negotiate."

Henry snorts. "You're not going to buy off the mother of my child."

A stabbing pain in my chest alerts me to the fact that the hypothetical knife is now buried several inches into my heart.

*Mother of my child.*

That's supposed to be *me*. We're supposed to be the ones building a family together, creating children, making memories and baking cookies and taking hikes. Not Henry and some stranger.

"And if she doesn't agree?" I say, ignoring the pain that is leaking out of me as though someone turned on a faucet in my veins.

"I'm confident we can get her to agree," Preston says.

Henry moves both hands to his hips, solely focused on Preston now. I notice he's still holding the photo of the little boy between two fingers. "There will be nothing manipulative about this arrangement. Invite her for a meeting, but that's it. If that is my son, the decision will be up to me and his mother."

A gulping cough that sounds embarrassingly like a sob breaks free from my mouth.

Henry turns instinctively at the sound, but keeps his eyes on Preston. "And my wife." He doesn't meet my eyes, which is good because I'm not sure what mine are communicating at the moment.

I drop them and assume a neutral expression, and only when it's firmly in place do I look back up at Preston. "How can we ensure this stays out of the news?" I ask.

"I will get her signature on an NDA before anything else," he says. "If that's okay with you, sir," he adds, looking at Henry. There's a cocky tilt to his chin.

"That's fine," Henry grumbles.

Preston turns to me. "Celia?" he asks, waiting for the final verdict.

What do I say? If I agree to this and we come to some kind of arrangement with this woman, the press will throw our family into a meat grinder, hastening Wesbourne's demolition of a three-hundred-year-old monarchy. But if I decline, Henry will go after it like a true-crime investigator on the trail of a serial killer. There is no way I can stop him from forming a relationship with this child that may or may not be his. Either we do it together and weather the storm the media throws our way, or he does it alone—a choice that will lead to the end of our marriage and leave me to deal with the media fallout from a love child *and* a divorce.

A *second* divorce.

I steeple my fingers together and take a deep breath. "Make the call."

Preston nods like I've made the right choice, but was there a right choice to make? Either way, I lose. "I will coordinate with Maisie on your schedule," he says.

A few seconds later, he's closing the door behind him, leaving Henry and me alone in a room full of tension so thick it could clothesline you.

"Why the hell do you allow him to call you Celia?" he says.

My nerves are strung so tightly, his words bounce right off me. "You just found out you've got a kid out there somewhere, and that's what you want to focus on?" I roll my eyes and sit down at my desk.

"It's completely inappropriate."

He leans over the desk, trying to crowd my bubble, but I pick up my phone and lean back in my chair, typing a message to Maisie. I will need her help drafting a plan for the conversation with this woman.

"Lots of people call me Celia."

"I'm talking about staff members."

I shrug. "Me too."

"Name one," he says.

I look up and sigh. "Maisie."

Henry rolls his eyes and looks off to the side. "She doesn't count. She's your friend."

"So is Preston." I return to my text. He will not guilt me into feeling bad about my familiarity with Preston, not with the possibility of two children appearing to disrupt our lives.

"He has a thing for you," he says.

I laugh and set the phone down. "Not everyone is trying to steal what's yours. And don't forget, you're the one with a ready-made family popping up like an annoying ad when you're just trying to live your damn life."

Henry steels his jaw, then moves toward the exit. "I'll take the east bedroom tonight," he says. The door slams shut behind him.

So this is what it's like to watch your world end in smoke.

# 10

# "Castle" - Halsey

HENRY AND I HAVEN'T spoken since yesterday, when he stormed out of my office after announcing he'd be sleeping anywhere other than in our bed. I have no doubt the reason he walks into the White Drawing Room only seconds before Elizabeth Gable is supposed to arrive has nothing to do with being late and everything to do with wanting to avoid any further conversation with me.

His eyes dart in my direction as he enters but quickly drop to the picture in his hand again. Even from this distance, I can tell it's the one Elizabeth sent. I want to know what's going through that head of his, to run my fingers through his hair and coax him to tell me everything.

I stand from the settee and walk toward Henry. He doesn't move away, but he also doesn't look at me.

"Hey." I place a gentle hand on his arm. "We don't know that the photo is authentic." Even though I'm pretty sure this is the same boy I saw downtown, I can't be certain.

His eyes snap up. "Don't start."

"You know how realistic AI is these days. I just don't want you to be disappointed."

"You're telling me you're concerned about *my* feelings?" He chuckles, but there isn't an ounce of humor in it. "You forget I know you better than anyone."

"I mean it. I want today to go well." I *need* today to go well.

"Then why are we meeting in your bloody intimidation chamber?" He shoves the photo into his pocket and glances around with an annoyed expression.

I study the room with its gilded everything and hard, reflective surfaces. Every object in here is either white, glass, or gold, including the giltwood sofa, which has ornately carved griffins on both arms. A glass chandelier the size of a large sedan hangs from the ceiling like a judge presiding over a courtroom.

"I meet people here all the time," I say.

"Yeah, people you don't *like*."

Before I have time to respond, the door opens, and a footman steps inside. *Here we go.* A blonde woman walks in behind him, holding the hand of a small boy dressed in school blues.

"Miss Elizabeth Gable and Mr. Axel Gable," the footman says.

The air crackles with a nervous tension as the pair approaches us. Elizabeth curtsies in front of me, and her son tries to imitate her gesture, causing his small knees to point out in both directions.

Laughter cuts through the awkward silence, my own included. "It's okay," Elizabeth tells him. Her voice sounds like music. To Henry and me she says, "Thank you for seeing us."

"Won't you sit down?" I motion to the sofa. I don't need to see Henry to know he's rolling his eyes behind me. When they precede us to the cluster of seats, I elbow his stomach. The only sound he makes is a quiet *umph*.

Elizabeth settles her son on the settee, then sits beside him, already breaking protocol by sitting before me. Henry and I take the chairs opposite them.

I study her, this vixen who has swept in to steal everything away from me. She is effortlessly cool, like she was air-brushed into life, the kind of woman it's impossible to like but also impossible not to.

She's wearing a soft blue oversized sweater dress that accentuates her striking eyes. The collar is trimmed in black fur, and it's belted at the waist. She looks delicate *and* confident. I didn't know you could be both of those at the same time.

Her strands are styled in loose waves, not unlike Bea's, but where Bea's are perfection itself, Elizabeth's are looser, more carefree, like she just spent the day at the beach and hasn't had time to freshen up. In short, she looks like a breath of fresh air, the kind of person who walks into a room and immediately garners the attention of every person in the place.

She pushes her hair behind her shoulder in a nonchalant move that would take other women decades to master. Maybe she's been practicing it for the past ten years. She alternates between glancing at me and casting doting glances at her little boy, who is busy gawking at the room. She studiously avoids looking at Henry.

"Are we in a castle, Mummy?" Axel whispers loudly.

"Yes, we are," she says. "And you, lucky boy, just met the queen for the second time in your life."

The heat of Henry's gaze scorches me as he processes this, and I know we will be having words later.

"Would you care for some refreshments?" I ask.

"What's that?" Axel whispers to his mum again.

Elizabeth laughs, a tinkling sound that makes you want to hit rewind so you can hear it again. "It means snacks."

His eyes grow large, and he pops his thumb into his mouth before glancing shyly at me and nodding. I press the button on the table beside me, and seconds later, the server who was waiting outside the door enters the room carrying a tray of tea cakes. She's followed by another carrying the tea service.

After everyone has been served and the staff have left the room, I turn to Elizabeth. It's time to get down to business. "Miss Gable, we'd like to hear what you have to say."

She flushes, something that might have made me look foolish, but it only adds a spot of color to her cheeks, emphasizing her California-girl vibe. "Please, call me Libby," she says. "All of my friends do."

I refrain from raising my brows and sneak a glance at Henry instead. His eyes are focused on the little boy on the sofa, feet dangling over the edge, stuffing tiny sandwiches into his mouth just like someone else I know.

The cup in my hand rattles against the saucer.

"I feel terrible about the article," Elizabeth says. "I was having a few drinks with some friends—at least I thought they were my friends—and I made the mistake of telling them about my letter." Her voice has a soothing cadence to it, the kind you long for when you're in bed with a fever or homesick at summer camp.

"One of them is a journalist," she continues, "and he's the one who published the piece." She wipes a bit of jam from Axel's face with a napkin. "Needless to say, we are no longer speaking," she adds quietly.

"You can imagine our shock at reading it." I cross my legs and wish, not for the first time, that I hadn't chosen this crimson pantsuit. Elizabeth does not appear to be the type of woman who is easily intimidated.

"I am truly sorry," she says. "Like I said, I had a few too many drinks. I had no intention of ever telling anyone about sending that letter. Or about . . . Axel's father."

"Do you consider it responsible behavior to get drunk when you're a parent?" I can't help asking.

Beside me, Henry shifts in his seat. His glare weighs heavy on me, but I ignore him.

"Axel was with his grandparents that night." Elizabeth runs her hand through her son's dark waves. They instantly spring back into place. She doesn't even have the decency to look annoyed by my question. "My parents adore him." She gazes adoringly at him, and he beams back up at her, and I've had just about all of the adoration I can handle in a single day.

"Maybe you could explain your motivation behind reaching out. As I mentioned, it was very unexpected," I say before Henry can join the fray of adoring fans.

"Like I said in my letter, I want Axel to know his father." She shoots a tiny look at Henry, and I catch my first glimpse of discomfort in this woman. I tuck this information away for future reference.

Henry's attention jerks away from Axel and onto Elizabeth as she says this. Trepidation trips its way into the recesses of my heart as my eyes flick between the two of them. Their gazes hold for just a second. Elizabeth drops hers back to Axel, running her fingers through his hair again, another nervous tick I can add to my list.

"Prince Henry is very busy. Perhaps we can come to some other kind of agreement," I say.

Elizabeth stutters out a laugh. "I'm not sure what you mean."

Before I can answer, Henry crouches down on the floor in front of the sofa. "What do you like to do, buddy?"

Axel stares at him, then pops his thumb into his mouth, sandwich forgotten.

"Go on." Elizabeth nudges him. "Tell him what your favorite toys are."

He watches Henry for several more seconds before slowly pulling out his thumb. "Cars." He immediately sticks it back into his mouth.

Henry chuckles and pats Axel's leg. "Me too, buddy, me too."

The scene is like a traffic accident. You don't want to look, but you can't tear your eyes away. You register the horror playing out in front of you, you know it's going to haunt your dreams, but there is nothing that could make you shut your eyes.

"I brought some pictures." Elizabeth rummages through her bag. She withdraws an envelope, which she holds out to Henry. "I thought you might like to see them."

He carefully takes it from her, and my pulse skids as their eyes lock again, with more confidence this time.

This cannot be happening.

Henry opens the envelope and pulls out the stack of photos inside. "Are these of you?" he asks Axel, who looks at the one Henry's holding out, then nods.

"Wanna look at them with me?" he asks.

Another nod.

Henry takes the empty seat on the other side of Axel, not so close as to be touching, but close enough that the three of them look like a bloody family sitting there, all perfect hair and perfect teeth and perfect fucking symmetry.

Nausea strains at the confines of my stomach, begging to be released in the form of the lunch I had earlier, but I shove it down with a fierce command to stay put. I need to get through this meeting.

"I think this is you as a baby," Henry says. "But you were pretty bald, so I can't tell for sure."

A small smile lifts the corners of Axel's lips.

Henry flips through a few more pictures, then says, "You had a race car cake for your first birthday? That's awesome."

The boy looks up at him, then back at the photos. He points to the next one in the stack.

Henry pulls it out. "You like this one?"

"What's that?" Axel pulls his thumb from his mouth to ask.

Elizabeth leans in for a closer look. Henry holds the snapshot out for her to see. "That's your present from Nana and Papa," she says. "A toy piano." She turns to Henry. "You play, don't you?"

My head is screaming now, screaming for this to end, for this damn nightmare to be over. For me to wake and find that Henry and I are still who we were two years ago, before he decided to ruin everything by wanting a baby and then producing illegitimate children when I didn't give him what he wanted.

Henry answers that he does play, although I haven't heard a sound from that piano in months. I tell myself that this is public knowledge, that all of Wesbourne is aware of his skills on the keys, of his once-promising future as a pianist—if only he hadn't been heir to the throne and more likely to be found in a club than behind a baby grand.

That she knows this small fact about him means nothing.

After all, Henry wasn't one for pillow talk before he and I became a thing. At least that's what he told me. But then again, he never told me he'd had sex with a beautiful woman named Elizabeth and that she was the mother of his firstborn child, a gorgeous son who looks exactly like him and is already promising to be the light of his life.

I clear my throat, not because it needs clearing but because my head and the air do. Henry and Elizabeth both look at me, matching smiles on their faces like they're parents at a soccer match and their little angel has just scored a goal.

"Shall we talk practicalities?" I force a smile onto my own face as if this whole scene isn't making me want to vomit all over Elizabeth's cutesy little ankle boots.

She gazes at Henry like she expects him to go to bat for her, but I'm his bloody *wife*. If he's going to go to bat for anyone, it should be me.

As though he understands what she's asking of him, he says, "Celia, maybe we can just play it by ear?"

My throat closes up, and tears prick at the backs of my eyes. Is he actually taking her side in all of this, pretending that he can cobble together a family out of the pieces of his past?

"If you just tell us how much you're wanting," I say, ignoring Henry and focusing my fake smile on Elizabeth, "we can get the check. I'm sure you have places you need to be."

Her gaze flickers between Henry and me. "I don't want any money."

*Sure you don't.* That's what they all say the first time.

"You don't need to be afraid of offending us. This is a delicate situation, and we want to make sure you are . . ." I fumble for the right words. ". . . taken care of."

Henry shoots me a look that all but screams, *Careful.*

She shakes her head and tucks her hair behind her ears. "Axel and I are doing just fine." At his name, the boy looks up from the photos in his lap. "I just want him to have a father." Her eyes travel to Henry again. She is quickly overcoming her previous discomfort. "If you're willing, that is."

He grins, first at her, then down at Axel. "Get to know this cool guy?" he says. "You betcha." He offers his knuckles to Axel, and the little boy pumps his own fist against Henry's.

Elizabeth beams at them. As her glow emanates to capture both of them in its rays, it smacks me across the face.

She's not here for fame.

She's not here for money.

She's not even here to sabotage me.

She's here to steal my husband.

# 11

# "Bring Me to Life" - Evanescence

Once Elizabeth and Axel leave, it takes Henry three seconds to turn on me. "What the bloody hell was that?" He throws his arm out, knocking over a sixteenth-century vase standing nearby.

"What was what?" I grab it before it can smash onto the floor.

"Offering her money. Saying nasty things. Acting like a bloody snob."

"I didn't act like a snob." I cross my arms over my chest. His eyes track the movement, making me instantly regret it, but I can't drop them now without drawing his attention again.

"Really? Then why did you use your posh voice?" He props an elbow on the mantelpiece behind him, faking nonchalance like a pro. He's wound as tightly as I am, and he can't hide it from me.

"I don't have a posh voice."

"'Would you care for some refreshments?'" he mocks.

I march over to him until I'm only a few feet away. His eyes flit across my face as if reading it to determine my next move. I start to laugh.

He couldn't have looked more startled if I'd started stripping and twerking right here in the Audience Room. His eyes narrow as he takes me in, and it only makes me laugh harder. I bend forward until I'm nearly doubled over, unable to suppress the guffaws wracking their way out of my body.

"C?" Henry asks, trepidation evident in his tone.

I'm laughing too hard to answer.

"Celia." He takes my arm and attempts to tug me upright. It takes a few tries before he's successful. He leads me to the settee.

"What is so damn funny?" he asks when my laughter finally subsides.

My stomach aches from all the laughing, but also from keeping the nausea at bay earlier, as they all acted like a picture-perfect family from an advert for omega-3 gummies. Without warning, the last few chuckles turn into sobs, wracking my body just as hard as the laughter did.

The sofa shifts beneath Henry's weight as he tugs me into his side. His arms wrap around me, holding me to him, and I bury my face in his shirt. His button-ups always look like they'll be stiff and starchy, but up close they're as soft as cashmere.

He smells so damn good, like whiskey and spearmint and home. Whenever I'm out of the country for a state visit, feeling homesick, this is the smell I crave. Not my freshly laundered sheets or hot chocolate chip cookies or the lavender in the East Terrace Garden or that incredible shea butter lotion Bea found in Paris, but *this*.

*Henry.*

Once I've thoroughly soaked through the cotton of his white shirt and my sobs have retreated to nothing more than sniffling shudders, I shift so I'm not leaning completely against him.

He pulls back to look down at me. "Wanna tell me what that was all about?"

I shake my head, not ready to meet his eyes just yet. "I'm a mess?"

"You've had a big shock," he says quietly.

I wait several beats in case he plans to add more, but he doesn't. "So did you," I say, picking at a small thread at his buttonhole. "You're not falling apart at the seams."

His hands gently stroke the top of my head like he's deep in thought. "Yeah, but this feels like a good thing to me." Several seconds pass. "I'm guessing it doesn't feel like that to you."

"You could say that." I keep my tone even, because I don't know where this is going. I don't want to restart our fight, but I won't be caught with my guard down either.

"I think this could work, babe." Musing lines his voice. He's already imagining a future with them, with all of us, as though he can just stitch us together into the fabric of his life simply because he wants us there.

"How exactly do you see this *working*?" It comes out icier than I intend, but it's no secret I don't always have the best control of my mouth.

"People successfully blend their families all the time," he says.

I push away from his chest. "We're the royal family, Henry." The cold rushes in as I stand, putting distance between his heat and my anger. "You don't *blend* royals!"

He shakes his head and looks off to the side in disgust. "You're back to being a snob."

"It's the truth. Everyone knows it, including Elizabeth, which is why she marched in here, intent on ripping our family to shreds!"

He pushes to his feet, and I take several steps backward. "If you had been paying attention, you would have noticed that she was trying to increase the size of my family, not rip it apart, which seems to be the only thing you're capable of doing lately!"

I flinch. He might as well have slapped me. "Is that really how you feel?" I say quietly.

"No." He runs his fingers through his hair. "Yes. I don't know. All I know is that I'm being offered the chance to be different from my own father, and I'm sure as hell not going to turn it down."

My breath hitches in my chest, stuck in place by the lump that has taken up residence there as well. The two compete for space, neither willing to give way to the other. "This isn't your only chance," I say.

Henry looks up at me, brows slightly furrowed. "I know. This would never take the place of any children you and I have together. But just in case . . ."

"In case what? In case I never give you what you want? This is your backup plan?"

"No." He sinks back down on the sofa and rests his elbows on his knees, his hands both buried in his hair now. "God, no. I just want to be happy. This seems like the only thing with even the slightest possibility of making that happen."

I close my eyes against the accusation. I no longer make him happy. Of course I don't. I can't give him what he wants.

"I want you to be happy too." I try to keep the tears out of my voice. I can't let him know how deeply his words cut.

"Then can you let me have this? Please?"

"How am I supposed to do that, Henry?" I spread my hands out in front of me. "This will destroy us. How can you not see that?"

He jumps to his feet again, never able to hold still for more than a minute. "It won't, C. I promise you that. You never even gave them a chance."

"Of course I did. I sat through the entire meeting, didn't I?"

He shakes his head and looks at the floor. "I could see the wheels turning in your head the whole time. You were trying to come up with a way to make it all disappear."

"I was trying to think of a way to save us all from going up in a cloud of smoke." Desperation yanks my voice up in both pitch and volume.

"The only person you cared about in that meeting was you. You don't care if I'm not happy, if I never get what I want. You certainly don't care about the two of them. It's always you and your image before everything else."

"How can you say that?"

His glare meets mine. "Because the only thing you can talk about is the way the press is painting you."

"That's not true." I blink hard to keep the tears from spilling over.

"You hid my own *child* from me."

"You don't know that he's yours."

"I can't believe you met him before and didn't tell me."

"I knew you were going to bring that up," I say with a sigh.

"Just like it came as no surprise when I found out. I thought, 'How typical, Celia.'"

I cover my face with my hands. I will not let this man witness me crying again. I do not want his sympathy or his pity. I inhale deeply and brush at my face, pretending I have dust caught in the corners of my eyes.

"So you're just going to accept everything she said? What if she's lying, Henry? You'd do that to us?"

"He looks just like me, C. Even you can't deny that. Which, I suspect, is why you tried to cover the whole thing up."

I stare down at my nails, pressing on my cuticles even though I got a manicure yesterday. "It's really just a matter of whether you slept with her or not." I look up as I say it, intent on catching him in any lie he tries to spin.

His face hardens into something I can't describe, and he says "I don't remember" in a tone that's so low I have to strain to make it out.

"You don't remember," I repeat.

He cuts me a glance. "That's what I said."

"How could you not remember if you had sex with her?"

I think about the only two men I've ever had sex with—Beck and Henry. I couldn't meet either of them in a corridor without the cells of my body remembering the cells of theirs, in spite of the fact that Beck is now happily married to my private secretary.

I was a virgin when Beck and I started dating, something my university friends loved to tease me about. I just didn't understand how anyone could blow off their studies for something that only lasted a few minutes. Especially since the only guy I had ever wanted had rejected me to date the entire female population of Wesbourne. And apparently get them knocked up.

My opinion on sex being a waste of time has changed since then, but that is entirely due to my previous misconceptions about what it could be. Of course, the guy who obliterated those misconceptions has obliterated them for a lot of other women as well.

"You wouldn't understand," Henry says.

"You mean because I never worked my way through entire university campuses by having meaningless sex with someone new every night?"

He paces to the other side of the room. There's no bar cart in here, or I'm sure he would be pouring himself several fingers of whiskey. "You never fail to bring that up, do you?" He turns and approaches me again. I move backward to get out of his way. "You just love to throw it in my face, like it's a fucking ball we're hitting back and forth. You know I did it to protect you."

I clench my jaw so hard it clicks. "Pretty sure you could have protected me just fine while finding a different hobby than rolling in the sheets. Not exactly the actions of a man who professes to have been in love with me."

"Says the girl who was engaged to *marry someone else*."

"How is that my fault?" I say. "You said you didn't want me!"

"Yeah, in order to protect you! God, Celia." He tugs on his hair. "How many times do we have to have this conversation?"

"As many as it takes for me to get over my fear of your past coming to bite us in the ass."

"That's ridiculous."

"Is it?" My eyebrows flick upward. "If you had just kept it in your pants once in a while, we wouldn't be facing the threat of fifty illegitimate children running around out there."

Henry shakes his head and gives me a look that says, *You are acting insane.* "I know you think I was a complete dipshit, but you of all people should know you can't believe everything the media puts out there."

"And yet we just came from a meeting with your supposed lover and child. Who, I might add, *you don't even remember.*"

"Have you ever had so much to drink you don't remember things clearly?" He raises his brows as if to say *Hmm*? "Remember Seychelles?"

My face heats at the memory: me, losing track after my sixth Mai Tai and waking to discover my mind a blank slate. According to Henry, I wandered the beach that night singing show tunes—which I hate—until a bird pooped on my head, which drove me to instant tears. I fell asleep before he could even get me in the shower.

"I didn't have sex with anyone that night," I point out.

"No shit," he says. "That would have been rape."

Thinking about our honeymoon is not good for keeping the tears at bay. I pinch the bridge of my nose. "We wouldn't be in this mess if you had just used a fucking condom."

He steps closer, making me press up against the mantle. "You know you're the only one I've ever not used a condom with."

"And yet we have evidence to the contrary." I'm breathless with him invading so much of my personal space. "Maybe you just didn't *remember.*"

The look on his face says he does not miss the sarcasm in my voice. "That fluke may be my only chance to have a child."

I flinch.

His face immediately turns apologetic. "I'm sorry, C. That was a shit thing to say."

"Yeah, no fuck." I sniff and push past him before he can mess with my emotions any further. "So what now? Are you going to ride off into the sunset with Elizabeth?"

He snorts. "Don't be ridiculous. But I do plan to stay in touch with her."

I straighten one of the pillows on the sofa. What I want to do is punch it, but that feels a little useless at this point. "What kind of name is 'Axel' anyway?"

"Well, for a guy that likes cars, I kind of dig it."

"Look how cute you two are. Naming your kids after your hobbies."

"Mock it all you want, but that's my kid we're talking about, so you won't do it in front of him or his mother."

I don't even have time to come up with a response before he's gone, as if he can't handle speaking to me for another second. I gape at the door that has already closed on him.

He left as though there isn't anything for him here anymore. Maybe there isn't. I won't give him a child, even though he doesn't know that. And I won't accept the one he found another way. I'm not leaving him much choice.

But he's not leaving me much of one, either. While he fights for the child he's apparently always wanted, I will be fighting for my family and for my country.

He's mistaken if he thinks I will go down without doing everything I can to stop the carnage that's coming.

# 12

# "Don't You Worry Child" - Swedish House Mafia

T HE NIGHT AFTER OUR fight, I don't sleep. Henry has decided the east bedroom of our flat in the palace is more appealing than the one he shares with me.

I miss his warm body spooning me until I get so hot I need to roll away from him. I miss the way he lets me put my chilly feet on him regardless of how cold he is himself. I miss the way he kisses my hair and nuzzles my ear, whispering, *You smell so damn good*. I try convincing Tundra to jump up next to me, but he just looks at me like I've lost my mind and plops onto his dog bed.

This morning, my eyes are heavy from lack of sleep, and the only thing I can think about is the Henry-Elizabeth-Axel scandal that's about to hit the newsstands. Which reminds me, I need to update Preston on how our meeting with her went so we can formulate a plan to deal with the wreckage to follow.

He'll be disappointed to hear my plan didn't work and that Elizabeth is refusing to be bought. Her claiming she only wants a father for her son is nothing but a ruse. Henry may be blind to it, but I'm a woman, and women can sniff out other manipulative women.

I should know. My younger sister is one of the best.

Speaking of Bea, I've got another crisis on my hands. I text Preston to meet me in my office later and decide to use the quiet of this early morning to do some research for her.

I'm about to type "abortion clinics Wesbourne City" into the search bar when it hits me that not only will Bea need to leave the city, maybe even the country, so that she's not recognized, but I should be using incognito mode for my search.

I start a private browsing session and widen my search to greater Wesbourne. The results are less than promising. I can't risk her going to some village clinic that may or may not know what they're doing. And there's no guarantee the secret wouldn't arrive back at the palace before we did.

It will have to be done overseas. I opt for England. The British are less enamored with royals from other countries due to having their own.

America went wild when Henry and I took a month-long tour there after our honeymoon. Every city we visited was stuffed with crowds, like fans at a Taylor Swift concert, all cheering and vying for the best spot to catch a glimpse of us. The thing that hit me most was the noise. They're so *loud*.

Henry was most impressed by the food. One night after a particularly lavish buffet, which offered every single dish known to mankind, he collapsed into bed beside me and pulled me close, then tucked my head under his chin. "We're never leaving," he murmured. "This is my food heaven."

I push that memory from my mind. It's no good dwelling on it now. I have too many crises on my hands at the moment.

I find a few state-of-the-art clinics in London that are both trustworthy and private. I print their brochures to show Bea later.

Next, I look for some luxury maternity resorts, also in Europe. Something tells me Bea might be more interested in this option, because she's terrified of doctors and will relish the thought of skipping off to a private resort for six months while the whole world misses and pines for her. She can put the baby up for adoption before coming home, and no one will be the wiser. There are a few promising options, and I print those brochures as well.

I'm just gathering the stack of materials and heading to my sister's room when a brisk knock sounds on my office door.

Maisie sticks her head around the corner. "Got a minute?"

Without waiting for my answer, she enters and closes the door behind her. Her hands wrap around her belly instinctively. She is the picturesque image of what a mum should be. I'd prefer to not have been about to marry her husband right before she did, but that is water under the bridge.

I quickly stuff the brochures beneath some other papers on my desk. She doesn't even notice.

"What's up?" I say, hoping she'll make this quick.

"We have a bit of a . . . situation," she says.

I raise a brow at this. "What kind of situation?"

"I'll just show you." She pulls her phone from her pocket and hands it to me.

I study it, but after a few seconds, I hold it out to her. "I don't know what I'm looking at."

"Look closer," she says. "That's my desk. Or at least that used to be my desk. It's currently buried under stacks of mail that are taller than I am. We are going to have to work around the clock to process it all, and that's if all three of us pull twenty-four-hour shifts."

I hand the phone back. "How do you normally handle it?"

"Normal mail stacks are half that size. And most of those are invitations, not letters."

"Why the sudden influx in correspondence?"

The breath rushes past her lips, and she sinks into the chair opposite my desk. "Oh, I don't know. Could have something to do with that article in the *Sun*."

"Could have or does?"

Maisie blinks at me. "Given the ratio of pastel-colored, floral-scented envelopes to normal mail, I'm going to go with *does*."

"You're kidding." My stomach curdles. "Do I dare ask what they want?"

"The majority are professing their love for Henry. The rest profess their love *and* claim to have had his child."

"Good god." I sink into my own chair.

"Yeah." The word rolls out of her mouth like a boulder down a hill. "I'll bring you a big stack of them. You can read them whenever you're in doubt as to whether you have the catch of the century or not."

I toss a pen at her head. "Not funny."

She moves to climb out of her chair, a cumbersome process. This right here is why I never want to have a child. You become a lumbering elephant for six months of your life.

"Hey, can you refill my prescription sometime this week?" I ask once she's upright.

"You got it. Same thing?"

"That's why they call it a refill."

Maisie sticks her tongue out and closes the door.

I give her a few minutes to head to her own office across the hall, then grab the pages from my desk and walk to Bea's suite.

"It's open!" she calls when I knock. She's perched on a chair in her sitting room, computer on her lap. She turns when I walk in. "Oh, darn. I thought you were Lavinia with my muffin." Her lips curl down in a pout, and she turns back to her laptop.

"Sorry to disappoint." I take a seat on the sofa, wondering if she was planning to eat the bottom of the muffin or save it for Henry.

"What do you think of the name Gemma?" she says without looking up.

"I'm sorry?"

"The name Gemma. If it's a girl. What do you think?"

"If what's a girl?" I say, genuinely not following.

"The *baby*, doofus." She pats her flat belly. "I'm hoping for a girl."

Air rushes against my eyeballs as they widen. "You can't be planning to keep it," I say.

She glances up for the first time. "I am." She turns her laptop so I can see the screen. "Look at this. Isn't that the most adorable thing you've ever seen?"

I'm about to point out that it's a baby romper, but something in her face tells me she's already acutely aware of that fact. "Bea, what are you doing?" I say instead.

"I'm just browsing, yeesh," she says. "I won't buy anything until I find out the gender. Which BabyCenter tells me can be done as early as fourteen weeks." She squeals and flips her screen again. "Oh my gosh, is this dress not to die for?"

I wouldn't even give a chipped nail for the thing, but that's not the answer she's looking for. I offer a tight smile instead.

"Just imagine a tiny little princess wearing that!" Bea says, still in rapturous over the floral-print outfit.

Is now a good time to remind her that her child would not receive a royal title, whether she chose to raise them or not? Based on the glow on her face, probably not. Plenty of time for that later.

"I did some research," I say as I pull the brochures from my bag.

"Me too," she says, eyes lighting up as she finds yet another gem from the baby boutique she's "just browsing." "It turns out there are a lot of foods pregnant women should avoid. Shellfish, cured meats, unpasteurized dairy. Alcohol, obviously. Do you know how well the kitchen washes the produce?"

"Uhh," I say. "Pretty well?"

"Because it's super important to get all of the bacteria and pesticides off. It can cause birth defects otherwise."

I'm questioning the integrity of the sites she's been visiting, but before I can voice my concern, she pipes up again. "Oh, and the electromagnetic rays from electronics can be so harmful to unborn babies." She lifts the laptop. "That's why I'm using this."

What I thought was just a blanket in her lap turns out to be a "radiation-blocking cover" for her belly.

God help us.

"Bea, why don't we talk about a few options." I slide the abortion pamphlets to the bottom of the stack. She's not in the right frame of mind for those. I hand everything over to her. "Look through these and tell me what you think."

She sets her computer aside and takes the brochures from me. "I can't thank you enough for helping me. It has taken such a load off my mind."

She opens the first brochure and skims through the info. It's for a maternity resort in Switzerland, complete with prenatal massages, personalized meals, and one doctor for every three patients on site. It's expensive, but in this situation, worth every penny.

"This place looks amazing," she says. "Do they have warm tubs?"

I furrow my brow. "Warm what?"

She looks up from the page. "Hot tubs are not safe for pregnant women, so they now make an alternative: warm tubs. It's basically the same thing, but the temperatures can't climb higher than one hundred degrees."

I nod along in agreement that this is a fantastic product to hit the market, but all I'm actually thinking is *What is happening here?*

Bea flips to the next brochure, one for a similar resort in Dubai. "Oh my god," she says. "Oh my god. Can you imagine giving birth here?"

I can't imagine giving birth, period, so that would be a no.

"It's Dubai for me, all the way. This place is fantastic," she says, still thumbing through the pamphlet. "I don't even need to look at the rest of these." She hands the stack back to me.

Great. Guess we're doing this then. Turns out those incognito abortion tabs weren't necessary after all.

"They work closely with an adoption agency to make that part of the process as smooth as possible too." It was one of the requirements I had when researching.

"Oh, that's nice." Her voice has a faraway quality to it. "I don't understand how some women can go through nine months of pregnancy *and* childbirth and then still decide to give their baby away."

"Plenty of women have strong reasons for doing so. Such as keeping their secret," I hedge.

Her eyes meet mine, a newly kindled fire flickering there. "I know what you're doing, Celia."

I smooth the lines of my skirt. "You do?"

"You're trying to talk me into giving up my baby," she says. "But you may as well give up now, because it's not happening."

I stare at her. "Bea, you asked for my help. I told you that you have options."

"I thought you meant for a birth plan or how to raise the baby. I didn't think you meant to give away my little girl."

"Bea, please listen to—"

"I'm surprised you didn't just drive me to a nearby abortion clinic." There's a sharpness in her voice that contradicts her soft femininity. "Or are there brochures on those in there too?" She motions to the pamphlets.

Heat climbs my neck and spreads to my cheeks. I close my eyes and lower my head, focusing on my breaths. "You can't keep this baby, Bea," I say at last.

She looks at me like I'm out of my mind. "Why not?"

"God, Bea. Do I really have to spell it out for you? You're not married. You're not even engaged or dating anyone."

"So? That way of thinking is super old-school."

I sigh. How is it possible that she is a member of the royal family and still so clueless about these things? "You are the Princess Royal. You can't have a baby out of wedlock." Frustration is leaking into my voice despite my attempts to maintain my cool.

"Plenty of single mums are raising their kids just fine." She lifts her chin with a haughty tilt. "I think I'll make a great mum."

No doubt she would, but— "You're still a royal."

"I know that," she snaps. "But I don't understand why you keep pointing it out."

"We're held to a different standard than the rest of the world, Bea. They look to us as an example of moral conduct."

She fiddles with the radiation cover on her lap, then tosses it onto the floor. "This isn't 1950. I'm pretty sure no one requires us to be married in order to have kids these days."

She's right, but what she's missing is the fact that the royal family is around fifty to one hundred years behind the times when it comes to morality. It's always been that way, and it's not changing anytime soon.

"So this whole thing—you looking into *options* for me—was just a way to get this baby out of the picture?" she says.

"I thought you were scared, Bea," I say, leaning forward. "You told me you were scared."

She looks down, rubbing circles over her belly. "I was scared." Her voice is so quiet I have to lean forward even more to hear her. "But then I thought about the miracle inside of me. Another human being chose me to give them life."

I don't think it works like that, but I can't bring myself to break her spell of wonder.

"I didn't think I was ready to be a mum. Sometimes I'm still not," she says. "But every day I feel myself growing more and more confident."

She looks up and meets my eyes. "I know I can do this, Celia. I'm sorry it throws a wrench in your plans for the family, but this baby is the best thing to ever happen to me."

After that, there's not much to say. She's not willing to listen, but I haven't given up. I'll wait until she's in the throes of morning sickness. When she's cut off from eating sushi with the rest of us, she may be more open to reason.

"I'm happy," she says as she hugs me.

I give her a smile in return. I have no choice but to come up with a solution. If she can't be talked out of this preposterous idea, it, coupled with the Elizabeth Gable scandal, will mean our entire image going up in smoke.

There won't be anything remaining. The whole thing will be ground zero.

# 13

# "I Found" - Amber Run

MAISIE WASN'T LYING ABOUT the letters. If anything—and this is the only time I'll ever have this particular thought—she may have been *under*-exaggerating. The box at my feet is stuffed full of envelopes, which she assured me is only a fraction of the stash in the correspondence office. It's only been a few days. How many more will flood the palace in the weeks to come?

Elizabeth Gable started a maelstrom when she got drunk and shared her deepest, darkest secrets with that reporter. Actually, it all started when she concocted this crazy fabrication.

How do we even know there was a greedy "friend" in the first place? It's just as likely—maybe even more likely—that she sold her story to the first journalist she could find. Any desperate person with half a brain could look at her son, see the resemblance to a young Prince Henry, and use it to their advantage.

Until we have hard, undeniable proof, I'm sticking with *guilty until proven innocent.* That might not be how the justice system works, but the justice system isn't holding the downfall of an entire monarchy in its hands.

I take out a small stack of envelopes and slice them open with my letter opener. The various scents wafting from the box are already giving me a headache, and I haven't even begun to read yet. I don't know how Maisie and her minions have been able to handle this so far.

The first one contains a single sheet of paper, written by an infatuated sixteen-year-old who hopes Prince Henry loves her as much as she loves him. It would actually be sort of sweet if I had any sympathy for the hormones of teenagers.

I toss it aside and pull out the next one. I promised Maisie I would help sort through these to relieve her staff, but something tells me I'll regret that choice. At least Tundra is keeping me company by sleeping on my feet.

The next one holds pages and pages of floral stationery. I skim them to get the general gist of what the letter writer wants—money, Henry's love, and the opportunity to bear him a child—before tucking them back into the envelope and tossing it aside.

Elizabeth Gable should be helping go through these. This is her mess after all.

Better yet, Henry should. He's the one they're all writing to. It would inflate his ego, but maybe he'd finally realize that his playboy stint didn't help him in the long run.

It takes several minutes to locate my phone, which I find stuffed under a sofa cushion. I send him a text.

> Can you come to my sitting room? I need your help.

I opted not to do this in our joint living room in an effort to avoid running into him, but making him suffer the consequences of his own actions is more tempting than avoiding him right now.

I have time to go through half a dozen more letters before he shows. Glad to know he'd be able to save me if I was in danger.

"Grab a stack," I say by way of greeting.

"Hey, boy." Henry leans over to pet Tundra, then nudges the box at my feet. "What's all this?"

"Missives from your mistresses. Although I'm sure they can't *all* be from your previous lovers. Even you aren't that prolific."

He shoots me a look that makes my toes curl, and not in a bad way. Tearing an envelope open, he scans the letter inside and tosses it onto the glass-top coffee table. "What are we doing, C?"

I don't know if he means physically at this moment or is referring to the tension between us every time we're in the same room, but I'm only willing and able to answer one of them. "We promise the people to open and read every letter we receive. I told Maisie I'd take 20 percent of them."

His eyes grow large as he stares at the box. "This is 20 percent?"

"Yep." I hand him a fat stack. "Better get started."

He takes it from me and sits in one of the chairs across from the couch. For a while, the only sound in the room is the rustling of paper and the slitting—or in his case, ripping—of envelopes.

I come across a gem too good not to share. "Oh look, it's Henry Junior." I hold up a photograph of a red-headed little boy with a large dusting of freckles across his cheeks. "He looks just like you," I say with a smile that could curdle milk.

Henry only glares and returns to the letter in his hands. He is giving them much more consideration than I am. Our current ratio is three letters for me for each one he reads. He is probably savoring every declaration of love.

There are a few more missives containing photos of Henry's supposed offspring. All of them also offer "proof" as to their claims—*same nose! look at the eye color! signature jawline!*—or even details about the night of conception.

"Gross," I say after reading the last one. "Did you really have sex at the top of a Ferris Wheel?"

"Only on weekends," he says without looking up.

I toss the descriptive letter onto the table. "If we're believing Elizabeth's story, why not all of them?"

Henry holds up a photo between two fingers. It's of a little girl of obvious East Asian descent. "Maybe because her child is the only one who actually looks like me?"

"And yet there's no denying the fact that you did sleep your way through most of the country. How do I know these women aren't all telling the truth? Maybe you have a selective memory where they're concerned too."

"It really bothered you that I said I don't remember."

"Of course it did."

"Would it have been better if I said I did?"

"Only if it's the truth." But would it? Wouldn't knowing that he still remembered kissing her mouth, holding her close, watching her orgasm, make this ten times worse?

"I'm sorry that I can't give you what you want," he says. "But why does it matters if I remember her? The issue is the same."

I take a deep, shuddering breath. "The issue is that sex is so meaningless for you."

He drops the bundle of letters in his hand. They hit the rug with a quiet thump, then gently slide out of their neat stack. "It's only meaningless if it's not with you," he says in a low tone.

My heart falters, skipping along like it's playing hopscotch in my chest. "I don't know if I believe you."

His eyes turn stormy. "Why are you so threatened by her?"

I allow several beats to pass before answering. "Because her claims could sink the entire monarchy."

He shakes his head. His hands twine together where they're dangling over his knees. "It's more than that. If you were only concerned about the royal family, you'd let me help. Instead you're throwing the past in my face every chance you get, like some kind of weapon."

"Your past is the reason we're in this mess."

"I thought we agreed to put it behind us."

"And yet it's not behind us, is it?" I toss the remaining letters in my hand onto the table. "It's right here, on display for the entire world to see. And instead of rejecting it and assuring me it's nothing, you're lapping it up like it's the best thing to ever happen to you."

Henry lurches to his feet and closes the distance between us in three strides. After nudging Tundra out of the way, he sinks to his knees in front of me and takes my face in his hands. "You know damn well you're the best thing that's ever happened to me. Anything telling you otherwise is a lie."

Tears are running down my cheeks. I don't even know when they spilled over. He brushes them away with his thumbs.

"I saw the way you looked at them." My sniff is loud and unladylike. "You looked at them like . . . like heaven met earth."

He shakes his head. "No. I was in shock, maybe even awe. And that kid is adorable and sweet. But that's all it is, I promise you."

I want to be reassured by his words, his touch, but when I close my eyes, all I can see is the image of the three of them on that settee. It is seared into my brain.

"You think he's your son," I say through my clenched jaw. It's tight from holding back tears, not anger, but the effect is the same.

"What choice do I have?" Henry sits back on his heels. "He looks exactly like me, C. You saw it, too. It's impossible to ignore. So until I have irrefutable proof that he isn't, I have to take responsibility as though he is."

"And what about Elizabeth?"

A flash of confusion crosses his face. "What about her?"

"You'll be spending a lot of time with her. Won't she get the wrong message?"

He takes my hands in his. "If she does, that's on her. It should be obvious by now that you are the only woman in the world I will ever have eyes for."

His platitudes sound so good, so comforting, and I allow myself to sink into them. He's my Henry, and if I don't want to share him with the world, I don't have to.

He straightens until his face is level with mine, then pulls me toward him with that gentle strength that makes me tremble. He takes my lips with his, and I sink into the ecstasy of him, of knowing that this man is completely and wholly mine.

He groans as I tilt my head, trying to get a better angle that allows him to push his tongue even further into my mouth. My hands tangle in his hair of their own volition. My chest arches to meet him, begging him to press into me. He complies, and my nipples pinch at the sensation.

One of his hands cradles my neck, guiding me where he wants me to go. The other finds its way under my blouse and teases my nipple into becoming even harder.

"Henry," I say, breathless and in desperate need of him. "Wait." Much as I want him right now, I can't do this with unfinished business between us.

He manages to pull back a fraction of an inch, still teasing my lips with the brush of his as he says, "Why?"

I do my best to lean back for a little distance from his intoxicating presence, but he still has his hands on my neck and chest. "Promise that we'll put this whole thing behind us." I stroke his cheek, all bristly from the stubble he lets grow. "It's not worth losing our marriage over, right?"

His brows pull together, and his hand stills beneath my shirt. "Exactly what do you mean when you say 'whole thing'?"

"All of it. Elizabeth and the press and the letters. All of it."

His hand drops. "You want me to walk away from them." The words come out in a breathless rush. There's no ignoring the coldness that has taken over his tone.

How do I say it so that it won't push him further away? "Just until we can confirm that Axel is your son."

He looks down at where his fingers grip my hip. "How can I make you understand that you have nothing to worry about? What if we meet with them again? You'll see that there is absolutely nothing between me and Elizabeth."

"No," I say with more force than I intend. "I don't want to see her again. Ever. And I don't understand why you choose to believe everything she says as gospel truth. How do you know she's not lying about the whole thing? You don't even *remember* having sex with her."

"Baby girl." He leans close until he can reach my neck. He nuzzles it, causing the nerves along my spine to prick to attention. "I remember each time I've had sex with you. Doesn't that count for anything?"

He reaches up to grasp my chin, then tilts it to give himself better access to the side of my throat. I moan as he peppers it with short, wet strokes of his tongue. "I could make you forget all of it if you let me." His voice is low and raspy against my neck.

He could. I know he could. But that's the problem—I'm not looking to forget. I need this problem gone. For good.

"Forgetting about it won't change anything," I say, struggling to retain my composure as he slowly unravels me.

"Maybe not," he murmurs, "but it sure would be fun."

I suck as much air into my lungs as I can and jump to my feet, pushing past him to round the coffee table. The abrupt absence of him is physically crippling, but I force myself to stand upright.

He pushes his fingers into his hair, and my heart crumples. Why can't any of this be easier?

"I'm sorry," I say quietly. "I just can't right now. Not until things are under control."

He looks over his shoulder at me, his eyes full of sadness. "At some point you have to realize that you'll never have control of everything."

# 14

# "Unbreakable" - Jamie Scott

T HEY TELL ME I'M an introverted extrovert, and maybe that explains why, when my plans to visit a senior recreation center are canceled as I'm walking to the car, I'm both disappointed and elated.

I was not looking forward to the honorary whack of hitting a tennis ball or needing to fake enthusiasm over sweaty gym lockers, but I was excited about seeing the work they're doing in the community and chatting about the possibilities of adding some new programs.

Davies escorts me back to my suite to change out of my tennis whites. He's filling me in on the camping trip he's taking with his son this summer but stops abruptly at the entrance to the White Drawing Room.

"Tourists," he says quietly when I come to a stop beside him.

Inside, a group of visitors are studying the room, necks craning to take in the ornate architecture and exquisite artwork. They're all wearing windbreakers, fanny packs, and trainers. One man is sporting a sweatshirt from the gift shop with *Wesbourne* printed across the front. The sight instantly takes me back to the day in Herrington Forest when my father asked a tourist to take a photo of us on our picnic blanket for my fifteenth birthday. It's the last photo I have of the two of us together.

"We'll go a different way." Davies places his hand under my elbow and steers me back out through the doorway.

The tourists haven't spotted us, and we try to keep it that way by moving slowly. We avoid random run-ins when possible and are usually successful. My canceled tour is the only reason we almost slipped up today.

Davies scans the gallery extending in both directions from where we stand. I can read his body language well enough by now to know he's scanning his mental map of the palace, looking for an alternate route that doesn't put us in the path of any more visitors.

"Audience Room." He motions down the gallery, and we walk in that direction. When we approach the jib door hidden in the wall, he holds up his hand, signaling that he will check the room before allowing me to enter. Even after three years as my PPO, he still thinks I'll forget.

I roll my eyes, but he's not looking at me. He has his ear pressed against the door.

"What?" I ask in a lowered voice. "Is someone in there?"

He swings his eyes to me, still listening. "We'll find a different route," he says, and straightens.

"Why?" I ask. "Who's in there?" I move past him to press my own ear to the door.

He's right. There are voices in there—two, specifically. I listen a few more moments. They're speaking softly, and I'm about to give up on identifying them when I hear the laugh.

My stomach lurches.

Why is Henry holding a private meeting in *my* Audience Room? Technically it's not off-limits to the prince consort, but he's never needed it for his own personal meetings before. Then again, with most of my engagements taking place away from the palace, I have no way of knowing how often he uses the room.

I look at Davies. "It's Henry."

He nods and averts his eyes.

"Who is he meeting?"

He takes a sudden interest in his shoes, leaning down to polish a spot on one toe.

"Davies." There's a warning in my tone, but we both know I pose no threat to him. It's not like I could ever fire him, not if it meant putting up with a PPO I can't stand.

He lifts his head, then stands upright. "I should escort you to your suite."

"Who is it?" I lean closer to the door.

Our eyes lock as I listen to the rise and fall of voices inside. The way Davies's are hooded tells me he knows who is in there with Henry and would rather I didn't. Which is all the more reason for me to find out.

There's another round of laughter inside the room. Once again, I recognize Henry's immediately, but I block it out so I can listen to the other. It's softer and harder to make out. There's a musical quality to it—

"No." It comes out as a whisper, but a desperate one. Tell me he is not meeting her after we agreed—

God, what is happening?

Davies looks concerned as he reaches for me. "Let's go," he says.

For a second I want to lean against him and tell him everything, the way Henry and I hardly speak anymore except to yell at each other and throw nasty barbs. The way sex has become a meaningless exercise in convincing him that I do want a baby when everything inside me is screaming the opposite.

I shake my head. "I'm staying."

"Ma'am, I don't think—"

"My husband is in there with another woman." I level my glare at him. "I'm staying."

Davies closes his eyes briefly but nods. "As you wish. There is a dressing screen on the other side of this door. They won't see you if you open it a few inches."

I didn't even remember that. I smile my thanks and slowly inch the door open. The voices get louder immediately.

"And then she says, 'Who's up for another round?'" It's Elizabeth speaking. "The room groans as everyone clutches their stomachs. Ten seconds later, she's passed out on the floor herself."

Henry's laugh commingles with hers again. The effect is sickening.

"I doubt she had any recollection of it the next morning," Henry says.

"I'd say not," Elizabeth agrees. "But the rest of us never forgot it."

I don't know who they're talking about, but at least their conversation isn't intimate.

"I'll never forget the time she found out how to say 'a coma.' She'd always thought it was one word: 'acoma.' Like, he's in acoma," he says.

Elizabeth roars with laughter. "That doesn't even surprise me."

They know the same people. This realization hits me slowly, in waves, as they continue discussing this mystery person. It's not proof that they slept together, or even that they knew each other before, but it's a step in that direction.

The invisible bands around my chest squeeze tighter.

I glance at Davies, who is patiently indulging me, standing at my side, hands clasped in front of him. I offer him a grateful smile and return to listening.

"Do you remember that one party? I think it was at the Quantum," Elizabeth is saying. "Clarice and Sabrina got on the table and couldn't get back down?" She dissolves into giggles. "It was hilarious. We left them up there for at least an hour."

"I'm not sure." Henry chuckles. "Was I there?"

"I think that was the night you had your tongue down the throat of some girl who looked like Sydney Sweeney."

There's a masculine groan. "God, don't remind me."

Revulsion curdles the contents of my stomach. I know he had a life before me, but that doesn't mean I want to hear the details. And now I know that he *does* know Elizabeth, something he thought he could hide from me.

Davies is looking at me. Can he hear as much as I can?

"Of course, you were hammered enough to not remember much of it," Elizabeth says in that soft, soothing tone.

I want to hit her.

I picture Henry rubbing his face the way he does when he's embarrassed. "Sounds right."

"I used to think things might have turned out differently between us if you hadn't been plastered every time we saw each other," she says.

I hold my breath.

Several beats pass. Then Henry says quietly, "I'm sorry, Lib."

*Lib.*

It's there, hanging out in those three letters—the truth I've been shoving away from myself every chance I get. Of course he had sex with her. Of course Axel is theirs. Of course he would've gotten into bed with someone as beautiful and toned and glamorous as *Elizabeth Gable*. Even her name sounds elegant.

I thought Henry was mine.

It turns out the entire world wants a piece of him, and he's more than willing to share.

Davies walks me back to my suite. I thank him at the doors, and I can tell that he understands it was for more than just the escort.

Inside, I wait in the living room for Henry. When he walks in a few minutes later, Tundra bounds over to greet him.

"Hey," Henry says when he spots me on the blue velvet sofa. "I thought you had an engagement this morning." He readjusts the jacket draped over his arm and scratches behind Tundra's ears.

"It was canceled." I don't look up from the vase on the coffee table. If I stare at it any harder, it might start to levitate.

"Oh." From the corner of my eye, I see him scratch his jaw. "How was the unexpected free time?"

"Enlightening."

He starts to move toward the bedroom, as if he's not sure what else to say.

"Why did you lie to me?" I ask.

He halts in front of the bedroom door, then slowly turns to face me. "What?" His face is a mask of confusion.

"You lied. About Elizabeth. Or should I say *Lib*?"

His chest inflates with a deep breath. "Celia, I can—"

"Explain? Oh, please do. Just give me a second to grab the popcorn."

He tosses his suit jacket over an armchair. "I didn't want to hurt you."

"You can mark that mission unsuccessful."

"C, I'm sorry," he says. "I hoped if you thought she was just some nameless woman I might or might not have slept with, you wouldn't feel as threatened."

"As opposed to what? Finding out you had a relationship with her?" I stand and move to the other side of the room.

"We weren't in a relationship."

"Could've fooled me."

He looks down and sighs. His tongue prods the inside of his cheek. "We were friends, a long time ago. More like acquaintances."

"It sounded like more than acquaintances in the Audience Room earlier."

His eyes flash up to meet mine. "You were eavesdropping?"

"Don't change the subject."

"I don't know what you want me to say. Yes, I knew her. Yes, we had sex. I didn't tell you because I didn't want to hurt you."

I cross my arms over my chest as though it will keep my heart from breaking all over again. "It would have hurt a lot less if you had just been honest with me."

"You mean the way you were honest with me when Libby first contacted the palace?"

"Stop calling her that!"

"Why?" He spreads out his arms like he's balancing on a precipice. "That's her name."

"You're not allowed to give her nicknames, and you're not allowed to see her again, either."

He has the audacity to laugh. "This is a marriage, Celia, not a dictatorship."

My nostrils flare as I exhale. "It feels more like a business arrangement at this point."

"Have you stopped to wonder why that is?"

"For starters, we're too busy putting out your fires to have time for anything else."

He just shakes his head and mutters something under his breath that sounds a whole lot like *unbelievable*.

"When did you sleep with her? Or was it more than once?"

His eyes cut to mine. "Just once. And I don't remember when."

"A ballpark idea is enough."

"I don't even have that, sorry."

"Your memory is not that bad. What aren't you telling me?"

His fingers plow furrows through his hair. "It was a rough year for me. I made some stupid choices. A lot of it runs together in my head."

"What made that year rougher than the others?"

His sigh is long and deep enough that the weight of the air shifts. He lifts his eyes, which are dark but flickering with heat. His voice is low when he finally speaks.

"You got engaged."

# 15

# "Roar" - Katy Perry

S OMETIMES I FORGET I'M an adult and can eat cookie dough if I want to. That's precisely why I'm standing outside Bea's door with a tub of it under my arm.

She opens the door in a silk floral robe. "This better be important," she says around a yawn. "I was napping."

"In the middle of the day?" I scoot past her and into the suite.

"That's normally when people take naps, yes," she says, closing the door behind me. "Why aren't you in a meeting or shaking the sweaty palms of forty-year-old men who look at you like they'd like to have you for dinner?"

I shudder at the vision. "I quickly approved everything the lord chancellor proposed." So I'd have time to brainstorm what to do about this particular dilemma.

"And you interrupted my nap for what? Sleep is good for the baby, you know." She rubs her still very flat belly.

"I need your help." I set the tub of cookie dough on the coffee table in the sitting room. "And I brought payment."

"I'm not sure I can eat—"

"Come on, Bea." I tug her onto the sofa next to me. "Once isn't going to hurt." I hand her a spoon.

"This is why, of the two of us, I will make the better mother," she says, taking it from me hesitantly, as if just looking at it might cause a birth defect.

I can't disagree with that, and looking at her stomach, I'm hit with the realization that the universe got it all wrong. Henry should have ended up with Beatrice, or even Elizabeth. Then he could have had all the beautiful babies he wants.

I clear my throat and pop the lid off the tub.

Bea leans forward and drags her spoon through it. "What do you need help with? And before you answer, remember that I am eight weeks pregnant and cannot help you move furniture or go on a drinking spree with you." She pops the soft dough into her mouth.

"I'm doing some investigating." I scoop my own bite of the sweet treat. "You won't have to move a muscle, except maybe your thumbs."

"I'm intrigued already. Who are we investigating?" she says, licking her spoon.

"Elizabeth Gable."

"Ooh, Henry's ex?"

"He claims they were never a thing."

"She had his kid though, didn't she?"

I stare at the spoon in my hand, cookie dough still perched on the end. "It would seem that way."

"A revenge plot," Bea says in her best Hannibal Lector voice.

"Not revenge. Sabotage." I scrape the dough off with my teeth. "I cannot allow her to destroy everything."

"Either one sounds like the exact diversion I need. What did you have in mind?"

"I need proof that she's not who she says she is. That she's after more than she claims."

Bea sits up straighter, and the cushion beneath her bounces. "I am totally down for breaking into her house. Do you know when she'll be away from home?"

I frown at my sister, wondering if I should take back my earlier thought about her being a good mother. "Uh, no."

"You mean we're doing a stakeout? Yes!" She pumps her fist into the air.

"I was thinking more along the lines of some social media stalking," I deadpan.

She blinks at me a few times, then sinks back into the cushions. "So more librarian grandma, less Blair Waldorf."

"Hey," I say. "This is pretty big."

Bea rolls her eyes and tosses her spoon onto the table. "Yeah, for someone who doesn't even know their way around their own Instagram profile."

I lean back beside her. "Come on," I say. "I need this. If I can prove to Henry that she's after something . . ."

Bea leans her head on my shoulder. "Don't worry. Your little sister is going to stalk the heck out of this woman."

"Why do you think I came here?" I press a kiss to the top of her head.

As though it propels her into motion, she rockets up from her seat, leaves the room, and returns a few seconds later, holding up her pink phone. "I've got the gear." She plops back down beside me. "I'm assuming her Instagram is private?"

"Uhh." I bite my lip. "Am I supposed to know that?"

She slowly turns her head to look at me. "You haven't checked?"

"Was I supposed to?"

She closes her eyes, and I get the same feeling I used to when Rosalind would read my essays and ask if I thought that was the way "hypothetically" was used. "Do you live in an actual cave?" She flips her long hair over her shoulder and taps away at her screen.

"I don't know her username," I say defensively.

Bea shoots me a side-eye, and a few clicks of her long nails later, holds her phone up for me to see. There are several profiles listed for *Elizabeth Gable*. "Which one is she?"

"How did you do that?" I point to the one that showcases Elizabeth's perfect face.

"I'm starting to think you were born in the wrong century."

"There are roughly a million and one things more important than fiddling with social media."

Bea mutters something under her breath that I can't make out, but her tone tells me I don't want to know anyway.

"So?" I ask. "Is it private?"

"No." It comes out as a sigh.

"But that's good, right?" I'm pretty sure private means locked.

"Sure. But I was looking forward to using one of my secret accounts."

It's my turn to stare at her. "Excuse me? Secret accounts?"

"What?" She shrugs, and her robe flutters across her back. "I have them for this reason. I can't stalk people using my own account."

God, the things I'm better off not knowing.

"Okay." I drag the word out. "So if she's not private, we can just start looking for dirt, right?"

"Yep. And my presence is completely pointless."

"Not true." I plant a hand on her thigh before she can get up. "I don't have a clue what to do."

"You really are a cave woman," Bea says, but I can tell she's secretly pleased to be better at something than me. "Pull it up on your phone too, and we'll both look."

I find Elizabeth's profile. A burble of excitement leaks into my chest right before I tap it. I doubt she thought we would check her out on social media, but she picked the wrong marriage to sabotage. I'm not going down without a fight.

Beneath her name, it says:

*Mum to Axel*

*Real estate agent*
*Health & wellness advocate*

How cute. Her profile picture is of her in a classic black pantsuit, arms crossed, head tilted as she smiles at the camera. It's your typical agent photo, except for the hot-pink background and the red lips she's sporting. They are vivid enough to draw the eye at first glance.

"Aww," Bea says beside me.

I peer over her shoulder. She's looking at a photo of a . . . baby goat? "What is that?" I ask.

"They went to the zoo." She scrolls sideways. "Look at the goats."

They're adorable, but even more adorable is little Axel sticking his hand out so the animals can nibble grain from his outstretched palm. I search for the photo on my own app. It's within a group of other zoo photos: Axel on the endangered animals carousel. Axel eating a bear-shaped popsicle. Axel standing near the flamingo enclosure. Elizabeth and Axel with their faces pressed close together, giraffes in the background.

I hit the back button to return to the collage of photos on her profile. It's a riot of color, nothing like the curated beiges and creams everyone else swears by. One of them catches my eye, and I click on it.

Elizabeth and Axel are standing in front of a colorful mural. They're both sticking out their tongues at whoever is holding the camera, heaped scoops of ice cream already dripping down the sides of their waffle cones.

Another one shows them in a theater with the caption, *Took the little guy out for his first Nutcracker performance! I have the best clients EVER!!*

There's a photo of Axel in an art gallery, shaking the hand of the man next to him. *I've admired Giovani de Luca for SO LONG and tonight Axel and I got to meet him!*

They've visited every museum in the city from the looks of these photos. They even went to the Historical Society. *He may not be able to read yet, but he already understands the importance of history!*

Hiking through the woods and up the mountainside, going slower than paperwork in a bureaucracy so that Axel can get his science education at the same time. Buying a pet goldfish in a bag, a giant grin on Axel's face. Cooking dinner together in matching aprons. Curled up in a blanket fort watching a movie.

Between these images are sprinkled professional ones too. Elizabeth Gable deems every moment worthy of a photo.

*The Castor family was so much fun to work with!*

*Late nights are worth it when you have the best team!*

*I just listed FOUR new homes this week! You do NOT want to miss them!!*

*When your co-workers decide to use their half-birthday as an excuse to bring cupcakes to work.* This caption accompanies a photo of Elizabeth holding a cupcake close to her face and pouting.

Between the professional-not-professional garbage and the adorably-too-adorable photos of her and Axel, there are also a bunch of health-focused posts. She apparently sells products in one of those network marketing things I've never understood nor cared to.

*I cannot believe how much better my skin feels since incorporating this smoothie into my day!*

*20% off sale on all of our products! Message me for details!!*

*You guys, this is the absolute best superfood blend on the market! If you are not already taking it, WHAT ARE YOU WAITING FOR?!*

"Find anything juicy?" Bea asks, startling me out of my trance as I watch Axel attempt to dance to something on the television, Elizabeth's giggles audible in the background as she tries to hold the phone steady.

"Huh?" I look up at her.

"Did you find anything we can use? You know, against Elizabeth?"

I glance at my screen once more, then lock it and toss the device onto the coffee table. "She uses more exclamation points than should be legal."

"Not exactly a crime," Bea says. "How about something useful?"

I think back over the photos I just spent the past hour looking at. "She's sickeningly perfect. She's so perfect my teeth are still aching."

"That's the cookie dough."

"I was hoping for cleavage and trashy clubs. Maybe an attempted bank heist or drug smuggling."

Bea's brows peak in the center of her forehead. "Pretty sure sane people don't post those things online."

"Did you find anything?" I ask.

"I did some digging, but I'm afraid it's not going to be what you want to hear."

"Terrific." I scoop another ball of dough. "Let me fortify myself first."

"She's a pretty open book on social media. That can be a bad thing, depending on what you're putting out there, but she does it in a genuine way that attracts people to her."

Of course she does.

"Did you see her follower count?"

I shake my head.

"Ten *thousand*," she says.

"So? I have like ten million or something."

Bea laughs. "You're the bloody queen. She's a nobody. Just a regular person who went viral and is quickly reaching influencer level."

"I have no idea what you just said."

"My point is that she's popular. Whatever she's doing is working."

I squint at her. "What is she doing?"

Bea pulls a comical face. "Being herself."

I let this sink in. I may have a thousand times more followers than her, but mine follow me because of my position. Hers follow her because of . . . her.

"Please tell me you found more than the fact that she's well-liked." If I can't find dirt on this woman, I don't know what I'm going to do.

"Her day job is in real estate, so I did a little snooping into the brokerage she works for. Their website shows that she's been their top-selling agent for the past two years."

"Okay. And?" I say. "If the brokerage is small, she can't make much."

"Except that this particular brokerage is known to handle some of Wesbourne's most prestigious clients."

"Meaning?"

"Meaning if Elizabeth is outselling her colleagues, and their deals are as high-dollar as they sound, she is bringing home some serious cash."

My brow puckers. That can't be right. "She's raising her son on her own. That can't be cheap. Besides, she probably has a lot of loans to pay off from university."

Bea bites her lip. "There's more. I also looked into that wellness company she sells for. She mentioned her rank in a recent post. According to the pay chart I found, she's making around five figures a *month* from those commissions alone."

"You've got to be kidding me." My head feels abnormally empty, as though my thoughts all saw the direction this conversation was headed in and decided to flee.

"I think it's safe to say this girl is not after money."

"Maybe she wants fame?"

Bea waves her phone in my face. "She doesn't need it, Celia. And I'm pretty sure she doesn't want it. From what I've read, she is as genuine and kind as they come. In fact, she's kind of repulsive with that wholesome, down-to-earth vibe. She's probably never even pirated a movie."

I squeeze my eyes shut and pinch the corners of them. There has to be another way.

"I can't let her steal Henry." I say it quietly, afraid that by giving voice to it, I'm admitting to the possibility.

"That's what you're worried about?" Bea says. "Henry is as much yours as he's ever been."

"I can't give him what he wants."

"You mean a baby? You just have to give it more time." She rubs her hand over my arm.

I shake my head. "The kind of mum she is. The kind of mum you'll be. I'm not—" I swallow and start again. "I'm not wired like that."

"Of course you are. How can you say that?"

"Have you seen me with kids?"

"Not very often—"

"Exactly."

"That doesn't mean anything," she says. "I've had even less experience than you, and I think I'll be a knockout mum."

I turn to face her. "You sure you don't want to consider the adoption route? I could go with you, take some time off, and—"

"Celia." She takes both of my hands in hers. "I want this more than I've ever wanted anything. I feel alive for the first time in my life. When I'm not puking out my guts, that is."

"I don't want you to get hurt," I say. *Or sabotage our family's reputation.*

"If I do, it will be worth it." She smiles, and there's so much joy in her eyes, so much lightness in her face. Maybe there's something to this motherhood thing that both she and Elizabeth have discovered.

I brush the thought aside and squeeze her hands in agreement. "I should go so you can rest."

"I'm sorry we couldn't find anything more helpful," she says once we're standing at the door.

I lift my chin. "I'm not giving up. There has to be something I can use to stop this woman from whatever devious plan she's enacted."

"You could always hire a private investigator to tail her like they do in the movies." Bea waggles her eyebrows at me.

"That's a brilliant plan," I say. Light bulbs are already flashing in my head. I should have thought of it sooner. "I'll bet Preston knows someone."

I call him on my way down the corridor, cookie dough tucked under my arm. His family has a list of political connections longer than the receiving line at my coronation. There must be a way for him to pull a few strings and hire someone quietly.

When he answers, I explain my request and the reason behind it.

"No problem," he says, as though I've just asked him to mail a letter for me. "My dad has a whole list of them."

"I don't even want to know why."

Preston laughs, a low chuckle that tickles my ear through the phone. "You mean not everyone keeps a section of their Rolodex devoted to PIs?"

"Only the sketchy ones."

"Well, in this case, I'm glad I can help out."

I thank him. "And Preston? I know it goes without saying that this is to be kept—"

"—in the strictest confidence. As always, my dear."

"Thank you. You're a gem."

"Anything for you."

# 16

# "Castles Crumbling" - Taylor Swift ft. Hayley Williams

"WE HAVE A PROBLEM," Preston says, entering my office without preamble. It's just after nine, and Maisie and I are in the middle of our morning debriefing.

I shoot him a look. "You know I hate that phrase."

"Fine. A *situation*." He stops in front of my desk. "One that's escalating quickly."

I glance at Maisie, but she looks as confused as I feel. "What is it?"

"Elizabeth Gable's name was leaked to the media. They just ran the story on the news," he says.

"How in the world did they get that?" I ask him, sitting up straighter in my chair. He's right. This is a problem.

"Who knows? My guess is the journalist who reported her story initially gave it up. What matters is how we handle this."

I drum my fingers on the desktop. "I assumed the way we always do: without comment."

Preston tucks his hands behind his back as he paces, looking like one of those barristers in old movies. "I think we should reconsider this time."

A frown pulls at my face. "I thought you said that once we take that step, it will be impossible to come back."

Maisie has taken a seat across the room, tablet on her lap and fingers scurrying over the keyboard. When I catch her eye, she mouths, *Do you want me to leave?* I shake my head.

"It's true that our usual method of approaching these kinds of stories is to say nothing," Preston continues. "But this situation is different."

"How so?" I ask.

He shoots me a look, then quickly returns his eyes to the floor in front of him. "For starters, it's true, isn't it?"

God, will everyone stop fixating on that? "How is that relevant?"

He coughs abruptly into his hand. "When the public finds out it's true and that we did nothing . . ."

He doesn't need to finish that sentence. We all remember what happened three years ago when the Crown refused to acknowledge the evidence pointing to the wrong bloodline being on the throne.

"And you're suggesting what?"

"Nothing but a simple press statement," he says. "A chance to tell our side of the story."

"Which is?"

"That we have spoken to Elizabeth Gable and are negotiating privately with her."

My left eyebrow inches higher than my right. "And you think that will appease them?"

"I'm counting on it."

"Okay." I nod. "Let's do it."

The problem with avoiding press statements is that when you actually give one, the pressure to get it perfect is amplified.

"Make sure you wear something that conveys the level of confidence and approachability we're going for," Preston says.

"I'll let my stylist handle that," I tell him.

We're still sequestered in my office, where we've been for the past three hours, and where it appears we'll be for the rest of the night if we don't get this nailed soon. Fortunately, the kitchen has been keeping us supplied with food.

"Are you sure you don't just want me to write this speech for you?" he asks after I pour my third cup of coffee. "You're dragging."

"I can handle it." I slump into the chair beside him, hoping the move away from my desk will help get the brainstorming juices flowing. "Where were we? Still trying to decide if we should use her name or not?"

"I think it clears up a lot of miscommunication that could arise if you just say it. It keeps the power fully in our court," Preston says.

"But aren't we submitting to her power by admitting that she's important enough for us to add her name to our official statements?"

"Not necessarily." He rubs his eyes with his thumb and forefinger. "We're showing that we're not threatened by her. Hiding her name sends the message that we're not ready to be open and upfront about the situation."

I let out a deep sigh that sucks me deeper into the clutches of fatigue. "Fine. Let's add it."

He jots a note on the pad he's holding. "We should also address—"

The door opens, and Henry sticks his head inside. His brows furrow when he takes in Preston and me sitting in the armchairs near the window. "What are you doing?" he asks.

"Working on a speech," I say, before turning back to Preston. I don't have time for Henry's theatrics tonight, not if I want to sleep before morning. "You were saying?"

The door clicks shut behind us, but instead of disappearing, I feel the weight of Henry's presence behind me.

Preston looks over his shoulder at Henry, then back at the notes in his lap. "I, uh, I was saying . . ."

I shoot a glare at my husband. "We're in the middle of something. Can it wait?"

He places his hands on the back of my chair and leans forward. I get a whiff of his piney scent, and my pulse jumps. "Maybe I can help," he says.

There's no use pointing out that he will only be a hindrance. He's already fully aware. I look at Preston. "Maybe we can finish it in the morning? It is getting pretty late."

"Good idea," he says, throwing one more glance in Henry's direction. "I'll see myself out."

After the door closes behind him, I stand and whirl on Henry. "What the hell are you doing? We were nearly done."

Hands still on the chair, he leans in. "I could ask you the same thing. It's almost midnight, C."

My eyes widen as I grab my phone. There's no way we were working on this for that long. But the clock confirms it's 11:38. Damn it. "I had no idea it was so late."

"If you would check your phone every once in a while, you would've. You would also have seen that I texted you three hours ago."

I look back down at the screen, and sure enough, I have several unread messages.

> **Henry**: Wanna watch something?

> **Henry**: I'll even watch Bridgerton with you.

> **Henry**: I promise not to complain. Very much.

I look back up to meet his eyes. "I'm sorry," I say. "I had no idea."

"Yeah, you looked pretty busy." His tone has a level of steel in it that sends off alarm bells in my head.

"We were working on a speech—"

"Always a good cover story."

"Are you implying that we were doing something besides writing a speech?" My eyes burn from holding them open and from the tears that are threatening to fall.

"Are you implying that you weren't?"

"Of course we weren't," I snap.

Henry's knuckles turn white on the back of the chair. "I'm sure it wasn't from lack of desire on his part. The question is, how do you feel?"

I shake my head in disgust and move to the desk to gather my things.

"You know he has feelings for you," he says, angling his body toward me.

Regardless of whether Preston does or does not feel something other than professional respect for me, he has not once acted on it. Which makes him a gentleman, and one I desperately need on my team.

I stick my planner into my handbag, then look up as something occurs to me. "Wait. Are you . . . jealous?" The idea is so outlandish I'm not positive it's not just the result of fatigue.

Henry's face flushes, and he crosses the room, keeping my desk between us. "Of course I'm fucking jealous. If he ever tries to make a move on you, so help me—"

"We were coming up with a way to address your secret love child, and you're upset that I was with Preston instead of with you?" I see his fists are balled up at his sides.

"I'm upset that he was keeping you up this late when you should be in bed," Henry says. It comes out as nothing short of a growl.

I can't help myself. "How do you know I wasn't the one keeping him up?" I zip my bag closed and sling it over my shoulder.

His glare is enough to melt the statue of David. Or my panties.

My press statement went the way we hoped and prepared for. I delivered the message in clear, concise sentences that proved we are not only willing to discuss the matter, but have already started to do so.

I answered two questions that Preston had prepared me for ahead of time, and then Davies whisked me back into the sanctuary of the palace. The whole thing was over in less than five minutes.

Regardless, those were five of the tensest minutes of my life.

Which is why I'm currently sitting on the edge of the sofa in our living room, watching both the clock and the television, waiting for the nightly news to come on. Tundra rests his head on my knee, and I stroke it as I wait. When the theme music starts playing, Henry walks in and sits beside me wordlessly. He props his arm behind me, and the warm weight of him flows into my shoulders.

The news anchor comes on, and after a few mentions of events going on around the world—another hurricane hit Haiti earlier this week, the strikes in Paris have been going on for two months—the screen changes, and the footage from the press conference begins playing.

They air the entire thing from start to finish. About thirty seconds into it, Henry's hand begins caressing my back, slowly rubbing up and down my spine. "You did great," he says.

I look a little stiff, wearing a mint-green power suit and reading from the notes in my hand, but my voice is strong throughout. I keep my chin up while offering a small smile to the reporters that swarm around me.

I turn just enough to give Henry a grateful smile before facing the TV again. The video clip ends and is replaced by the news anchor.

"Developments in this story continue to become more interesting," he says. "Not only did we receive a press statement from the royal family today, but our team was also able to secure an interview with Miss Gable herself. Here she is now."

I swing my eyes back to Henry. Did he know about this? He looks frozen in confusion.

They are now showing a video taken in downtown Wesbourne. I recognize the street the Historical Society is located on. Elizabeth's disgustingly perfect face fills half the screen, mic shoved in front of her, wind blowing strands of her hair like it's been orchestrated by a modeling producer.

"Tell us, Miss Gable," the off-screen reporter says, "is it true that you met with Queen Celia and Prince Henry?"

"It is." Her voice is as musical as ever, like high, clear notes on a freshly-tuned piano.

"And what did they have to say? Did they agree to your terms?"

She chuckles nervously and attempts to tame her hair. "They were wonderful. I didn't come with any terms. I just want Axel to know his father."

"How does Prince Henry feel, knowing he has a son?"

Henry is no longer reclining against the back of the sofa but leaning forward, elbows on his knees. Even Tundra sits up and stares at the screen.

Elizabeth manages to look both flustered and composed at the same time. "I think he's in shock, mostly. We haven't talked about it much yet."

"Can you tell us more about your relationship with the prince?" the reporter says.

A single, surprised laugh falls out of her mouth. "I believe that information belongs to me and Prince Henry only." Henry relaxes with relief beside me. "But the only relationship we have with each other now is as it pertains to Axel."

"How does your son feel knowing his father is the prince consort of Wesbourne?"

The interview continues, but I block the rest of it out. I've seen enough to establish several things in my mind.

First, left alone, my press statement would have been fine. But paired with Elizabeth's interview, I come off as cold, unfeeling, and buttoned-up. She *glowed* for the camera.

Second, between her musical laughs and that enchanting smile, she has charmed the socks right off the entire population of Wesbourne—I'm sure of it.

Third, gauging by the look on Henry's face as he sits mesmerized by her on the screen, I'm going to need to find a way to imbue myself with some of that same warmth, or I will lose him forever.

# 17

# "Royalty" - Egzod + Maestro Chives

**"Y**OU'RE SURE THIS IS going to work?" I say.

"I'm sure," Preston says from beside me in the car. "The info went out last night."

"And you're sure it won't look like an intentional leak? Because if they find out the palace—"

"Relax, Celia. It will work."

My eyes drift down to the hand he's just placed on my leg. The knot of unease in my stomach increases. "Okay," I say quietly.

He continues staring out the window. "The press tends to be too busy scooping the story to question where the scoop came from. But just in case, I covered our tracks."

After the catastrophe that was my air time on the news a few nights ago, made so by Elizabeth Gable's flawless interview that followed, Preston decided that we needed to remind people of just how much they adore their queen. Most of the engagements I attend are private, allowing those I'm meeting with my full attention, and they are easier to maintain from a security perspective. But that doesn't mean the public isn't hungry for a secret spotting of the queen herself.

That is what Preston is counting on. By leaking the details of my engagements today, he hopes to draw at least a few members of the press to the events, where they will be able to get prime footage of the queen at her best, serving water to invalids in the hospital and molding things out of clay with children.

"You've got this," he says, increasing the pressure of his hand on my leg before releasing it. "You're the queen of Wesbourne. Is there anything you can't handle?" A lopsided, boyish smile lifts one side of his mouth.

A hysterical chuckle trips past my teeth. Does he want me to start a list?

Davies shifts in the seat in front of us in the limo. There's a flash of annoyance on his face as he looks at Preston, but he masks it quickly. "We'll need to delay our exit just a bit longer, ma'am," he says. "We need more time to secure the grounds."

He doesn't need to explain. I finish the sentence for him in my head. *Since we're expecting company.*

Davies balked at Preston's plan when he was informed of it this morning, but by then it was too late. He hides his disdain for the press secretary better than Henry does, but I recognize the tension in the set of his shoulders.

Despite their less-than-eager acceptance of our press secretary, without him, the entire royal family's reputation would be in shambles, and Wesbourne would no longer have a monarchy.

I nod and offer Davies a small smile. He remains stoic for a few more seconds, but his facade slowly crumbles, and he gives me a minuscule smile in return. No one's going to accuse him of being a teddy bear, but neither are they going to accuse him of ever dropping the ball on duty.

The car slows, and we pull up to the back entrance of Billings Memorial Hospital. Davies shoots me another look, which I know is his reminder to stay in the car. He doesn't bother with Preston. He'd probably welcome a bullet in the back of my press secretary's unsuspecting head.

Preston scrolls on his iPad. "Anything you want to go over before we do this?"

"I think I'm all set." I take a deep breath and smooth down my skirt. When I told Renaldo that I needed something soft and feminine for today, he pulled out a teal midi dress with loose lines and a small floral print.

He was right. It's perfect. It's the exact thing someone like Elizabeth Gable would wear.

The public needs to be reminded that I can also be warm and nurturing. In spite of how in control I feel in a suit, they don't do me any favors in that department.

I steel myself as we approach the back door. This has gotten easier with time, but it has yet to be something I can do without holding my breath and shielding myself from the memories.

I glance at Davies. As though he's attuned to even the movement of my eyes, his own jerk sideways to meet mine. I don't have to ask if he remembers our little adventure to the hospital three years ago. That was one of the stupidest decisions I've ever made, and one that cost him his job.

"It's not too late to turn around," he says without moving his lips.

I lift my chin. "They're expecting me."

The doors open, and we step into the aggressively air-conditioned room. The security team leads us down corridors lined with supply closets and offices. Even those smell like antiseptic. I remind myself to breathe through my mouth.

The staff has given us the service lift for our private use today, and we take it to the top. The plan is to work our way down, stopping on each floor to greet one or two patients and to give the press plenty of time to find us.

Preston has done the recon work of figuring out which patients afford the best opportunity for a visit that may or may not coincide with press coverage. I admit to feeling a little queasy about the way we're turning something that should be a kind gesture into nothing short of a political move, but I also can't deny that Preston's plans have had a 95 percent success rate so far. The man is brilliant, and he understands politics and swinging public opinion in our favor.

The press office gave each selected patient notice that they would be receiving a special visitor and warned them they might be caught on camera.

Preston taps away at the map on his screen. "Room 1086," he says.

After the room is swept by the security team, Davies leads me inside. I tug at the rubber gloves I've been issued, making sure the bands are securely in place around my wrists. The least I can do is keep from making these patients any sicker.

There's a young woman in the bed at the center of the room. She has lovely thick auburn hair that frames an even lovelier face. Neither of those is as radiant as her smile, though. Her entire being shines with it, like it's a crack in the sidewalk, letting in light to help everything in its path grow.

"Hello," I say. "You must be Samantha." I return her smile, but there's no way mine has even half the wattage hers does.

"Your Majesty." Her voice is a little throaty and breathless, as though she just raced down the halls to reach her room before I did. "It is such an honor to meet you."

"The honor is all mine." The words slip out by instinct after all this time.

"If you say so," she says with a laugh that's just as throaty as her voice. "I had to ask Harry Styles to wait until tomorrow to visit."

Her unexpected humor is exactly what I need to help me relax. My eyes travel around the room. It's like being inside a flower garden. There are bouquets on nearly every surface, and the walls are papered with incredible drawings of summer blooms. The curtains on the window overlooking the city are thrown open as wide as they'll go.

Even the balloons floating above a few of the bouquets don't bother me. They're not the sad *Get Well Soon* ones the gift shop specializes in but invigorating reminders to *Rock On!* and *Slay 'Em, Bae!*

I turn back to Samantha, who is still bestowing that heart-stopping grin on me. She's covered in a fleece tie-dye blanket rather than the standard hospital-issue sheet.

I gesture to the room. "It's so colorful in here."

"I adore color, so my friends made sure I had some." She inclines her head toward the wall opposite her bed. "My friend Emilia painted that one."

I turn to admire the painting she pointed out, giving it the requisite oohs and aahs it deserves, all while wondering what Samantha is doing here. She appears perfectly healthy. Her skin has a peachy glow that makes her look like she just came back from the coast. Her hair didn't get that lustrous on its own, and she's even wearing makeup.

I'm asking myself if it's possible that Preston planted her here for optimal optics and simultaneously telling my stomach to calm down when she says, "Do you like flowers?"

I startle out of my concentration. "I do," I say. "Hydrangeas in particular."

"My favorites are chocolate cosmos. They're hard to grow, but if I could, I'd plant a giant patch of them outside my bedroom window. They smell just like chocolate." She closes her eyes for a moment, as though she's remembering the scent of them, and then her eyes flutter open and she laughs. "Well, I'd have someone else plant them. Don't think I'll be kneeling in the soil again."

My brows tug together in the center of my forehead. I remind them to relax. "Can I ask why you're here? You don't seem . . ."

"Sick?" she says. "Technically, I'm not. But they're still monitoring my spine. The doctors thought there was some activity a few days ago, but it looks like it was a fluke." Her smile isn't as large as before, but it's still brighter than most people's.

"What are they monitoring it for?" I ask.

She blinks at me like she's unsure what I'm asking. "To see if there's a chance of correcting it?"

I tilt my head to the side. I want to follow what she's saying, but I am completely in the dark here. "Did you injure it?"

"I broke it in a car accident. I'm paralyzed from the neck down."

Davies's steadying arm remains solid behind me as I take an instinctive step backward.

"Oh, fudgesicles," Samantha says. "You didn't know. I didn't mean to startle you. I'm so sorry." She directs the last sentence to Davies, who is still offering support around my waist. "I just assumed they told you."

I shake my head. "But you're so . . ."

"Normal-looking?" She laughs. "Fate decided to steal my movements and leave my face." She tilts her head to the side, and I imagine her hands coming up to meet her chin like she's posing, but they'll never do that again.

"Happy," I say.

"Oh." There's a beat that I think she would fill with a shrug if her shoulders were able to move. "I try to be. Some days are harder than others."

How is every day not a living hell, I want to ask. "How do you do it?" I say instead.

"My response to life is the only thing I can control." She says it like it's an obvious thing, understanding what is and isn't within your control.

"What happened?" I say quietly, not trusting my voice.

"My boyfriend got distracted while driving. We were fighting over the radio dial. He ran off the side of the road, and the car rolled down the incline. The passenger side took the brunt of the impact." She tells it like she's rattling off events for her history teacher. "I'm fortunate it was only my spine that broke."

Fortunate? God, is she delusional?

"I don't know how you do it," I say meekly. I've had nothing like the struggles she has, yet my happiness looks as fake as a smiley-face bumper sticker next to hers.

"I still have so much to be grateful for. Focusing on that and not on my problems helps a lot."

I shake my head and the thoughts in it, trying to get them to fall into a place that makes sense.

Preston nudges my elbow from behind. "We need to be moving to the next room," he says under his breath.

I step toward Samantha's bed and place my hand on the blanket next to her. "You are an inspiration." I reach to wipe at the tear dangling from my eyelashes before remembering I'm wearing rubber gloves.

"Thank you for coming." Her smile beams into the center of my soul. "This made my year."

As we leave the room, Preston whispers, "Hold on to that tear. The press is waiting for us outside."

I school my features into as much casualness as I can and follow him into the hall, Davies at my side. "See to it that someone interviews that dear girl," I say. "Her story needs to be nationally broadcast."

As promised, there are several reporters lining the corridor of the hospital when we step out of Samantha's room. Cameras are already running. We duck into the next patient's room like we're trying to escape, but all I can think is that I hope all this effort is worth it. Even if it's not, I will never forget the girl in room 1086.

Drayton Center for Young Learning is a primary school located in the Junction, a neighborhood of Wesbourne City known for its gang violence and crime. The brick front of the building looks tired and depressed, as if it's seen more than its fair share of life. The concrete steps leading to the doors are cracked, weeds sprouting through them. A large oak tree sits in the front yard, shading a good portion of the school from the afternoon sun.

Preston prepped me for this visit on the way over. Most of the information was unnecessary, but we're trying to avoid what happened in Samantha's room. It doesn't look good when the monarch doesn't know anything about the people she's meeting.

We've arranged to visit several of the classrooms. There won't be time for all of them, but Preston agreed to an assembly with all of the children in the gymnasium so they can at least get a chance to see me and wave before we need to leave.

Davies seems on high alert as we enter the school. With unemployment and crime high in this section of town, the boredom and depression can lead to devastating consequences. He didn't want me to come here, but Preston insisted it was important for my image.

As expected, the press has followed us here, although I doubt they'll be allowed inside. Two security guards inspect our bags when we enter. The click of cameras penetrates the glass of the front doors.

There is a cluster of faculty waiting for us inside. They bump each other as politely as possible, all wanting to be the one to "fetch you some water, ma'am" and "if you need anything, please let us know." I greet them and shake their hands before Preston says we need to move on to the children if we're to keep to our schedule.

The headmaster leads us down the corridor. It smells of mildew and chalk. The floors are bumpy, and the tile is cracked in multiple places. I'm surprised the city hasn't deemed it unsafe for kids. If someone were to trip and go down on this tile, the bruises would be significant.

I'm scheduled to visit Mrs. Humphrey's first-grade class first. The headmaster pops his head in to let them know I've arrived. When we step inside, the students are deathly quiet for a group of six-year-olds. Every child has stopped what they are doing to stare, around thirty sets of eyes glued to me from each corner of the classroom.

A little girl holding a giant collection of plastic dinosaurs in her arms is the first to move. She walks up to me, stops right before she treads on my toes, and says, "Are you the queen?"

I laugh and crouch down in front of her. "I am. Pleased to meet you." I'd offer to shake her hand, but hers are a little preoccupied at the moment.

"I'm so sorry." A woman in her early fifties approaches and both bows and curtsies. "I meant to have them all lined up and teach them to bow but"—she waves her arms around her in a circle—"it's like corralling circus cats around here. I'm Mrs. Humphrey."

We shake hands, then she allows a few of them to ask me questions. After I tell them that no, I don't know Santa Claus, no, I've never ridden a dragon, and yes, I have a real crown, Mrs. Humphrey has them all sit down while she passes out coloring pages.

Their tiny plastic chairs look older than the ones I remember using in primary school. The children settle into them like a hungry mob, grabbing crayons and markers from the baskets in the middle of their tables.

I use my hand to fan my face. The air is practically stifling in here. The extra body heat we brought with us doesn't help.

"I'm so sorry. The air conditioner's broken." Mrs. Humphrey gestures to the unit in the window. "They were meant to fix it last summer but . . . well, you can see they didn't." Her laugh is tinged with resignation.

"The school doesn't have a central unit?" I ask. Preston and Davies must be sweltering in their jackets as they stand against the wall.

"Oh, no. The building's too old for that, and it would cost too much to put one in." She scoots around the table to break up a fight between two girls who both want the same pink crayon.

I move over to where the men are waiting. "Please make a note," I say to Preston. "There has to be something we can do to help."

He nods his agreement.

Mrs. Humphrey smiles at me from across the room as I move to rejoin her. "What would you say the biggest needs here at Drayton are?" I ask.

She bites her bottom lip and scans the room. The compassion in her eyes leaks out and touches every single child she looks at. "Right now I would say funding for our food programs."

"Food programs?"

"For children who don't get enough to eat at home. We provide breakfast here at school and stick a few things in their bags for dinner."

I blink, searching for appropriate words. "That's incredibly sad. How is it currently being provided if the funds aren't there?"

She gives me an embarrassed smile. "The teachers have been pooling their money together to help the neediest ones. It's not much, but we can't send them home with empty tummies."

A crack like the ones in the concrete steps out front splinters across my heart. One thing is certain: I may have come here with the intention of boosting my own reputation, but I will not leave without doing everything in my power to help these children.

"That's noble of you," I say. Of course I can't promise her anything because we have to keep the giving anonymous. If we didn't, we'd be completely inundated with requests. But that doesn't mean I'm going to turn a blind eye to the needs here.

The kids in front of us are scribbling away, big, bold streaks of every color of the rainbow splashed across their pages.

"I guess they haven't had the lesson on staying inside the lines yet," I say with a light chuckle.

Mrs. Humphrey beams over the head of the little boy in front of her. "That lesson isn't in the curriculum. We don't believe in controlling their creativity."

I look for the joke on her face, but it holds nothing but sincerity. "Then how do they learn to become artists?"

"Oh." She laughs, a deep, husky one this time. "We don't need to worry about that. Let me show you something."

She leads me over to the windows along the back wall. "There." She points outside. I stoop to look beneath the half-pulled blinds.

The school is a square-shaped brick compound. In the center is a large playground, similar to the quadrangle at the palace. On all four walls surrounding it is the biggest mural I've ever seen. It spans the entire perimeter of the quad and reaches to the top of the first-floor classrooms. The pictures are detailed and clearly drawn by multiple artists. There are wild animals, people of every size and race, mountains, lakes, and other images too small for me to make out.

"It's amazing," I say. "Who painted it?"

Mrs. Humphrey looks back at her students, still hunched over their drawings at the table. "Students from the upper years. Many of them sat at these very tables and colored to their heart's content. Every year, several of them add more to it."

I can't stop staring out the window at the wild and beautiful art in front of me. "It's so . . . *good*."

"It always turns out more beautiful when we let them go."

When I retire to our suite that evening, I want to tell Henry about Samantha and the Drayton school. We used to share things like that with each other all the time, but I can't remember when I last talked to him about something I was passionate about.

He's sitting in the living room when I come in. The television is turned to the news, and he doesn't look up when I walk over to the sofa. "Hi," I say softly.

"Hey."

I look around for the evidence of whatever crime I've committed this time. When it becomes apparent that he isn't planning to say anything else, I change course and head for the bedroom. Looks like tonight won't be the night things change after all.

"It's a good thing you never planned to be an actress," he says right as I reach the door.

I turn back to face the living room, but he's still focused on the television. "Excuse me?"

"Your acting sucks."

"What acting?"

"I'm watching the news. You can probably figure it out."

"And you think what? It was all a big act?" I shouldn't let him swing my emotions like this.

"I think you and Preston cooked up a big plan to make sure you were caught on camera."

When I don't respond, he turns to look at me over the back of the sofa. "Am I right?"

"I'm not having this conversation with you." I open the door to our bedroom, the one I fully intend to have to myself tonight, but his voice filters in before I can shut it.

"You may have fooled them, but I know what surprise looks like on your face."

# 18

# "Rise" - Katy Perry

I SPENT LAST NIGHT tossing and turning. Sleep was a mix of hyper-realistic dreams and that liminal state it's hard to wake from. Bea had had her baby, and she kept saying things like "Isn't she beautiful?" But when I looked at the tiny bundle in her arms, all I could see was Axel's face. Henry's face.

I knock on my sister's suite before heading to my office. I can't let this go without trying once more to change her mind. She's too young to be a mother, especially a single one.

Her lady's maid, Christa, opens the door, stepping aside so I can come in.

"Who is it?" Bea calls.

"Just me, but I can come back later," I say. It's not like I can risk the staff overhearing this particular conversation.

"You're fine. Come in."

When I enter, she's sitting at her dressing table, a large and ornate piece from King William I's reign. The dark wood gleams against the mauve walls. She meets my eyes in the mirror as Christa resumes her position behind her, curling Bea's glossy strands into loose waves.

"To what do I owe the honor?" Bea says, toying with a fat makeup brush.

"I was just"—my eyes shoot to Christa—"checking up on you. It's been forever since we've talked."

Bea cocks a brow in the mirror. "You were just here last week. You interrupted my nap, remember?"

"There was that one thing you were dealing with, and I wasn't sure how—"

"For god's sake, Celia. She already knows."

"Knows what?"

Bea rolls her eyes and turns on her stool, tugging her hair from Christa's hands. The maid gasps and fumbles to keep hold of the curling iron without singeing Bea's curls off.

"Christa," Bea says. "She knows I'm pregnant, so you can stop tiptoeing around like the palace will explode if a single soul finds out."

My eyes flicker to Christa, who, to her credit, appears completely immersed in salvaging Bea's hair and oblivious to our conversation. I'm not stupid, however.

"Can we talk somewhere . . . privately?" I say.

Bea whirls back around to face the mirror, sending Christa into yet another tailspin. "This *is* private. And I already told you, Christa knows I'm pregnant. Who do you think bought the test for me?"

I don't miss the way Christa's eyes flit to mine, then immediately back to her work.

"Bea, are you sure that's wise? No offense, Christa, but if you're telling staff members, Bea—"

"Everyone's going to find out eventually," she says.

"They don't need to," I tell her.

"Why are you so determined to hide this?" She tosses the makeup brush onto the table, where it lands with a loud clatter.

"I'm trying to protect you."

"I don't need protection. Babies are wonderful things." Is she aware of the way her hand floats to her stomach? A few gestures like that in public, and this whole thing blows up in our faces. "Miracles."

I step closer to the dressing table and rest my hand on Bea's shoulder, careful to stay out of Christa's way. "I know that. But think about what you'll be giving up if you go through with this."

"Parties. Drinking. *Work*." She rolls her eyes again. "I don't like those things anyway."

"*Men*," I add, raising my brows.

She shrugs my hand away. "I'm tired of them too. Besides, the right guy will love me *and* my baby."

"Then think about what this will do to our family's image."

A harsh sound flies from her mouth. I think it's meant to be a laugh, but it sounds more like a cackle. "You mean *your* image."

"All of ours," I say. "What one of us does affects the others."

Bea smiles so sweetly in the mirror, it hurts my teeth to look at. "Then your good deeds can make up for the rest of our naughty behaviors."

It's getting harder to breathe. There's a tightness in my chest that wasn't there when I came in. I need to get out of here, to get back to a place where I'm still holding the reins on what now feels like a team of wild horses, stampeding toward the edge of a cliff.

Just before I turn on my heel and march toward the door, I remember that I hold a trump card of sorts. I take a deep breath, keeping my eyes trained on Bea's face in the mirror.

"Does Mum know?"

My sister visibly jolts, her eyes flying up to meet mine. We stayed locked there for several seconds, then she drops her gaze back to the earrings she's scooting around the table. "I'm planning to tell her," she says, her voice as quiet as the strokes of the brush Christa is dragging through her hair.

"And how do you think she'll take the news?"

It's no secret that Rosalind is not only traditional in her views, but as old-fashioned as they come. I have yet to convince her that "Alexa" is simply the voice activation prompt for our smart devices and not the name of a woman on the other end listening to all of her conversations.

"I think she'll be excited about a grandchild." Bea lifts her chin.

It's a farce, and we both know it. The only grandchild our mum will be excited about is the one who will someday be sitting on the throne of Wesbourne.

Before I can reply, my phone rings from inside my bag. I fish it out and check the screen. It's Preston. I glance at Bea once more, but she is adamantly ignoring my gaze. I move toward the door. "I need to take this. But we are not done talking about this."

"Or we could be," she says.

I click to accept the call and close the suite door behind me.

"Good morning," Preston says. "Sleep well?"

"I did, thank you. What's going on?" He never calls me unless it's a serious. "Please don't tell me they did another story on Elizabeth."

He chuckles. "No, nothing like that. The coverage from the other day was splendid, though. The press is raving about you."

"That's good to hear." Maybe it will help buffer the news of Bea's pregnancy.

"I'm calling to relay a message from the private investigator you asked me to hire."

My eyes dart up and down the corridor to make sure no one is around. "Shh!" I hiss. "I hope you're alone."

"Relax," he says in an amused tone. "I'm alone. Are you?"

I scan the corridor once more. "For now. What is the message?"

"One sec." Papers rustle on the other end. "He wants to know how far you're willing to go for information."

I pause. Is it like a sliding scale, or . . . ? "What are my options?"

"He didn't give options per se."

"I'm not willing to kill someone, if that's what he means."

A hoot of laughter erupts, and I hold the phone away from my ear. "He's a PI, not a mob boss, Celia. He's not going to threaten anyone with murder."

"I don't know how these things work," I say in a loud whisper.

"He said he's struggling to find anything on Ms. Gable. He wants to know if you're okay with him approaching the little boy."

"Axel? Why would he do that?"

"Probably to see if he can get the kid to confess to something."

"He's three years old," I say. "It's not like he's out committing crimes."

"No," Preston says slowly, "but he might be able to tell us if he has a daddy somewhere. One who *doesn't* reside at the palace."

"Right. Okay." My head is spinning. It does make sense to talk to Axel, if he'll ever take that thumb out of his mouth long enough to say anything. "I don't know how he'll get the chance to talk to him alone. Elizabeth's pretty protective."

"That's what we're paying him to figure out. He'll find a way, don't worry."

"Okay," I say quietly.

I take a deep breath. The ethics of this are questionable at best, but I need to know what her end game is and find a way to stop her. If cornering her son is the only way to do that, then I don't have another choice.

"Tell him to go ahead," I say.

I'm sticking my things back into my handbag at the end of the day when the door to my office flies open. I suppose I shouldn't be surprised to find my husband standing there—after all, he's the only one with the propensity for flinging doors open like he's God Himself.

"Hello to you too." I slide my phone into an exterior pocket. I cannot wait to take a long, hot shower and fall into bed. This day has been a rollercoaster I can't wait to disembark from.

Henry stalks over to my desk and places his palms on the glossy surface. The heat from his body pulses between us, but I don't look up. Whatever he's upset about now will have to wait.

"I'm extremely tired." I sling my purse over my shoulder. "Maybe we can talk tomorrow?"

He doesn't budge or give any indication that he's heard me. I stupidly dart a quick look at him. Deep divots line the space between his brows, and a scowl pulls the corners of his mouth down. Desire pulses through my belly.

"We'll talk now," he says. His voice is as hard as steel. "Does terrorizing children wear you out? Is that why you're so tired?"

I return my eyes to his face in confusion. "What?" I was invited to watch thirty minutes of preteens doing gymnastics this afternoon, but no one seemed terrorized by my presence.

"Did you hire someone to talk to Axel?"

*Fuck.* I completely forgot about the phone call with Preston this morning. I search my brain for a way out of this. How can Henry possibly know about that? Was Preston telling people? I'm going to kill him if he was.

"Answer the question, C."

"Technically, I didn't hire him for that—"

"Damn it, Celia! What the hell were you thinking?"

"You left me no choice." I toss my bag back onto the desk.

Henry flinches as though I've slapped him. "What are you talking about?"

"You and Elizabeth! I am trying to save our family, our marriage, this whole damn country, while this woman is doing everything she can to get her claws into you and tear the whole thing apart."

He blinks several times. "She's not trying to destroy anything. She just wants Axel to have a father."

"Then why did she wait three years to tell you?"

"Because she was scared." He shakes his head like he can't believe we're even having this conversation.

"Scared of what?"

It takes a long time for his eyes to lift from the floor. They slowly climb the length of my body until they finally reach my face. The heat soaking into me has more to do with anger than lust, but I won't deny there's a little bit of that too. When he finally looks at me, he says quietly, "You."

I can't stop my mouth from falling open. "Why would she be scared of me?"

Animation leaks back into his features. "Because she was afraid you would do something like this."

"Something like what? Protect my family?"

"Like stalk Axel at school to get information from him. He was *terrified*, C."

Regret pangs in my chest. I never meant for Axel to get hurt, and if I'd thought there was even the slightest possibility of that, I would've told Preston no. "How did you even find out?"

"Elizabeth called me, demanding I get my wife to back off."

This stings, but I keep my face from flinching the way it desperately wants to. "Why does she have your number?"

"I gave it to her." Henry paces over to the window and looks out, as though it's an ordinary evening and he isn't tearing my heart to shreds.

A slow bleeding has started in my chest. "You're the bloody prince consort. You can't give out your numbers to random women." *You're my husband.*

He slowly turns to face me. "She's the mother of my child, Celia."

The room is quiet, his words floating around and bouncing against the walls. What is there to say after that proclamation? He doesn't see how this information is going to tear our family and our country apart. Or maybe he does see it and just doesn't care.

There's a brisk knock on the door, followed by Maisie sticking her head inside. We need to work on her waiting-for-an-answer-before-entering thing.

"Oh good, you're still here. I got your—" She takes a few steps into the room before spotting Henry. "I'm so sorry. I thought you were alone." She glances down at the small package in her hand and carefully lowers it to her side. I recognize the blue-and-white bag.

"You can just stick it in my purse." I nod at it on the desk and turn back to Henry. "I'm going to take a shower and head to bed. We can talk about this tomorrow."

By the time I turn around, Maisie has left the room. I grab my handbag and leave Henry still staring out the window.

# 19

# "Stay" - Rihanna + Mikky Ekko

I toss my handbag onto the bed and walk into the closet. My nostrils flare at Henry's blatant disregard for hanging things where they belong. All it would take is a simple toss onto a chair or drop into the laundry hamper, but he insists on discarding his socks and pants on the floor. I guess that's what happens when you grow up with maids just one step behind you, cleaning everything up.

I kick aside his leather jacket and grab a set of cotton pajamas from my drawer before heading to the bathroom. He's damn wrong if he thinks I'm dealing with more than one of his messes right now.

The hot water of the shower feels good. If I close my eyes and tilt my head back, I can imagine that everything is okay. That I didn't just have a fight with the love of my life, that that isn't what every conversation dissolves into these days, that we're not both keeping secrets from each other and telling lies in the same breath.

The tension in my shoulders slowly ebbs. I picture it swirling around and spiraling out through the drain, the way my therapist suggested. *Stress begone.* As if that's all it takes for it to disappear.

If I could just get Henry to understand what allowing Elizabeth and Axel into our lives is doing to us. He's so blinded by his desire to have a child that he can't even see what's happening. Elizabeth Gable knew exactly what she was doing when she swept in with her vanilla-scented wrists and her saltwater waves and her vegan leather ankle boots.

I pump a puddle of body wash into my hands, then add a second one for good measure. Rubbing my palms together, I let the aroma of peppermint and basil fill the air. I allow myself to appreciate the softness of my curves under the lather, something I rarely take time for these days.

When Henry and I first got together, I rarely took a shower alone. He was always there, rinsing the shampoo from my hair, stroking my back with his strong hands, letting them explore other parts of my body. Nine out of ten showers ended with an orgasm against the cool tile.

But it's been a long time since he slipped in here with me, since either of us initiated sex for a reason other than trying to get pregnant. It's become difficult to climax lately, and I find myself faking it more and more.

My fingers have wandered down between my legs of their own volition, stroking first the soft skin of my inner thighs, then moving higher, to my apex. By leaning against the wall of the shower, I can almost convince myself it's not my hand down there but his.

A noise startles me out of my trance, and my eyes fly open. The shower door is yanked open, and Henry is standing on the other side.

At first I think he's going to come inside, but that's before I notice that he's still in his clothes, the same ones he was wearing in my office thirty minutes ago. Moisture runs down the glass door, and several drops land on his suede shoes.

It's when my eyes are traveling upward again that I see what he's holding. My heart lurches from my chest and bounces across the slippery tiles beneath my feet.

"What the bloody hell is this?" His voice is a study in quiet, menacing control. He holds it up so that I can't possibly claim ignorance about what he's talking about.

I open my mouth, but no matter how hard I try, no sound will come out.

I've been so careful up until now, always moving the pills to my dispenser and tossing the packaging away in one of the public bathrooms downstairs. I stand there like an idiot, water streaming over my breasts, my flat and empty womb, my frozen face.

"I—I can explain," I manage to stammer out.

I've never seen his face this hard and cold, not even minutes ago when he confronted me about the private investigator. He drops the small pink compact unceremoniously to the floor. It cracks, part of the lid splintering off and skidding across the tile.

"I don't want your soddy excuses," Henry says. He leaves the bathroom—just walks away before I can offer a word of explanation.

I slide down against the shower wall until I hit the floor. I don't bother turning off the water. I pull my knees up against my chest, curling myself into as tight of a ball as possible. It isn't until my face is securely planted in the small hollow that forms that I allow my tears to fall.

Huge, wrenching sobs, the kind I haven't cried in ages.

Months.

Maybe years.

It wasn't supposed to be like this. He wasn't meant to find out. I was going to quit taking them as soon as the timing felt right. I thought it would just be for a little while, until we got things sorted with the monarchy and the press.

But then one thing led to another, and here we are.

I was planning to choose a month on the calendar, the one that would be our "baby" month. I read summer pregnancies are especially brutal, not to mention that summer is the busiest time for the royal family, what with garden parties and walkabouts and parades.

I was leaning toward a spring or even winter delivery. Either one would have gotten me out of carrying an extra twenty pounds during those rough months when you're already sweating buckets. My doctor said it might take some time for my body to conceive after stopping the pills, so I was planning for that as well.

Originally, I earmarked this month as *the one*, but when my calendar filled with more events than ever before, I decided to wait. It's not like I told anyone but myself anyway. My first duty is to my country. I can't let her down. Things will slow down eventually.

When next month's calendar grew as full as this month's, I decided we could wait another year. Better that than risk the summer pregnancy thing. No one wants to see me walk the streets of Wesbourne with a watermelon under my dress.

And now Henry knows my secret.

God, I should've hidden it better, should've never kept the pills in my bag in the first place. How did he even find them? Was he going through my things? Did he suspect something? Maybe Elizabeth planted an idea in his head. She might be the reason behind all of this.

I get to my feet. That woman will not win. She is not getting her claws into my husband or my life. Whatever she thinks will be the outcome of this whole scandal, she's wrong. If she thinks she can beat Celia Chapman-Payne, she's about to find out differently.

I turn off the water and step out of the shower. It isn't until I'm squeezing the moisture from my hair that I discover I forgot to grab underwear from the closet.

"Henry?" I call out.

There's no answer.

I try again, but I can't hear anything. The bastard's ignoring me.

Grabbing a fluffy white bathrobe from a hook, I wrap it around myself. I walk through the bedroom, which turns out to be empty. My handbag is on the bed, tipped onto its side. I have a sudden flashback of tossing it there on my way to the closet. It must have fallen over and spilled its contents across the duvet, including the prescription refill Maisie stuffed inside earlier.

*Bloody hell.*

I walk through the closet to get a pair of panties, but something feels different. Missing. As I'm turning to leave, I'm struck by what feels off in the room.

Henry's jacket isn't on the floor anymore. He must have finally decided to act like an adult. I open the doors of his closets to make sure he hung it up properly, but I can't find the bloody thing. I search every single cupboard, but it's not there. I even check my own on the off chance he got disoriented.

Confused, I wander back into the bedroom. The jacket isn't here either, and neither is Henry. I check the rest of the apartment as a choking sensation grabs hold of my throat. I refuse to acknowledge it.

He wouldn't leave.

When the apartment proves empty, I try calling him. It goes directly to voicemail. I send him a message. *Where are you?* Several minutes go by, and he still hasn't opened it.

I return to check the nightstand on his side of the bed. Dread claws its way from my belly to my throat. I clamp a hand to my mouth to keep from vomiting it across the carpet.

His personal car keys are gone.

I don't have a second to lose. I sprint down the corridors in nothing but my cashmere bathrobe, hoping no one will see me, but trusting that if they do, they won't recognize me.

Getting to the quad requires navigating two flights of stairs and a maze of corridors to the back exit. I know I'm going to be too late, that he's already long gone, driven off into the night by my deception in that rumbling black car of his.

I run into the quad anyway, not realizing until I do that it's pouring outside. I scan the lot for Henry's vehicle, knowing I won't find it. When I spot a pair of taillights near the Ambassador's Entrance, I almost don't register them, but when I do, I bolt across the wet grass and soggy gravel to where he's just sliding into the luxurious onyx interior. He doesn't see me at first, but when I slap my palms against the slick window, he jolts and lowers it.

"Celia, what the hell are you doing out here?"

"Are you going to her?" I say, raising my voice over the rain.

"What?" His brow wrinkles in confusion. "To who?"

"Elizabeth!" I shout. The wind whips at my robe, and I clutch it tighter around myself.

"Why the fuck would I be going to her?" He looks at me as though I've lost my bloody mind, and maybe I have, but all I know is that I can't lose him, can't do this without him, and if that means accepting that he has a son, fine, because I'll do it. I'll do anything if it means keeping him, keeping what we had and what we don't have anymore, for the hope that we might someday find it again.

"You need to go inside," he says, facing the windshield and not me.

"We can do DNA testing," I say. "On Axel. Find out if he's really yours."

Henry's voice is quiet, and I have to lean closer to the window to hear him, grasping the car door for balance. "I already ordered a kit."

"Great, then." My thumbs press against the weather stripping.

"The test will almost certainly prove I'm his father. This isn't some magic wand you can wave to make it all go away."

I swallow, willing the emotion back down into my chest, where it belongs. "I know. I'm willing to accept it. Just please don't go."

He turns to look at me then, and I wonder which version of me he sees—the girl he fell in love with two decades ago or a madwoman in a sopping bathrobe with hair dripping in her face. "You don't think I'm leaving because of Axel?"

"I don't know why you're leaving," I say, throwing my arms wide.

Henry shakes his head and drums his fingers against the steering wheel. "I can't do this anymore, C."

A pause, a beat, until I bring myself to say it. "Can't do what anymore? Us?" My voice cracks as I speak the word.

He just hangs his head like he's bearing the weight of the world on his shoulders. The rain is coming in through the window, leaving puddles in the creases of his jacket sleeves.

"Is it because of the pills?" I ask.

At first I think he's not going to answer this either, but then he lifts his head and says quietly, "It's because I don't know who you are anymore."

His words slap across my heart. I can physically feel their sting. I open my mouth to respond, but the hinge on my jaw isn't working. It just trembles there, not allowing me to fully open or close it.

Henry won't look at me, is embarrassed or repulsed by me—either or both, I don't even know anymore. I can't stop staring at him, this man I love with every cell of my being but also find myself despising more and more every day. How is it possible for love and hate to live together in the same space?

"You promised to stand by me through better or worse." My voice surprises both of us. "This is worse."

"I don't think even God Himself would blame me for leaving," he says.

"You said I could trust you." My voice wobbles. "Now you're leaving at the first sign of trouble?"

"The first sign?" He lets out a loud laugh. The sound is chilling. "I have dealt with so much from you for the past two years. The fact that you don't even recognize that says a lot."

"You think I haven't gone through a lot?" How can he possibly think the past few years have been easy for me?

"Most of that was your own doing," he snaps.

"I am trying to lead this country!"

"No one asked you to sacrifice who you are."

Is that what I've done? Lost myself in this effort to be everything Wesbourne demands of me, everything she deserves from her monarch?

"I'm still me," I say, but it sounds weak even to my own ears.

"Why did you do it?"

I don't have to ask. I know what he means. "There were a lot of reasons," I say.

"Give me one."

I dig my nails into the rubber strips around his window as though I can attach myself to his car and keep him here. "I'm not ready to be a mother."

"You could have just told me that."

I shake my head, flinging wet strands of hair across my face. "You wanted this so badly."

He whips sideways to stare at me. "You think I wanted it if you didn't? God, Celia. Am I some kind of monster that you would think I'd put my own desires above yours?"

Tears are blinding me, or maybe it's the rain, but I shake my head again. I clamp my lips together to hold back the sob rising in my chest, but I have to speak. Otherwise he'll leave and it will be all my fault. "I hated to let you down."

"So you *lied*?" He turns away, disgust leaking from his pores.

"I was going to stop, as soon as—"

"As soon as what? Everything fell into place? The stars aligned and the universe gave you a sign? It doesn't work like that, C! There's never a good time to have a baby!"

I gnaw at my lip, wishing I could go back and erase time, undo the past two years. Maybe if we had just talked about it . . .

He slowly turns his head, the wheels in his brain clearly spinning as he puzzles through something. Finally he says, "That's not it. You didn't hide this from me because you weren't ready." His jaw flexes, setting in place like concrete. "What's the real reason you don't want to have a baby with me?"

I grit my teeth against the sob that is dangling at the back of my throat. I cannot tell him. If I acknowledge this black hole, we will only get dragged into its depths, and I cannot allow that to happen.

"Celia, answer me." That familiar warning tone triggers my jaw to relax. The sob bursts forth. I cover my face in shame.

Henry lets me cry, but his warm fingers snake around my wrist. After a few minutes, he tugs my hands away. "Tell me," he says softly.

I open my eyes and focus on that handsome face, the one that has seen me at my worst, has loved me anyway. If I tell him, will he still love me? Or will he drive off, my heart stowed in the boot of his car like a piece of luggage?

Those eyes probe the depths of my soul like a fireplace poker discontent to let the fire go out. I've never been able to resist them, and I can't start now. "I'm scared," I say.

His fingers are still wrapped around my wrist, and he squeezes gently. "Of what?"

I shake my head, willing the words away, the ones I know will hurt him even more than they hurt me. How could they not, when I'm attacking the essence of who he is?

"I'm afraid . . ." I take a deep breath and wipe the wet strands out of my face, even though the wind just whips them right back into place. "I'm afraid you'll become like your father."

With the words out, I feel lighter. But at the same time, a searing pain replaces their weight, like I've been released from beneath a fallen beam only to catch on fire.

The rain thrums all around us, a sound I normally love because it means cozy fires in the library and musty old books in an armchair. But this rain feels different. It's too cold, too spiteful, its drops hitting me like tiny pebbles hurled by an angry crowd.

Henry stares straight ahead like I haven't said anything. For a brief interlude full of relief, I think maybe he didn't hear me. But the way his jaw has tightened tells me he took in every word.

"I used to be scared of the same thing." His voice comes out quiet and clipped, his words chopped apart by scissors. "That I would turn into him, do to my own children what he did to me."

I wrap my arms around my middle and tuck my hands over my elbows in an effort to retain some warmth. My robe is thin and became saturated within ten seconds in this downpour. If he would just come inside, we could talk about this somewhere dry and warm. Now that everything's in the open, we might even end the night—

"The fact that you loved me in spite of everything . . ." His voice cuts through my fantasy of our warm bed. "That's what gave me faith that I could be different. Rise above all of that."

Something in his tone frightens me. The finality of it. Panic flutters in my chest, a trapped butterfly desperate to get out. "I do love you," I say. "More than anything."

He closes his eyes and swallows, his Adam's apple bobbing with the movement. "I never thought you wouldn't have that same faith in me."

# 20

# "Almost Lover" - A Fine Frenzy

T HE GRAVEL IS COLD and sloshy with rainwater, the tiny pebbles sticking to the soft flesh of my legs like barnacles to the hull of a sailboat. My robe is completely sodden and hugs my limp frame. I don't even remember what being dry feels like. Around me the rain pounds, taking its vengeance on me, the woman who's lost every man she's ever loved.

My father.

Beck.

Henry.

When I close my eyes, I can still see the red of Henry's taillights as he drove across the quad. The flash of white as he braked for the gates, fading back to red as he drove through them and out of the palace grounds.

Where did it all go wrong? Was it the birth control? The dishonesty? Not accepting Elizabeth Gable's story the first time? Or the second? Hiring that bloody PI? Was it the fact that I'm not ready to be a mother?

Was it my deep-seated fear that I'd married a man who might turn into the monster his father is?

This isn't the way the story goes. It can't be. Being in control of the situation is meant to alleviate regrets. I had it all handled.

Until I didn't.

If I could just pinpoint the moment it all spun away from me, the moment I dropped the plate, knocked over the first domino. If I could just figure out what went wrong, I could fix it.

I hear Adelaide's voice in my ear. *Controlling others is what weak people think power looks like.* I knew she might be right, but I expected him to get mad, maybe storm out of the room to fume. I never thought he would leave.

I don't know how else to live. Giving up control means giving up the future. That's not something I'm willing to do, no matter how weak it makes me. I have a duty to this country, and I cannot let her down.

But if retaining control cost me Henry, it did nothing to minimize regrets. Watching him drive away rivals only one other regret in my life: seeing my father's cold body in that hospital bed.

So maybe Adelaide is right, and there is another way. Maybe . . . but I'm too tired to think about it anymore.

The rain feels warm now, and my teeth have stopped clattering together like a snapping turtle's. I lean over until my head touches the gravel. I'll just take a short nap, and when I wake up, I can figure out all of this.

Someone is lifting me. The scent of cloves and laundry detergent fills my nostrils as I bury my face in his starchy suit jacket. It's warm, which only makes me aware of how cold the rain is.

"I've got you, ma'am," my guardian angel says. His voice sounds familiar.

I blink my eyes open, but the rain is still coming down in torrents. I can just make out a chin with a deep dimple in it.

Once we're inside, the brightness of the corridor hits me like a stage light. I shift upright and recognize Davies. Heat flames to my cheeks.

"You can put me down now," I say. I'm suddenly alert and all too aware of my sodden state.

He gives me a once-over before carefully lowering me to my feet. "You sure you're okay, ma'am? I don't know how long you were out there."

"I'm fine." I press a hand to the wall to make sure I don't topple over. "It wasn't long." Time has eluded me, so I have no idea whether this is true or not.

"I can call your doctor or—"

"No. I'm okay." The less time spent being analyzed by a doctor, the better.

"I'll help you upstairs, then," Davies says.

He leaves me at the door of Henry's and my suite.

Inside, the rooms don't look any different. I expected them to have changed when Henry decided to leave, to have lost their luster or something. But our giant bed with its silk and velvet tapestries is still as lavish as ever. The gilded glass chandelier sparkles like a child at her first piano recital.

It's not fair. Henry leaves and I'm . . . what? Meant to carry on like nothing's changed? What am I supposed to tell people? What is the press going to say when they get wind of this?

I peel off the robe, now stuck to my body like a glove to a wet hand, and drop it into the bathtub. Putting on some dry clothes, I am planning to slip into bed, but when I look at it, I can't bring myself to climb between the sheets, knowing I will be alone there for god knows how long.

Instead, I swipe a bottle of red wine and a corkscrew from the bar and head down the hall. The only thing to take my mind off what just happened is work, and I've got a lot of it at this point.

I reach my office without running into anyone, since most of the staff has gone home. Hopefully we can keep all of this a secret. Preston should be able to help me with a story to explain Henry's disappearance, just until I can formulate a plan to get him back.

I forgot to bring a glass with me, so after uncorking the wine, I tilt it back and drink directly from the bottle. My desk has too many memories tied to Henry for safety, but I would be hard-pressed to find a single room in this place that isn't haunted by the ghost of him.

Everything is already shut down for the day, so while I wait for my computer to fire up, I pull out my phone. There's a reminder on my home screen of a memory from two years ago. When I open it, I see it's a picture of Henry and me playing Monopoly.

Technically, we must have already finished playing, based on the look on his face. We were so happy back then, in spite of the faux scowl he's wearing in the photo. I can't remember the last time we played a game together. These days we're lucky if we go to bed at the same time.

Of its own volition, my thumb begins scrolling right, sifting through more photos, carrying the weight of a thousand words and even more memories.

Henry on the sofa, wearing those obnoxiously sexy glasses and study-ing something in his lap, right before I tackled him and we made love on the floor.

The two of us deciding to cook breakfast together and nearly burning the entire palace down when we got too distracted by each other to keep an eye on the eggs.

Hiking through a small forest an hour from the city when we just needed to escape for a while.

A tear splashes onto my phone screen.

What happened to us?

What Henry and I have is bigger than us; it's bigger than life. We can't just throw it away as soon as things get tough.

But I know, even as I'm thinking this, that things have been tough for a while.

There's something so comforting about the knowledge that another human being loves you more than you love yourself. Not everyone gets the opportunity to experience that, no matter how much they may deserve it. But what does it mean when that person no longer deems you worth loving?

It can't be true. I know Henry still loves me. He has to. One doesn't just turn off love like it's a faucet. I learned this lesson years ago when I tried to stop loving him. It's impossible.

Which means he'll come back. I'll make sure of it.

He said he'd already ordered a DNA test kit, so maybe it's just a matter of waiting for the results. I know in my bones that they'll be negative. There is no way that Axel is Henry's son. None of it makes any sense. I would *know* if Henry had a child.

It's nothing but a tactic to tear us apart. But we're stronger than that. He'll do the test, and when the results come back negative, he'll see that I was right all along.

The sound of knuckles rapping against the door jars me from my thoughts. I set the bottle of wine onto the desk. I didn't expect him back so soon.

"Come in," I call. My heart has jumped into my throat. It quickly flits back home to my chest when Preston sticks his head into the room.

"I just wanted to check that you're okay," he says, concern in his voice.

"I'm fine. Or at least I will be." I hold up the bottle of wine, which is already half gone.

He grimaces and steps inside. "Davies told me what happened."

"He shouldn't have done that," I say, frowning. Davies rarely bucks protocol.

"He was afraid word would get out and wanted me to have a plan in place in case it does."

I deflate in relief. Of course he was just looking out for me. "Is that why you're here? To hide my latest scandal?"

"I'm here," Preston says, helping me out of my chair, "to be of assistance where I can. If that means listening while you pour your heart out over that bloody bastard, I'll do it."

He leads me over to the sofa. I snag the bottle from the desk, chugging from it on the way over. He gives me a glance but doesn't say anything. Henry wouldn't have been able to keep his mouth shut.

"I don't know what happened," I say like a pathetic child as I sink into the cushions. "We were so happy one minute, and the next . . ."

Preston takes the seat beside me, leaving several inches of space between us. "Did I ever tell you I used to be married?"

I shake my head and take another swig of wine.

"We were happy for a few years. Had the typical honeymoon phase that everyone goes through, I suppose. Then one day she decided she preferred her coworker over me." He slaps his hands against his thighs. "And that was that."

"Is this meant to make me feel better?" I ask.

His eyes shift sideways. "Sorry. I'm not good with emotions."

"Me neither, apparently." I hold up the bottle.

"You want to talk about it?" He says it like he's not sure whether it's the right response or not.

I turn to study him. That lock of dark hair has fallen over his eye again, making him look younger than he is. "Not really," I say. Not because I don't think he'd make a good listener, but because I don't know if I can bear to face what went wrong between Henry and me. "But I'll have to eventually, won't I? Wesbourne isn't going to sit silently while they lose their beloved prince consort once again."

Preston clears his throat and rubs his hands up and down his thighs. "They care about you, you know."

"Who?"

"The people." He turns to meet my eyes. "The staff. Everyone."

I force a laugh. "I hardly think that's true."

His hand lifts and settles on mine. "You're the best monarch this country has seen in a long time, maybe even forever. People love you."

I tilt the wine back to guzzle a few more mouthfuls, then look down at our entwined hands. "But if he doesn't, what does the rest of it matter?"

Preston's fingers squeeze mine. "Maybe his opinion isn't the one that counts."

Warmth flows from his hand through mine and into my arm. It's nice sitting here, having actual physical contact with someone without the pressure of wondering whether it will lead to an orgasm or conception.

He brings his other hand to wipe away a tear trailing down my face. His fingers linger on my skin, heating it and causing goosebumps to rise on my back.

He leans in and presses his mouth against mine, and I freeze, my body like a block of ice. When he pulls back, his eyes immediately search mine.

"You should go," I say with a frown.

"Of course," he says quickly, then stands up. "We'll talk more about how to handle all of this in the morning."

After Preston leaves, I set the bottle of wine in the rubbish bin. No more of that tonight—it already led me to do something stupid. I can't believe I let Preston kiss me. Of all the foolish things I could have done, that one might be at the top of the list. I am not only his employer, but his queen. And a married woman, even if my husband might be in bed with Elizabeth Gable at this exact moment.

Will he tell her they shouldn't use birth control? It's what he wants after all, and she's the type to give him anything, including another baby.

I know it's a toxic road that can lead to nowhere good, but I picture them together. Does he thread his fingers through her hair the way he does mine? Does he kiss her as thoroughly as he does me, like the world is going to end if he doesn't consume me?

I touch my lips, where the press of Preston's is but a faint memory, nothing like Henry's, which leave me scorched for hours afterward. Is he using that same mouth to seduce her, to ravish her the way he used to ravish me before we let everything get between us?

The thought splinters through me, and I sink to the floor. I've lost everything that matters. What good is any of it if I don't have him anymore?

# 21

# "right where you left me"
# - Taylor Swift

THE NEXT WEEK PASSES in a blur, aided by the three glasses of wine I allow myself to have every evening. I don't see Henry even once. He must have sent his valet to grab some clothes while I was gone. Either that or he went out and bought new ones.

He doesn't answer his phone when I call, and his only response to my dozens of text messages is *I need some time.*

I don't know what that means. How much time and for what? Is he filing for divorce? Sorting everything with Elizabeth first? Planning to leave Wesbourne? I discreetly question several staff members, but no one knows any more than I do.

Preston and I put together a statement in case any rumors start circulating. We'll say that Henry was called away on business but that he will be returning to the palace soon. So far, we haven't needed to issue it.

Preston has been keeping an eye on the tabloids for pictures of Henry and Elizabeth together, shopping at the farmer's market or collecting Axel from school, but there is nothing as of yet. They are wisely keeping a low profile.

We don't mention the kiss. Things between us don't seem to have changed, and for that I am grateful. I cannot afford to lose Preston and his brilliant handling of the press, especially over something as ridiculous as a kiss that was mediocre at best.

After a long day of appearances, I'm turning off the lights in the suite before bed—I'm finally able to sleep in it alone—when there's a knock on the door. Switching on the lamp in the living room, I go to open it. I assume it's a staff member and am completely unprepared for the sight of Henry standing on the other side.

My legs weaken, and I sink against the jamb as I drink in the sight of him. He's in a T-shirt and jeans, which both look incredibly soft. A dark shadow covers his jaw, and his eyes are pinched in sadness.

I want nothing more than to fall into his arms. He must share the same thought, because he pushes into the room, presses me up against the wall, and takes my mouth with his. His hands bury themselves in the roots of my hair. I moan as he angles his head, his tongue invading my mouth and eradicating all thoughts from my mind. His hands find their way along—

"C?" Henry's voice breaks through my daydream.

I blink, but he's still standing right outside the suite.

"Can I come in?" he says.

I move back, holding the door open for him, as if this isn't his home too, as if we're strangers meeting for the first time. He steps inside and watches me.

I don't know how to bridge this chasm between us. It feels too vast. Looking at him now, I'm not even sure he wants to bridge anything.

"I wanted to tell you myself," he says. He looks down at the manila envelope I just now notice in his hands.

Oh god, oh god, oh god. Are those divorce papers already?

"I got the DNA test results back."

He extends his hand, holding out the packet. I stare at it, then lift my gaze to him. Why can't he just tell me what it says? I try to read the answer in his eyes, but he is intentionally keeping them masked from me.

I take the envelope and pull out the sheet within. A bunch of scientific jargon and numbers fill the page, but none of that matters, because across the top in big, bold letters are the words *Probability of paternity: 97%.*

Something that feels remarkably like a real knife burrows its way into my heart. I try to inhale, but the cold steel keeps me from catching a full breath.

I hand the report back to him, keeping my eyes averted from his. He must be ecstatic and hiding it from me. He's a better actor than I am, I'll give him that.

"Ninety-seven percent?" I say after he takes the envelope back.

"They never issue 100 percent. The 97 is because boys only inherit 47.5 percent of their father's DNA."

I nod as though I understand, as though hearing him spew this scientific mumbo-jumbo isn't weird, as though he hasn't been learning all this stuff while I've been here alone, trying to clean up this mess and salvage what's left of our reputation and this country.

"Congratulations." My tone is flat.

He clears his throat. "I know you were hoping—"

"I'm happy for you." I force the words out. They taste bitter on my tongue.

I don't want him to have a child, not with another woman. That was something we were meant to share together, a first for both of us. We've missed so much already. Can't we have this one single thing?

"I want you to know that while I'm excited to be a dad, I never wanted it like this."

I lift my eyes to his. He's staring at me intently, like it's essential that I understand what he's saying.

"Do you believe me?" he asks.

My eyebrows inch upward, and I take a quiet breath. "I think so."

Maybe this isn't the way he wanted it, but he isn't balking at it the way I am. He isn't balking at all. It's as if it hasn't rippled his life plan in the least.

I study the sleeve of his shirt, where a tiny rip has formed at the cuff. He's been working out. It's only been a week, but the muscles in his arms are more defined. Or maybe it's just been a while since I've seen his bare arms up close.

"Celia." He says it so softly, at first I think I imagined it. But when I look up, he's gazing at me. For a second, I think he's going to pull me into his arms, apologize for everything, and tell me he'll never leave again.

He doesn't. He just looks at me with those droopy eyes, his heart filling them. There's so much pain. Why is he hurting? How is it fair for him to be hurting when he has everything he wants? I'm the one left standing alone and broken.

"Are you okay?" he asks.

I lift my chin, demanding it not to tremble. I will not break in front of him. I can't afford to. "I'm fine."

He pulls his bottom lip between his teeth and nods. "That's good. Listen, I wanted to ask—"

I brace myself for what's about to come.

"What do you think about Axel joining us on a few public outings?" he says.

I reach for the console table behind me. The smooth wood beneath my palm keeps my heart from jolting out of my chest and skidding across the floor. I search for the word I'm looking for, but it stays just out of reach.

"C?"

I drag my gaze from the rug. "Hmm?"

"I know it's sudden, but I think it would be good for the people to see us as a solid family unit."

"Is that what we are? A family unit?"

Tundra pads into the room and stands at my side.

Henry crouches down to greet him. "I'd like to think so."

"So you still consider yourself part of this family?"

He looks up at me as if I've lost my mind. "Of course I do."

"Your absence this past week has left some of us in doubt."

"I told you I needed time."

I gesture to the envelope still clutched in his hand. "So what? Now that you got what you wanted, you're back? Ready to become *Full House*?"

"I am trying to find a way through this for all of us."

"And what does Elizabeth think about that idea?"

"I haven't said anything to her yet." His voice is quiet. "I wanted to talk to you first."

"I assumed this was practically pillow talk for the two of you."

The mailer in his hand crinkles as his fist tightens around it. "Why do you insist on believing there is something between us?"

"Because I've seen the way she looks at you!"

The room grows still. The lamp casts shadows over Henry's face. He feels like a stranger to me, but nothing can erase the line of that jaw from my memory. I will never forget the way it feels beneath my fingers, beneath my lips . . .

"That doesn't mean I look at her the same way."

My throat closes. "How long until you do?"

Henry looks away and rubs his nose. "I have no feelings for her whatsoever. You can choose to believe me or not, but I have done nothing to give her the idea that we will ever be together."

*Except leave your wife.*

"Does she . . . know?" I gesture to the gaping space between us, space neither of us would have tolerated a few years ago. Space that was always filled by our bodies pressing together, never able to get close enough.

He shakes his head. "This is between us."

As comforting as it is to know that he isn't unloading our marital problems on Elizabeth's willing bosom, it doesn't answer the one question my heart can't stop asking. "Are you here to stay?"

He moves to shove both hands into his pockets before remembering that he's still holding the DNA test in one. Instead, he drops them back to his sides, where they hang limply. "I think it's best if I don't just yet."

I desperately want to clutch at my chest to contain all the pieces of what must surely be my heart splintering apart. I force them to remain where they are. "How soon?" My voice breaks on the last word.

He shakes his head. "I don't know. Maybe in a week? Two?" He runs his fingers through his hair. I long to feel its softness with my own hands. "I need time to process everything, to figure out what I want."

He doesn't need to say it. It's there in his words, hanging on like a chimp on a trapeze.

*To decide if I still want you.*

I nod, because I can't trust the words that will come out if I open my mouth.

"I wanted to tell you about this in person." He lifts the envelope like he's seeing it for the first time. "And to grab a few more things. Is that okay?"

I gesture to the bedroom as if to say "be my guest," but inside I'm screaming "of course it's not okay, how could it be okay for you to come back here to rub that in my face and grab your toothbrush while you're here like we aren't married and I don't still reach for you in the middle of the night or turn to tell you something while I'm getting dressed before remembering that you're not there you're never there and I'm not sure you ever will be again?"

Henry retreats to our bedroom. When he returns several minutes later carrying a small leather bag, I still haven't moved.

"Got everything?" I say sweetly, as if he's only going on a guys' trip and not walking back out that door and my life.

"Yeah." It's nothing more than a whisper.

*What about me?* I want to scream. *Am I no longer something you consider necessary for survival?*

We both move to the door, our bodies drawn by the magnetic force field between us. They haven't got the memo yet that this isn't something we do anymore.

I tilt my face up to his, waiting for him to say something, anything, to give me hope that he'll be back, that this isn't goodbye.

*Stay stay stay.*

He pulls the door open. "Will you please think about the Axel thing? I think you'd love him if you got to know him."

I want to ask how he knows this, if he's been spending time with them, if that's where he's been when he hasn't been with me.

I don't. I don't say any of it. I just nod. "I'll think about it."

He offers me a tight smile. "I'll see you later."

*Will you?*

I want to beg.

I watch him walk down the corridor, his gait so familiar it causes a pang of homesickness. He doesn't look back.

# 22

# "Paper Crown" - Alec Benjamin

I'M DUE AT OLIVIA'S apartment in fifteen minutes. Normally, I look forward to the break and the chance to catch up. Today, my stomach is a pit of dread.

What do you say to your mother-in-law when your husband is no longer living with you, can't even bother to tell you what it is he wants, and just expects you to sit back and wait patiently while he sorts through his life?

I don't know how much Henry has told her—if he's told her anything at all. I'm walking into the situation blind, and I'm placing the blame squarely at his feet, where it belongs. I may have made some mistakes that led us to this place, but he is acting like a coward by running away.

For five minutes, I debate blowing off the meeting, but when Maisie sticks her head into my office and asks if I remembered I'm seeing Olivia, I decide not to risk it. The more I stick to my normal routines, the easier it will be to sell the story that Henry is simply away on business.

"I'm on my way," I tell her, grabbing my handbag from beneath my desk.

Olivia's suite is on the third floor of the residential wing, and like many of our private apartments, has several entrances. I use the one right off the private kitchen, where I know the powder room is. I've been at various engagements all morning, and I forgot to use the restroom before heading over here.

Slipping inside, I finish my business, then inspect my face in the oval mirror over the sink. Daphne has been doing a good job hiding my puffy eyes. If she wonders about them or the half of the bed that hasn't been slept in, she has yet to say anything to me.

I smooth the bodice of my dress and pinch a little color into my cheeks. By the time I'm done, even I can't notice a difference from my usual appearance.

Assuming Olivia is in the kitchen preparing tea, I head in that direction, but when I walk in, the room is empty. The kettle is cold, and there are no cups sitting next to the stove. Did she forget? I haven't seen any signs that her memory is failing.

Then it hits me squarely between the eyes. *Henry told her.* And like any adoring mother, Olivia chose to take her son's side.

Should I confront her or leave before she discovers I'm here?

I'm still frozen with indecision when voices float over from the other side of the apartment. Following them, I walk through the dining room and stop when I get to the living room doorway.

Inside, sprawled on the floor, are Henry and Axel. Henry is wearing a pair of jeans that hug his backside so nicely, my nipples harden on principle. He's propped up on his elbows, arms straining at the sleeves of his shirt. Axel is directly across from him, mimicking his posture.

A dozen Hot Wheels are scattered between them on the rug. The whole scene is punctuated by booms and crashing noises as they push the toys around. Axel drives a car over Henry's arm, and Henry pretends the motion fatally wounds him, which sends Axel into a fit of giggles.

There's a pang in my chest, something I'd normally call longing, but I certainly have no desire to get down there on the floor and smash cars into anything, so I don't know what it is.

Henry reaches over and tickles Axel's stomach, which only makes the boy laugh harder. They roll around on the floor, Axel's shyness at their first meeting completely gone.

Henry is *happy*. Blissfully happy. The thought lands in my gut like a punch. I haven't seen his face light up like this for ages. This is what he wants, what he *needs*. He needs to know that he isn't the man his father is. That he could never be that man.

I shouldn't have doubted it. Of course he won't turn into William. There's no way in hell the man I love could become that kind of monster. In the few short weeks he's known Axel, he's been more of a father to the boy than William ever was to him.

I long to reach for him, to tell him I was wrong and that I'm sorry. That I messed up by letting my fears get the best of me.

A movement from the sofa reminds me where I am. Olivia moves to the doorway, her eyes fixed on the two boys still wrestling on the floor. Laughing at their antics, she asks, "How about some cookies?"

A high-pitched "yay!" pierces the loud cacophony of masculine sounds coming from the mass of limbs.

Realizing that Olivia is headed my way, I scoot back into the kitchen before she spots me. Unfortunately, I'm not fast enough.

"Celia. Is it . . . ?" Olivia halts in the doorway and glances at her watch. "Oh dear, I had no idea it was already this late."

"It's fine. I have a lot of things waiting for my attention, anyway." Heat flares across my face as I head for the back door.

"Celia, wait. Come here." She crosses the kitchen and pulls me into her lavender-and-cookie-dough-scented embrace. She's the only royal I know who bakes her own cookies from scratch. Hugging me tighter than you'd expect for such a small woman, her collarbone digs into my shoulder. It should be noted that she doesn't *eat* the cookies she bakes.

I know she's offering me comfort, and as much as I love her for it, and for all the ways she's been the mother to me that my own mum wasn't, I don't allow myself to relax in her embrace. I can't, not knowing what Henry must have told her and what this all looks like from the outside.

She reads my stiffness and pulls back. "Come sit down so we can talk."

"I should be going. I don't want to intrude," I say.

"Nonsense." She bats away my objection as though it were a fly. "They didn't even notice I was in the room. Besides, I have something for you."

She retreats into the kitchen, leaving me no choice but to follow. A quick glance toward the living room confirms that Henry is still unaware of my presence.

Olivia pulls a small bowl from the refrigerator and sets it on the table in front of me, along with a spoon. I pop the lid off.

"I know you prefer the dough," she says with a smile.

Olivia's cookie dough has always been the best, and even when I was a kid, she would save me several spoonfuls. The small gesture cracks something inside me. She could easily have chosen to shun me over whatever story Henry has told her, but instead she's saving me dough and letting me hide in her kitchen.

"Thank you," I say quietly, spooning some out.

She uses a spatula to move cookies from a baking tray to a hand-painted china plate. "Let me just take these to them before they come to hunt me down." At the doorway to the dining room, she turns back. "Please stay. I would really like to talk. Just for a few minutes."

I bite my lip as she walks back to Henry and Axel. I briefly consider fleeing, but I can't, not after that look she gave me. This is Olivia we're talking about. It would be like kicking a kitten. I pull out a chair at the table and take a seat.

When she returns a few moments later, I watch over her shoulder to make sure Henry isn't following her. The last thing I need is him throwing me out of his mum's apartment.

I can't tell if Olivia's surprised to find me still here. I incline my ear to the living room, hoping to hear what they're doing in there, but it's quiet.

"Munching their cookies, I'd imagine." She keeps her voice lowered. He can't have told her everything if she's willing to keep my presence here a secret.

"He asked if I wanted to meet Axel," she continues. "As if I could ever say no to meeting my grandchild."

That grandchild should have been Henry's *and* mine, but I don't think she's intending to be cruel. "What do you think?" I say. "Of Axel?"

She beams and begins stacking the rest of the cookies in a tub. "He's a darling. So handsome and sweet, just like his father."

I murmur in agreement and shove another spoonful of cookie dough into my mouth.

"I know how difficult this must be." She reaches across the table for my hand.

*Do you?* I want to say. As far as I know, William never had any former lovers claim to have had his child, although the thought isn't far-fetched.

"It isn't fair that everything happened this way, when you haven't been blessed with a baby of your own, but don't give up, love. It can still happen."

I blink at her. So he didn't tell her everything. At least not the part where I've been taking birth control for the better part of two years while letting him believe I want a baby as badly as he does. "I'm not so sure," I say.

"Of course it will. Perhaps if you slow down a little, maybe take a vacation. The tropics always help me relax."

"Did Henry tell you that we—" The right words vacate my head.

"He mentioned that this has all been very hard on you." She looks at me thoughtfully. "I did notice your color's been a little off recently."

So Daphne's makeup jobs aren't quite good enough to fool the former queen. I can't even make an accurate guess as to whether I've been more pale or flushed recently. I seem to alternate between the two with alarming regularity. "That would be an understatement," I mutter.

Olivia sets down the spatula and massages her wrists. "This has all been hard on him, too. He's been struggling for a while."

"He told you that?"

"He didn't have to. I've watched him change little by little over the past few years."

I pick at the hem of my dress. "Isn't change good?"

"Sometimes. But not when you watch the light go out of someone you love."

An ugly fist knots itself around my stomach. "Is that what you think? That I stole his light?" I can hardly bring myself to ask the question.

Her eyes dart up to find mine. "Not at all. But I think watching you become someone he didn't know you were has changed something in him. It's not easy for a man to play second fiddle to his wife."

I drop my eyes to the wood grain in front of me, remembering the day Henry and I sat at the table in the Green Drawing Room with our families, listening to our worlds get turned upside down. When Parliament presented their idea of an arranged marriage to us, they intended for us to reign together as king and queen.

But that's not the way fate left things.

"I don't know how to change that," I say.

"No one expects you to, least of all him." Olivia waits until I look up. "But give him a chance to be the man you deserve. The man you know he is."

I want to shout at her that I'm not the one who left, I'm not the one with the secret past and the secret lover and the secret child. I'm not the one who is threatening to blow our family and our reputation sky-high with dynamite to cater to my own whims.

"Mum?" Henry's voice comes from the living room, sending my blood hurtling through my veins at breakneck speed.

I jump up from my chair and dart from the room. He can't know I was here.

Olivia stops me as I'm closing the door. "He loves you, Celia. It's breaking his heart to see you hurting like this."

I nod and force my lips into a tiny smile that feels more like a grimace and head down the corridor. I want to believe her words, believe that this is nothing more than a blip on the radar of our marriage, that fifty years from now we'll look back at this time and roll our eyes at how ridiculous we were.

But regardless of how badly I want to believe her, I can't.

Because she doesn't know everything.

She doesn't know that I've been faking infertility for years or that I lied to Henry about it. She doesn't know that I let my press secretary kiss me. She doesn't even know that Henry moved out.

So how could she possibly know if he still loves me?

# 23

# "I Can Do It With a Broken Heart" - Taylor Swift

T HE REST OF MY afternoon turns hazy. Preston and I are working on a strategy to handle the press once the news of Henry's DNA test results make headlines. The people will eat this up. They don't care about the nature of the news, as long as it feeds their ravenous appetite for drama.

I'm confident they favor Henry over me. He's always been Wesbourne's sweetheart, their golden boy. They live vicariously through him, fantasize about him, and envision what their lives might look like if they had his luck rather than their own.

They're happy enough to greet me at social outings and when I'm presenting a plaque, but they don't lie awake at night dreaming of the possibility of a night with me.

"I wouldn't be so sure," Preston says when I voice that last sentiment out loud.

We're both sitting on the floor of my office. Maybe I was inspired by Henry playing with Axel earlier, because an hour into this meeting, I kicked off my heels and sat down on the rug in front of the fireplace. After an arched brow that pointedly questioned my sanity and a shrug that said "what the heck," Preston joined me.

His legs are splayed out, one knee bent and supporting his elbow. That thick, dark hair is once again breaking the rules by flopping over his forehead. He brushes it aside and meets my eyes. "I mean it."

"I am the equivalent of a bucket of ice water on anyone's fantasy." I read over the notes in my hand once more.

Preston laughs abruptly, as if I've said something surprising as well as ridiculous. "Why do you say that?"

"Have you read what they say about me?"

"That's my job."

"They call me the Ice Queen. Ring a bell?"

He smiles and shakes his head, causing his hair to move back into its favorite position over his eye. "So you don't show emotion easily in public. Who cares?"

"Everyone, apparently."

He lowers the pages he's holding to the floor and scoots closer. "Just because the press takes particular pleasure in ripping your reputation to shreds, does not mean the people share their views."

"You don't need to try to make me feel better."

"Maybe I want to." He reaches out and toys with a strand that has fallen over my shoulder.

Goosebumps spring up along my spine. I don't need this. I don't need some cheap validation to make me feel like a better queen, a better person. But that doesn't make it any less nice or appreciated.

"They don't judge you for the actions of your family, you know," he says, still twisting the hair around his finger.

I keep my eyes lowered, not wanting to look at him. "Have you watched the news recently?"

"I'm not saying the press doesn't lump you all together before flaying you, but the average Joe out there doesn't think of you like that."

"You can't know for sure."

"Sure I can." He drops my hair and lets it fall back against my shoulder. "I'm one of them, after all."

"You are hardly a commoner," I say with a smirk. Preston's family has immense political connections, part of the reason the press office has benefitted so greatly from having him on board.

"My mother's family runs a small grocery in the village of Laurent. Ever heard of it?"

I fiddle with a thread on my skirt. "No, but that doesn't make you an expert."

"Maybe not," he says quietly. "Maybe I'm just speaking for myself, then."

There's something in his tone that causes my heart to pick up speed. It's not that I long for adoration from a man. It's more that I haven't felt worthy of it in a long time. Preston is the first man to look past the garbage of the past few years and recognize who I am at my core.

He places a finger below my chin and gently lifts it. His eyes are full of warmth and something else I don't want to think about. He moves his hand to my neck, and heat spreads where our skin touches. "You're an incredible woman," he whispers. "And so beautiful."

He lowers his head and presses his mouth against mine. Like last time, my body goes rigid. This isn't right, but I don't know what to do. His tongue traces the seam of our lips, encouraging me to open and allow him to explore my mouth. I resist, keeping my mouth closed.

When his hand slowly slides down on a clear path to my breast, I push him away. "No, I'm not doing this."

He hangs his head and nods. "I can wait."

Wait for what? For Henry to divorce me? For me to fall out of love with him? For it to feel anything other than weird and revolting to taste someone else's mouth?

I'm not sure why I'm the one who's been cursed with a moral code. While Henry is probably sleeping with Elizabeth, I can't even kiss another man without guilt eating away at the base of my spine.

Who cares if Preston and I don't have feelings for each other and this could never be anything more than an inappropriate workplace romance? I need something to get my mind off the mess my life has become, and he is offering the perfect distraction in an attractive package.

But I know that the real reason things could never progress between us has nothing to do with physical attraction, the fact that I'm married, or the inappropriateness of sleeping with an employee. It has everything to do with the fact that Henry has ruined me. I will never be able to look at another man and feel desire that even comes close to rivaling the tsunami of what I feel for Henry.

This is why the people will relentlessly cheer for their prince consort. Not because he has a strong moral code or brings about change for the betterment of everyone, but because he's a magnetic powerhouse. He has a way of winning over the most adamant of naysayers with nothing more than a flash of that trademark grin and a wink of those dark, bottomless eyes.

It's completely unfair.

There's a knock on the door, and Preston lurches backward. We're both still on the floor, attempting to scramble to our feet when it opens and Henry walks inside. If there was any doubt in my mind as to how this looks, it's cleared up the minute I see his face. His eyes narrow, and his nostrils flutter as he looks over Preston's rumpled appearance and my shoeless feet.

A jolt of something I can't quite identify shoots through my body. Fear? Excitement?

I look down at the papers strewn around on the floor. "Maybe we can finish our meeting later?" I ask as Preston scoops them up.

Nodding, he shoves the stack under his arm. "Just let me know what time."

It isn't until he's walking through the door that I regret not asking him to stick around. The look on Henry's face is terrifying.

"Meeting?" he says, closing the door. There is a distinct mocking tone in his voice.

"Yes." I smooth down my skirt. "We have those occasionally."

"And do you always have meetings with your staff on the floor?" He takes three steps closer. His presence is so *full*, like he's the ocean and there are millions of organisms finding life inside him.

"Only the ones I particularly like."

His eyes narrow even further. "You are walking on thin ice, Celia."

"Funny. I wasn't aware I'd left the fight ring."

My desk presses into my back. Visions of Henry laying me across it choose this moment to remind me of the way it feels to have him skirting his hands over every curve of my body, whispering my name like a prayer into the soft spots.

I wish desperately that I could busy myself with something—any-thing—to keep my eyes off him and my hands from wanting to reach for him, but I can't. His powerful magnetism is at play, keeping me pinned right where he wants me. My heart pounds.

"Is he getting more than a paycheck?" There's a steel backbone in each of Henry's words.

"You mean other than a nightly massage and his own private suite?"

A muscle in his cheek twinges, and his jawline becomes even more defined, if that's possible. "This isn't funny."

"I couldn't agree more." Crossing my ankles, I lean back against the desk.

Henry comes closer, close enough that I can see the tiny scar on his chin from falling out of our shoddy excuse for a treehouse when we were little. "Do not fuck with me, Celia. Did you sleep with that pig?"

Biting my lip, I keep my eyes focused on him. His brow is furrowed with deep lines, and I can almost smell the anger rolling off him. I know he's analyzing the tiniest of my movements, so I give a barely perceptible shake of my head.

His eyes close, as if he's trying to control his emotions before he speaks. But when he finally opens them, he doesn't say anything.

"Would it matter if I had?" I ask.

He blinks several times. "What kind of question is that?"

"A serious one?"

He shakes his head like he's trying to figure out who I am and what's going on. "Of course it would matter. You're my *wife*."

"Could've fooled me." Before he can respond, I add, "How's Elizabeth?"

"How the fuck should I know?"

"Maybe because you left me for your new family?"

He shakes his head again and turns toward the window. "I'm not having this conversation with you."

"You're the one who started it with your ridiculous accusations."

"I have been telling you for a long time that your press secretary wants nothing more than to get you out of your clothes, but you never believe me. And now I walk in and find you two on the floor in a position that left little to the imagination."

"We were working," I snap, guilt eating at me.

"So you're telling me he didn't make a single move on you?" Henry steps close enough that I can smell the spearmint on his breath and the pine of his deodorant.

"Did Elizabeth?"

He looks genuinely confused. "Did she what?"

"Make a move on you!" Why does he insist on being so utterly clueless? The woman would have married him the first time he looked at her; I'm sure of it.

"I don't have any bloody idea. I'm too busy trying to keep my wife from sleeping with her secretary."

I cross my arms over my chest. "That's ridiculous, and you know it. I would never sleep with Preston." The thought makes me want to be violently ill.

"I don't know anything anymore," he says.

"You can't come in here and accuse me of things like that." My mouth fills with the bitter taste of shame.

"Yet you've been doing the same thing to me ever since our wedding. With Libby in the picture, you finally have a face to put with your empty accusations."

I hate the way he says her name. I hate the memory of her perfect teeth and her perfect skin and her perfect hair. I hate that he's right.

"Why are you even here?" I say.

His eyes soften just a fraction. "My mum said you were at her flat." When I don't say anything, he adds, "I'm sorry you saw that."

"Elizabeth lets you have Axel?"

"I asked if I could introduce him to my mum. She had to work, so she arranged for me to pick him up from school."

"That's nice." There's a tightness in my throat I'd do anything to eradicate.

"The last thing I want to do is hurt you, C," he says.

A sad smile works its way onto my lips. "Too late."

# 24

# "Confident" - Demi Lovato

I BUSY MYSELF WITH the myriad of papers Maisie left that need my signature. Nothing like scrawling your name at the bottom of hundreds of documents to get your mind off the fact that your marriage is on the rocks and there's little you can do about it.

Just when I think my hand is going to officially turn in its resignation, my phone rings, prompting me to throw the pen down in relief. It's a number I don't recognize. My first instinct is to decline it, but this line is monitored pretty heavily. If the caller got through, they must be a legitimate person and not one of those creepy robots.

When I pick up, there's gruff male voice on the other end. "I have intel for you."

I pull the phone away from my ear to frown into it. "Who is this?"

"Jack Reacher." There's a pause. "I was asked to look into someone for you."

This must be the PI Preston hired, but I thought I'd made it clear to Preston he was to handle everything. "Why are you calling me?"

"I told you, I have intel." Open-mouthed chewing comes through the line, and I gag. My press secretary and I will need to have a chat about the suitability of the PIs he hires in the future.

"That information could have been relayed to the person who hired you."

"Yeah, well I was told you'd want to hear it straight from me."

I'd like to tell this churlish SOB what he can do with his information. "I'm not sure what you've been told, but I no longer need you to trail the subject."

"Suit yourself." I picture this slobbering mess of a man shrugging in his rumpled suit. "It was a boring job anyway. Lady never did nothing interesting."

I grit my teeth. Of course she didn't. She's Elizabeth Gable, perfect mother, perfect real estate agent, and perfect future wife. "After your uncouth attempts to get information out of a three-year-old, I decided we no longer need your services."

"Hey, I was given orders to do what was necessary. Talking to that little brat was creative and innovative."

I'm surprised he even knows the meaning of innovative. "It was un-ethical. I don't care how badly you are in need of information—you will not do something like that again on my dime."

"Whatever you say, Mrs. Queen."

The nerve of this man. "Good day to you, Mr. Rea—" I pause, con-sidering. "Your name isn't Jack Reacher, is it?"

He cackles. "And here I was, thinking you wasn't so quick on the uptake."

"I'll see to it you're paid, but do not expect my business in the future."

"If you're paying anyway, do you at least want to hear what I found?"

I pause, my thumb already hovering over the disconnect button. Hir-ing this ridiculous pathetic excuse of a person was an idiotic idea, but I won't deny there's a small grain of curiosity in me that wants to know if he gained anything valuable from trailing Elizabeth. Henry will blow a fuse if he ever finds out, but if this information leads to us prying that woman from our lives, it won't matter how I obtained it.

"Or I could sell it to the highest bidder," he says when I don't answer. The sound of his crunching comes through in the silence.

"Just tell me what you found." I clench my jaw. "And if you could put your crisps away for the rest of what I hope will be a very short conversation, it would be greatly appreciated."

He laughs as a wrapper crinkles on the other end. "You're as charming as they say." Mockery coats his tone like oil.

I'm going to fire Preston, if I don't murder him first.

"I've been trailing your girl for a week," the PI says. "She did the usual—grocery shopping, library with the kid, yoga class. I did enjoy that one quite a bit."

He laughs lewdly, and I swallow the bile rising in my throat.

"Went to a god-awful amount of houses. She's a real estate agent, and she's constantly bobbing around the city to meet people at these big ol' mansions. I wasn't always able to get super close to those. They had gates, you know."

"Would you please get to the point?" I snap.

He waits a few breaths, probably just to irritate me. "Well, today, she did something different." He pauses again, and now I know for sure he is dragging this out to make me pay for being rude. When I don't give him the satisfaction of a reply, he continues. "Drove out of town on that road that leads to Summersville. I thought maybe she had a big, fancy house showing out there. But she just kept right on driving."

Does this man think I care that Elizabeth took a day trip out of the city? She probably went to place flowers on a forgotten grave in the middle of the heath.

"I followed her, being sure to stay out of sight. You know, slowing down and letting a few cars get between us so she didn't get suspicious and all that."

"I am aware of how to properly follow another vehicle without detection," I deadpan.

He ignores this. "So anyway, about two hours out of the city, she finally pulls off onto another road. That's when I realized where we were."

I raise my eyes to the ceiling as I wait for the inevitable seconds to pass as he drags this out.

"Staggart Prison."

I'm familiar with the name, although I've never been there. It happens to be where Henry's father is incarcerated, not that he's ever visited him. And while a part of me knows Elizabeth was probably taking cookies to the prisoners in a sweet little basket with a gingham napkin, there's a tiny spark of hope that she was there on a more nefarious mission. To visit her murderous brother, perhaps, or to trade confidences with an old roommate?

"Is this the part where you say she went inside, but you can't tell me any more?" I ask, sick of this wild goose chase.

"This is the part where I tell you that she went inside, and I got the name of the person she visited. But it will cost you another ten grand."

"Piss off. We've paid you plenty." The words fly out without thought, and I immediately regret them. This information could be vital to bringing Elizabeth down. I'm on the verge of blowing the whole thing just because a bumbling idiot of a man got under my skin.

Fortunately for me, he laughs and says, "I'm just messing with ya. Told you I'd include this information free of a charge. Kind of like an upgrade to first class."

The man wouldn't know class if it slapped him in the face. I don't point out that this is the first information of any kind that he's been able to supply, and we should actually be receiving a refund.

"You sure you want to know who she was visiting in the ol' slammer?"

I pinch the bridge of my nose. If I had a gun, I'm not sure whether I'd shoot him or myself first. "Positive," I bite out.

"Alrighty then. Don't say I didn't warn you." He waits again, and I picture him picking at something in his teeth while smiling devilishly as he makes me squirm.

"She was visiting King William. Oh, beg your pardon. The *former* king. You know, your father-in-law?"

I don't address his absolute lack of propriety or manners. I don't tell him that the only way to refer to him these days is as William Sutherland, since he lost his title and his dukedom when his crimes came to light. I simply end the call and lay my phone on the desk, trying to process this information.

What the hell was Elizabeth doing visiting William?

# 25

# "Small Bump" - Ed Sheeran

I'M STILL ROLLING THAT obnoxious excuse of a PI's words around in my head when my phone rings again. I flip it over to reveal Bea's name and face on the screen, then drop it back down unanswered. Her current drama will have to wait.

Why would Elizabeth visit William? Is she trying to get information from him? Trying to win favors with Henry? If the latter, she should have done her homework better. Visiting his father will only drive Henry further away, not closer. Maybe they're working together on a plan titled "How to Wreck the Entire Nation."

My phone lights up once more. I sigh at the sight of Bea's name and connect the call. I know my sister well enough to know that she'll keep calling until I answer.

"Hello?"

There's only silence.

"Bea? Are you there?"

She lets out a noise of surprise, as if she didn't realize I was on the other end. "Celia?"

"Yes. Is everything okay?"

"I—I don't know." Tears percolate in her voice.

I fight the urge to roll my eyes. She probably broke a nail.

"Can you please explain what's wrong? I can't help you if you don't tell me." I do my best to tamp down my irritation.

A hiccuping sob fills the phone, and I shift it away from my ear. "Bea, what's wrong?"

Another wail comes through the line. I switch on the speaker.

"Bea, you need to calm down and tell me what's wrong." The sooner I can tell her what a loser her latest boyfriend is, the sooner I can go back to figuring out what's going on with William and Elizabeth.

"It hurts," she whimpers.

I have a flashback to my own experiences with heartbreak, lying sick in bed, feeling as though the world was ending and leaving me behind. I soften my tone. "It's going to be okay. Want me to bring some wine?" I say before remembering that she's pregnant.

She mumbles something I can't make out.

"I can't understand you," I say. "Can you say that again?"

"There's . . ." Her voice sounds distant. "There's so much . . . blood."

The words make my own blood freeze. "Bea?" Panic laces my voice. "Bea, where are you?"

There's no answer.

I try again. "Bea! Talk to me. Where is the blood coming from?"

She still doesn't respond, and I'm not going to waste any more time trying to get info from her. I use the location finder Henry installed on all our phones. Bea's red dot shows she's inside the palace, probably in her suite.

I dart out the door, nearly colliding with Maisie as I do so. "Sorry!" I yell over my shoulder. "It'll have to wait!"

The corridors are blessedly empty as I make my way to my sister's apartment. I don't have time to stop and greet staff members or explain why I'm running like a crazy person down the three-hundred-year-old galleries.

Her door is unlocked, another relief. I was planning to call Davies to break it down if necessary. I rush inside, calling her name as I go. There's a sound coming from the direction of the bedroom, so I head there first.

The room is empty, save for the huge bed hung with purple tapestries and gold brocade. The scent of vanilla and plum fills the air.

"Bea?" I call.

A moan sounds from the bathroom. When I push the door open, what I see brings me to my knees. My sister is crumpled on the floor, half leaning against the tub. She's wearing a satin bathrobe that exposes her tanned and toned legs. Her head is bowed to her chest, and she doesn't look up when I enter.

I register these things distractedly. What my eyes can't stay away from is the blood. A dark red stain is seeping out from beneath her robe. It's spreading across the floor, growing larger the longer I look.

I shake myself out of the stupor I'm in. "Bea!" Grabbing her shoulders, I give her a shake. I know I can't let her go into shock. Her head lolls backward, and I place my hands on either side of her face. "Bea, look at me."

Her eyes remain closed.

"Oh my god," I whisper desperately. "Beatrice, answer me!"

She still doesn't move or open her eyes.

I fight against my tears as I pull out my phone. Davies's contact card is still pulled up, and I press the call button.

When he answers, I explain the situation. As soon as I hang up, I call an ambulance. Davies arrives less than two minutes later. I'll never know if he silently follows me around the palace in case I'll need his help or if he has superhuman abilities when it comes to movement. Whatever the case, I've never been more grateful.

As soon as he spots Bea, a guttural sound slips past his lips. I've never seen him express emotion, but the look on his face is enough to make me blink a few times. "Is she—" His voice breaks.

"She'd better not be."

He drops to the floor beside her, paying no attention to the blood beneath his knees. "Bea!" he says urgently. "Beatrice!"

"I've already tried that. An ambulance is on its way."

Davies doesn't seem aware of my presence. His eyes remain focused on Bea, and he's clutching her hand as if she'll slip away if he doesn't keep a firm grip on her. While we wait for the EMTs to arrive, he checks her pulse, lifts her eyelids, and gauges the amount of blood on the floor.

"Do you know what's wrong?" I ask.

"I think she's hemorrhaging," he says. "Which is highly unusual, un-less—"

"Unless what?" I need to know what is wrong with her, nothing spared.

He glances at me, Bea's wrist still pressed between his fingers. "The most common cause is miscarriage. But she's not—"

The floor seems to drop out from beneath me, the world slowly tilting me forward.

"Celia?" Davies reaches his other hand toward me. He's never called me by my name before.

"She's pregnant," I whisper.

His face grows even more ashen. We both turn our attention back to Bea, looking for a way to make her more comfortable, even though we both know that it will take more than a pillow to fix her now.

A bustle of activity in the suite announces the arrival of the emergency personnel. They make their way into the bathroom, which has shrunk to half its usual size, pushing a stretcher between them. They lift Bea's still unresponsive form onto it, then strap her in as they listen to Davies update them on the situation. As if he's asking for permission, his eyes cut to me before telling them she's pregnant.

It hadn't even occurred to me to keep this secret. If my sister's life is hanging in the balance, there is nothing I won't do to save her—including throw away my crown.

They whisk her away, and I attempt to follow, but Davies pulls me back. "I can get you there just as fast," he says.

I try to pull away. "But I should be with her."

"I know. We'll be there soon."

Our ride to the hospital is quiet. Davies must sense that I want to be left alone with my thoughts. I consider calling my mother, but since I'm not sure Bea has broken the news of the pregnancy to her yet, it seems best to wait. Of course, rumors of the Princess Royal being taken to the hospital by ambulance are bound to be circulating the halls of the palace within minutes, and it would be better if she heard it directly from me.

I settle for a text, but in true Rosalind fashion, she calls me immediately. I fill her in as best as I can, leaving out the part about the blood and the baby, instead telling her that I found Bea passed out in her bathroom and that we're taking her to the hospital.

"I'm on my way," she says.

"Mum, that's not necessary. I'm sure she's fine. We'll probably be home in a few hours." If there's a way to save Bea *and* keep my mother and the rest of the world from discovering her little secret, so much the better.

"Nonsense," she says. "She's my daughter."

Davies has managed to arrange a private entrance for us at the hospital, and we're led up to a private waiting room where a nurse assures us we'll be notified as soon as there is any word on Bea.

Time takes forever to pass. I keep my eyes glued to the clock on the wall, watching each second tick away. The loud clicks each time the hand moves are the only thing keeping me sane.

Davies hands me a cup of tea, and I accept it with a confused grimace. I didn't realize he'd left the room. He points to the small kitchenette pushed against the back wall, complete with kettle, tea bags, and suspicious-looking biscuits.

After what feels like a bazillion hours, a youngish-looking doctor steps into the waiting room. He bows his head and murmurs, "Your Majesty."

"How is she?" I bolt out of my chair when I spot his clipboard. Those things mean updates.

"She's doing fine now," he says. "Unfortunately, she had an early-term miscarriage. I'm afraid she lost the baby."

I slap a hand over my mouth, refusing to fall apart in front of this man. Davies will make sure the entire hospital staff signs an NDA, but I don't care about any of that right now. Bea is going to be devastated when she finds out.

"She's resting right now," the doctor adds. "We performed a D and C to remove any pregnancy tissue from the uterus, and she's sleeping off the general anesthetic."

I don't know anything about miscarriage, or pregnancy for that matter, but this sounds serious. "Is she going to be okay?"

He nods. "She'll be fine. We'll keep her here for around twenty-four hours, just to ensure there are no further complications, but recovery only takes a few days."

My mind is whirling. How can Bea have come in pregnant and be leaving without her baby? It's the exact thing I was trying to pressure her into doing, and the universe intervened, granting my wish and stealing hers.

"The main concern is heavy bleeding and infection," the doctor says. "We'll prescribe a few antibiotics to help avoid that."

"Will she ever be able to have—" I can't finish the question.

The doctor's brows lift. "To have another baby? I don't see why not. At least 80 percent of women who've had a miscarriage go on to have normal pregnancies. I haven't seen anything in this case that leads me to believe this would prevent a future pregnancy."

"Then why . . . ?"

He shakes his head and flips the pages of his clipboard back into place. "No one really knows. Sometimes the body decides it's not meant to be. Sometimes the baby isn't viable."

*Sometimes your sister wishes your baby away.*

I thank him, and he leaves, assuring me that I'll be notified as soon as I can visit Bea. When my mother arrives, I fill her in on everything the doctor said, including the fact that Bea was pregnant.

"Oh my god," she says, pressing her hand to her mouth. "My sweet girl."

I can't stay here any longer. Davies follows me down the hall, looking as ripped apart as I feel.

"You okay?" He stands just behind my elbow, ever the watchdog.

I clench my jaw in an attempt to stem the tears. I can't fall apart now, not when Bea needs me. "I will be," I say.

Bea is awake an hour later, but the nurse says she's still groggy and that I shouldn't take more than a few minutes. I nod and step into the room. Davies paces the hall outside.

"Hey." I force a smile. "You gave me quite a scare."

Bea looks at me, her eyes already regaining their sparkle. "Sorry 'bout that." Her voice is slightly slurred from the medication lingering in her system.

She looks so fragile in that bed, so delicate and feminine. Even in a hospital gown, she manages to look beautiful. She has an essence about her, not dissimilar to Elizabeth's, that draws people in.

"Is Henry the father?" The words are out before I can stop them.

Bea blinks rapidly. "What?" she squeaks, then clears her throat and tries again. "The father of . . . what exactly?"

"Your baby."

Her eyes go wide, a picture of horror and innocence mashed together. "Oh my god, Celia. Are you serious?"

"Just answer the question." I may regret asking, but now that it's out there, I need this answer like I need air.

"You cannot seriously think I would sleep with my brother-in-law."

"Stranger things have happened."

She fixes me with a glare. "No, Celia. Your husband isn't the father of my illegitimate baby. *God*." Crossing her arms over her chest, she turns away from me.

I feel equal amounts relieved and stupid right now. It was ridiculous to think they might have slept sleeping together, but when my brain started spiraling, it just made sense.

"I'm sorry, Bea. Things have been really crazy lately. I should have known you wouldn't do something like that."

Her eyes tell me that yes, I definitely should have, but my apology softens her a bit. "You've been under a lot of stress, what with that hoyden claiming her kid is Henry's and all."

The corners of my mouth tug up in a small smile.

"Trust me," she says. "My baby is *not* Henry's, and I have no intention of exploding your life with my choices." She rubs her belly through the hospital sheet.

It hits me like a freight train. The strong set of her jaw, the spark in her eyes, the way she's already bouncing back to her usual self. The way she's rubbing her belly and using the present tense . . .

They didn't tell her. They didn't bloody tell her about the baby. They must have decided that as queen, I'm more than qualified to be the one to inform my sister that the thing she loved the most in the world is gone.

"Bea . . ." How do I even start? I don't have a clue how to break news like this to anyone, let alone someone I love.

My eyes must convey something my mouth can't, because the smile drops from her face. "What is it?"

"Do you know why you're here? In the hospital?"

Her brows scrunch together. "I had some pretty bad pain in my stomach. There was a bunch of blood on the floor. I assumed it was my gallbladder or something, but I haven't talked to the doctor yet."

*Gallbladders don't bleed like that.* "It's a little more serious," I say, fighting to keep my words from wobbling.

"What are you saying?"

"I'm sorry, Bea." I press my lips together to keep a sob from slipping out. "The baby's gone."

# 26

# "Kiss Me Like You Do (Movie Version)" - Ellie Goulding

L IKE A CONVICT, I escape the clutches of Bea's grief. The nurse admonishes me for getting her blood pressure up. No wonder they didn't tell her about the baby themselves. I'm halfway back to the waiting room before I remember that my mother is waiting, ready to pounce on me for knowing about Bea's pregnancy and keeping it from her.

I can't handle that. I can't handle much of anything at the moment. In fact, the only place I want to be is the exact place I'm not welcome. I ache to feel Henry's arms wrapped around me, imparting his strength and comfort. I imagine the press of his lips against mine as he chases every thought that doesn't contain him out of my head.

I stop abruptly in the deserted hallway, causing Davies to turn and look at me, concern in those striking blue eyes. "You okay?" he says quietly.

"I can't go back in there." I motion to the waiting room up ahead.

"I'll take you home, then," he says, placing a gentle hand on my arm and escorting me to the lift.

I don't know what I would do without this strong giant teddy bear always looking out for me. I consider telling him so, but I get the distinct impression he'd rather I keep it to myself.

As I sit alone in the backseat of the car, emotion threatening to suck me under, I'm reminded of another car ride a few years ago. Henry pulled me into his lap after the shooting, holding me against his chest while I shook. Later, at his penthouse, we did other things that still cause my skin to heat when I think about them.

God, what I wouldn't give to have those hands on me right now. The way his intense gaze sinks into me until it scorches my toes. The way he says my name like a prayer into my neck. The way he uses his mouth to make me tremble.

I lean forward in my seat. "Can we stop at the Atlantis instead?"

Davies shoots me a look in the rearview mirror. When he has satisfied himself that I haven't completely lost my mind, he nods. "Sure." It sounds tight, and I regret how often he's been required to cater to my whims.

"Thank you." I settle back into my seat. Or rather, I try to settle, but now that I've made the decision to go see Henry, a new kind of nerves takes over my body. What if he's not there? What if he doesn't want to see me? What if he's busy?

What if he has company?

I stare out the window and try not to be sick. We pull into the underground parking garage of the Atlantis minutes later—not nearly enough time to talk myself out of this or convince myself it's the right thing to do.

Security is a lot lighter than it was the last time I was here, when I was being hunted like an animal by William. Henry still owns the Atlantis, although he donates all the profits to a charity that helps underprivileged kids make it through school. It's a tiny thing to make up for the effects of insidion he helped bring into the country, but at least those in the program have much lower chances of getting addicted to drugs.

Davies has me wait in the car while he scans the garage, although who could possibly be here to hurt me is unclear, since we just decided to come a few minutes ago. Once the coast is clear, we head for the top floor, and I'm scared my heart is going to jackhammer through the bottom of the elevator car.

I'm not ready to step into the dripping luxury of the penthouse. It now serves as extra lodging for high-ranking guests of state—as well as Henry's crash pad when he'd rather not share my bed, apparently.

Despite the fear clawing its way up my throat, I enter. I am not ready for the soft T-shirt and worn jeans Henry's wearing or the way his hair falls into his eyes or the way he looks up from his phone in surprise as he walks into the foyer.

He is home to me, and life, and certainty, and everything good in the world. He is the sun and the moon and every twinkling star. He is every beat of my heart, all the oxygen in the room, and every surge of blood in my veins.

I want to launch myself into his arms, soak up every ounce of him, take him into myself, and breathe again. My heart has been waiting for this—for him—and now that he's right in front of me, I want nothing more than to bury myself in the folds of his shirt and sob until it's drenched.

If we crowd out the rest of the world, the pressure and the expectations, the talk of babies and families, the secrets and the lies, the Elizabeth Gables and the Preston Ansleys—if it all disappears, and we're just Henry and Celia again—everything will be okay. We'll be okay. We'll be more than okay. We'll set the world on fire and never look back.

He looks so enticing, standing there like a human popsicle, just waiting to be enjoyed. I can already taste his mouth, feel his tongue gliding along mine, that sweet spearmint flavor bursting against my taste buds like little fireworks.

"What are you doing here?" he says, shaking his head as he breaks into my fantasy.

I blink like an idiot. "I just came from the hospital."

"My god. Are you okay?" He moves toward me, concern etched into his brow.

"I'm fine. Bea isn't."

"What's wrong?"

"She had a miscarriage," I whisper, my voice hardly strong enough to get the words out.

"Oh my god." He pulls me against his chest, and I can't stop the endorphins that race through my bloodstream. We fit together perfectly, like two puzzle pieces. "I didn't even know she was pregnant."

I inhale a deep lungful of his whiskey-in-the-forest scent. "She wasn't very far along."

Keeping his arms fitted around me, he tightens them ever so slightly. "Who knocked her up?" He sounds as if he'd like to rip them a new one.

I use my shrug as a subtle way to get closer to him. "She wouldn't tell me."

His hands stroke my back. I can't tell if it's intentional or if he's doing it without realizing it. "How is she?"

"She was pretty wrecked about it, but the doctor said she'll be fine physically."

"That's a shitty thing to go through."

We stand there quietly, wrapped in each other and our own thoughts. Finally, I break the silence. "It was my fault."

Several beats pass, then Henry pulls back to look down at me. "What do you mean?"

I squeeze my eyes shut, as if that will erase my blame in the whole situation. "I pressured her to give up the baby. I didn't want—"

"—another scandal." Stiffening, he drops his hands, leaving me cold and empty.

"She's not ready to be a mother." I reach for him, but he steps backward.

"Sounds familiar."

"Henry, please. I'm sorry for the way I've screwed everything up. With Bea and with you." I take several steps toward him, and this time he doesn't move away, just looks down at his feet.

"You can't blame yourself for Bea's miscarriage. Even you don't have that much power," he mutters.

I place a hand on his chest. It's warm and solid beneath my palm. Goosebumps scurry over my skin. "But I'm the reason we fell apart. And I'm sorry." I take one more step, bringing my nose back to the softness of his T-shirt, which does a poor job of masking the strength beneath it.

He doesn't say anything, but his inhale catches. He's breathing harder than he was a few minutes ago.

"Will you let me make it up to you?" I raise my face to his.

He looks down at me and swallows. "What did you have in mind?" His voice is strained, and I inwardly rejoice at seeing I still have this effect on him.

I loop both arms around his neck, tugging his mouth closer to mine. "You could get me pregnant," I whisper. I lift my mouth, eager for that first taste of him. His lips are soft and full, and I arch myself against him, knowing it will never be enough.

He pulls back and breaks off the kiss. "That isn't funny."

"I wasn't trying to be."

"Then what are you doing?" He lifts his head again, but I keep my arms around his neck.

"I want to have a baby with you."

His face grows tired. "We're not in any position to be having a baby."

"We could get there."

"C, we're currently separated."

His words hit me like a slap. Is that how he sees this . . . arrangement? "I thought you said you needed time."

"I do. That's what a separation is for."

Everyone knows a separation is to make the final split easier. Few couples come back from one with a stronger relationship. "Maybe a baby is what we need," I say, even though I don't believe it.

"Fuck that, Celia." He thrusts both hands into his hair and steps backward, breaking my hold on his neck. "Don't say what you think I want to hear."

"I'm trying to hold on to what we have. What is so wrong with that?" My tears threaten to spill over. Why does he have to make this so hard?

Henry shakes his head, eyes on the floor.

"Can't we at least try?" I feel as small as my voice sounds.

His strong edges soften the way a cloud softens the light when it moves in front of the sun. "You're on birth control, remember?"

"So I won't take the pill tonight."

"That's not how it works."

I know that, or at least I did up until the minute I decided throwing myself at my husband's feet and begging him to have sex with me would be a good idea. "Right." I take a deep breath. In for an inch, in for a mile. "Then can we just have sex? I miss you."

Meeting my eyes, he shakes his head. "I don't think so."

A giant crack splinters my heart in two. "Why not?" I fight to keep control of my voice.

"Because it's a bad idea." He doesn't look like he believes it for a single bloody minute.

"How could it be? We're married," I remind him.

"I don't want you to get the wrong idea."

I gape at him. "And what idea would that be? That you still love me? That you still want me? That you're coming home?"

He doesn't say anything, and I have my answer.

My god, I've been such a fool. He's never been mine. That was only an act he played until he got bored with it.

A sob-heavy "oh" is the only thing I'm capable of getting out, because what else is there to say when the person you've spent your entire life loving decides they don't want to love you back anymore?

"God, C. Of course that's not what I meant." Henry moves toward me, hands spread wide.

My face feels like it's met the inside of a blender at high speed. I struggle to keep the tears at bay. They badly want to go to battle for me. "I get it." I hold up a hand to keep him from coming any closer. "Someone better came along, and you want to explore your options."

A muscle in his jaw jumps. "Someone *better*?" It's practically a snarl. "You think there's 'someone better' out there for me?"

"It doesn't matter what I think."

"How long are we going to keep having this conversation?" His tone cuts across my skin like shards of glass.

"Until I believe you!" I say. "I don't understand why you won't have sex with me."

"I told you. I don't think it's a good idea."

I stare at him, at this Greek god in front of me, all muscle and delicious-smelling skin. I know how much he enjoys sex, how much he *needs* sex to be able to focus. He denied seeing Elizabeth, but maybe he's been fulfilling his needs elsewhere.

"Are you sleeping with someone else?" I say through a haze of rage and tears.

His eyes narrow dangerously. "I cannot believe you just asked me that."

"I cannot believe you've dragged me to the point where I need to."

"Let's get one thing straight." He steps closer, then grasps my chin. "You are not only my wife, but the love of my life. I don't take a single breath without being aware of my need for you. I'd say I'll tell you the second that changes, but I suspect I'll be dead."

I can't breathe. I literally can't catch my breath, can't form a single thought as he gazes at me with those dark eyes, his words hanging between us like gauze. Any thought or breath I was about to claim darts away as he yanks my mouth against his.

This isn't like the kiss we shared a few minutes ago. This one is a fevered madness, a grappling mess of limbs and teeth and lips, proving that I was right in guessing his need is as great as my own. Done holding back, he attacks me like it's his job to consume me.

He bites my lip hard, then kisses it better. "There will never be a day I don't want you, baby." He backs me up against the wall.

"But you said—" I start, but he cuts me off with his mouth. His tongue slips past my teeth, and I groan. How is it possible to desire someone so badly that you want to tear them limb from limb?

I press into him. He's already rigid beneath me. My core tingles in anticipation. I greedily reach for the zipper on his jeans, but he pushes my hands away.

"Why not?" I slide my palm against that hard, flat stomach, then down to his waist.

He grabs both my wrists with his left hand and pins them above my head. "I'm in charge, that's why."

My pulse leaps. Henry continues his assault with his mouth, leaving a trail of kisses down the side of my neck and across my collarbones. I squirm, unable to dig my fingers into his thick hair the way I desperately want to.

He placates me with another scorching kiss, but he doesn't let go of my hands. I arch against him, eager for more, but he pulls back, leaving only our faces connected.

"Henry, please," I say.

He only deepens the kiss, diving into my mouth like he'll die if he doesn't explore every inch. Our tongues perform a slick, hot dance over each other. He uses his free hand to pinch my nipple through the fabric of my dress.

I gasp into his mouth, feeling his smile as he does it again.

"I would do anything for that noise," he says, sucking on the tender skin behind my ear.

I gasp again and arch into him. "Please tell me you're going to do more than torture me." I'm completely breathless already, and we haven't even started yet.

He hums against my neck, his breath hot and electric. "What more do you want?"

I let out a small cry as he bites my nipple. He hasn't even bothered to pull my dress off yet, and already he has me at the edge. "I need you inside me," I pant.

"Oh, I'll be inside you all right."

*Sweet mother of god.*

"But not with my cock."

My heart plummets, and the fog momentarily clears. "Why not?"

He gives one more tug on my breast, then lifts his head to meet my eyes. "Because I need you to understand that you can't control me. I will fuck you senseless with my hands and my mouth, but only because there's nothing else I want in this entire bloody world than to watch you come apart."

I want to argue, to say that's not fair, but his mouth is on mine again, even hungrier and greedier than before, if that's even possible. He drops my hands and leads us to the bedroom without removing his lips from mine even once.

Once inside, he kicks the door shut. "Take off your dress."

I want to tell him to take it off himself, but I don't dare, not with that look in his eyes. Instead, I reach for the zipper at the back. I turn to show him that I can't reach it, and he scowls as he tugs it down. He mutters a quiet "fuck" under his breath as he stares at my bare skin.

Once the dress is puddled on the floor and my bra and panties have been tossed aside, he points to the bed. "Go lay down." I obediently crawl onto it and lie on my back, but he shakes his head. "On your stomach."

My heart races as I roll over. I can't see him after he climbs onto the bed. He straddles me and places both palms on my ass. Goosebumps cover me from head to toe.

He begins massaging both my butt cheeks, rubbing deep into the tissue. It feels incredible and deeply sexual. His thumbs skim the line of my ass, gently moving closer and closer together.

He lifts his pinkie finger to my mouth, and when I open it, he slips it inside, prompting me to suck on it. I do, and several seconds later he pulls it back out. It's warm and wet as it slips between my ass cheeks and inside. The sensation makes me clench tightly. He swirls it there for a bit, and when I think I can't handle the wait any longer, he pulls it back out.

Using his thumbs, he gently pulls me apart, splaying my legs out further. His fingers run lightly over my entire seam, and the feeling is both too much and not enough. I inhale sharply, causing him to chuckle.

"Like that?" he murmurs. The bed shifts as he moves behind me. I have no idea what he's doing until the all-too-familiar heat of his mouth is upon me. I cry out as his tongue strokes me, then pushes into me, slow and deep.

He alternates between tiny flicks along my entrance and deep thrusts into my core. I shudder beneath him, but he doesn't relent. The gentle pressure of his fingers joins the softness of his tongue. Two of them slide into me, and I arch at the sudden invasion of pleasure.

"Easy," he murmurs in amusement, and presses me down into the mattress with his free hand. With the other, he teases my anal opening, then slides a finger inside.

I am going to explode. He uses both hands to thrust into me, setting a steady rhythm I can follow. The bed provides an unmatched amount of friction as I slide back and forth over it.

When I think there's no way I can handle another minute of this, his mouth joins his hands in some sort of circus trickery. His name leaves my lips in a scream. This is all the encouragement he needs, and he continues fucking me with his mouth and his hands as promised.

White-hot pleasure pops at the edge of my vision, and I clutch the pillow beneath my head in desperation as the world's biggest climax rips through me. He doesn't let up as I scream and thrash, ignited by feelings so intense I'm afraid I'll be nothing but ash when it's over.

He is still licking me and playing with my clit when I reach the other side. I can't handle any more. If it were possible to die from feeling too much, I would already be dead.

"Please," I say, nearly in tears. "Please stop."

He presses one last kiss to me before extracting his fingers.

"How am I still alive?" I say into the pillow.

He growls against the small of my back. "You should feel more alive than ever."

"I do." It comes out dreamily. With some effort, I manage to roll onto my back. "Your turn." I reach for the button of his jeans.

He darts up from the bed faster than I've ever seen him move before.

"Where are you going?" I say. Normally I'd prop myself up on an elbow, but I have the strength of a newborn right now.

"I told you," he says through clenched teeth. "None of that this time."

"But—"

"I said no." He leans over me on the bed, and it takes everything in me not to reach up and grab his shirt. "You want the power back, but you're not getting it."

I frown. "This isn't about power. I just want to make you feel good too."

"That's the thing," he says, straightening. "It's always about power for you."

"How can you say that?"

"Did you forget I know you better than you know yourself?"

My scowl deepens. "This was not a power play. I just missed you."

"Then tell me: how does it feel, climaxing and not being able to give anything in return?" He walks out of the room, leaving me alone in the bed after the best orgasm I've ever had.

He's wrong. Sure, I want to return the favor, but more than that I just want to feel—

Bloody hell. He's right.

I feel completely powerless.

# 27

# "Little More (Royalty)" - Chris Brown

I FORBID HENRY'S WORDS from haunting me. Unfortunately, they're not good at following instructions. I hate that he's right. If I'm just after power, what does that make me?

I refuse to let this be the legacy I leave. When future generations of students read about this period in their history textbooks, they will not read about a queen who sacrificed everything to maintain her power.

The question is, what can I do to prove to Henry that I don't want to be that person?

The answer comes when I'm scanning my schedule for the day as Daphne finishes my hair and makeup. The opening of a new children's farm in the southern part of the city is slotted for eleven o'clock. I'll shake a few hands, pet a few animals, and let the photographers do their thing.

I just need to convince Henry to come along and bring Axel.

He answers after a few rings. "Hey," he says, his voice breathless. I picture his hands on his hips, a sweaty towel draped around his neck.

"Hey." Heat rises to my face as I picture what happened yesterday in his bed. That experience is going to become a permanent part of my dreams from now on. "Please tell me you're free today."

There's a slight pause. "That depends."

"On?"

"What kind of favor you're about to ask."

I'm momentarily distracted imagining which kinds he'd be open to. I shake those thoughts. "I'm attending the opening of a new children's farm this morning. I was hoping you'd come too."

"To a children's farm?" He sounds skeptical.

"With Axel."

"Just to clarify, you want me and Axel to come with you to a petting zoo."

"Yes?" I say it like it's still a question.

A long sigh floats through the phone. "Why?"

"What do you mean why? He'll love it."

"C, you haven't cared before. Why now?"

"I do care. I've always cared."

"Is this about yesterday?"

As if I need another reminder. I squeeze my thighs closer together in hopes they will stop tingling. "Of course not. Look, you asked to do some events in public with him, and I thought this might be one he'd actually enjoy."

"Then why do I get the feeling you have an agenda?"

Needles of apprehension prick my spine. "I don't. I just miss you."

There's silence on the other end. I picture Henry raking his hand through his hair. "So you want me to call Libby and say what? 'My wife wants to borrow your son for a few hours'?"

Hearing him call her by her nickname still sends a bolt of pain through my abdomen, but I'm comforted that he says "your son" instead of "our son." My brain hums with the words "my wife."

"Do you mind?" I say.

He sighs again. "I guess not. Is she invited too, or just Axel?"

My muscles clench. I never considered inviting Elizabeth. She'll ruin the vision I had for today, completely stomping all over the whole thing in her adorable little dress and sneakers that shout "I am the personification of a cool mum!" It'll be an absolute nightmare.

"Sure!" I say, too brightly. There's no way I'm fooling him with that.

Sure enough, he snorts. "Okay. I'll see what she says."

This will be good, I remind myself. The press will see that there's no animosity between us, it will squelch any rumors that may be circulating about Henry and me, and it will hopefully prove to him that I'm willing to do what I can to save us—even spend time with his sickeningly perfect ex.

Henry and Axel arrive at the palace right before we are due to leave for the farm. I note the absence of Elizabeth with an overwhelming sense of joy that contributes to the enthusiastic kiss I leave on Henry's cheek.

His hand slides around my waist as if by muscle memory, and I linger there as long as I dare. After a few seconds, I sense him growing uncomfortable, and I pull back.

I squat down next to Axel. "Are you excited to see the animals?"

Smiling, he pops that ever-present thumb into his mouth and nods before glancing up at Henry. Henry ruffles the kid's hair and takes his hand to lead him to the limo.

"Elizabeth couldn't make it?" I ask once we're in the car.

He studies me for several seconds, creases forming at the edges of his eyes. "She has a closing to attend."

"That's too bad."

"Like you're not relieved," he says under his breath.

"The more the merrier." I shrug and smile at Axel, who is watching us with wide eyes. *I'm trying, Henry.*

The children's farm boasts over thirty different animal species for families to visit. Other visitors have been limited to a small handful in order to decrease the amount of security needed.

The press is here too, of course, and even though I know this will provide some great footage, I'm a little annoyed by their presence. We won't have even a modicum of privacy.

Axel votes we visit the goats first, so that's the enclosure we head toward. He walks solemnly beside Henry, clutching his hand tightly as PPOs and photographers surround us. It must be terrifying to be thrust into the spotlight like this, and even though it's his mother's fault, I feel sorry for Axel. It's not like he's had any say-so in the matter. Elizabeth bloody Gable should have thought about what she was doing to her son before starting this whole drama.

Once we're inside the enclosure, I get a handful of food from the machine and take it to Axel, who is staring at the goats with much less enthusiasm than before. "Do you want to feed them?" I ask.

He shakes his head and sticks his thumb into his mouth again. We'll need to work on that, or else Elizabeth will have my head for allowing him to catch some animal-related disease.

"You sure? They're nice, especially if you feed them." I hold out my hand and show him the pellets.

This catches the attention of several nearby goats, and they immediately head toward me. I don't typically consider myself scared of animals, but when three large goats start heading for me, looking at me like I'm going to be their next meal, I'm as terrified as the next girl.

I remind myself that Axel is watching, not to mention the cameras all around, and force myself to stand my ground. I hold the food out to the goats, and one of them scarfs it down before the others can get any.

"See?" I say to Axel when my palm has been licked clean. "That's all there is to it."

"Um, C?" Henry is standing next to Axel, his son's small hand tucked inside his large one, but he's looking at the animals now swarming me, all begging for a handout.

"What?" I push a particularly obnoxious goat off my shoes.

A smile spreads across Axel's face. He pulls his thumb out of his mouth in order to point at me. "Look!"

I look around for the source of their entertainment. A huge white goat stands several feet away, a piece of yellow fabric hanging from its mouth. Glancing down at my lemon-colored blazer, I see a large section has been torn from the side.

"No!" I yell. "Bad goat!" I start to chase him or her across the paddock, then think better of it. The entire country does not need to be amused by the sight of their queen running after a goat.

I turn back to find Henry and Axel both bent over in laughter. "Glad you found that so humorous," I say, heading for the hand-washing station.

By the time they join me, I have to admit it was slightly funny. My blazer won't recover, but if that's what it takes to put a smile on Axel's face, bring it on.

We head to the geese next. Axel was attracted by their squabbling and general chaos, which can't be a good sign. By the time we're done, the boy again refusing to pet anything, my trousers are less "glacier white" and more "barnyard brown."

Back on the asphalt path, Henry studies me, paying special attention to my mucked-up pants, destroyed jacket, and disgusting sneakers. "At what point did that outfit seem like a good idea?" There's a twinkle in his eyes I'd have to be blind to miss. Is he *flirting* with me?

The thought sends a warm tingle through my veins. I slip out of the blazer and toss it into a nearby rubbish bin. I don't miss the way his eyes linger on my bare shoulders. "Good ideas are overrated." I swoop up Axel's free hand. "Where to next, buddy?"

I can feel Henry's gaze on me as we head to the miniature ponies. The weight of his attention feels heavier than that of any of the cameras following us. I lean down to whisper to Axel, "Race you there."

He offers me an open-mouthed smile and drops Henry's hand. We sprint toward the ponies and arrive in a mad dash of giggles. When Henry joins us, the grin on his face is worth everything.

A guide inside the pony enclosure helps Axel into one of the saddles. Henry and I watch from the wall as they walk circles around the pen.

"You're good with him," he says.

I look up, waiting for the barb. He returns my gaze, a faint smile hiding in the corners of his eyes.

"Thank you," I say, meaning it. His sincerity is like a cool breeze on a hot day.

He turns his attention back to Axel, but I can't tear my eyes from him. The sun is hitting his face just right, throwing that ridiculous jawline into even deeper shadow. I want to run my tongue over it, feel the stubble of the five o'clock shadow he always has these days.

His arm is perched along the wall behind us, and I take a tiny step closer, just enough to be inside its embrace. After a few more minutes, I find the courage to place my head against his shoulder. I wave as Axel makes another loop on his pony, then rest my fingertips on Henry's stomach.

His muscles tighten beneath my hand. "What are you doing?" he says quietly.

I pretend not to hear him and nod at Axel. "Look at him, actually smiling. He's a natural on that horse."

A few seconds later, Axel decides he's had enough and tries to lurch off the side of the pony. The guide manages to grab him in time, but Henry and I both rush over.

"Hey, buddy," Henry says. "Go a little slower next time, okay?"

Axel wants to see the llamas next and—still high from his ride—skips ahead of us down the path. I'm still high from being in the circle of Henry's aura. I have to admit, there's a part of me that is incredibly turned on watching him with Axel. A mothering instinct, I suppose, trying to find the best mate to help raise my children.

I'm not sure if it's the hormonal tempest going on inside me or the remnants of yesterday's sexcapades, but I reach for Henry's hand, entwining our fingers as I point to the zebra enclosure on our left. "Look," I say, a little breathless at being so close to him. "Aren't they stunning?"

He merely grunts in agreement but doesn't pull his hand from mine. I desperately hope it isn't just for the cameras.

The llamas aren't too interested in us, even when Henry hoists Axel up to offer them a handful of grass. We eventually give up and keep moving down the path. The cameramen follow behind, giant monstrosities mounted over their shoulders as they document our entire excursion.

"You think they ever get tired of lugging around those big things?" I step closer to Henry and slip my hand back into his.

He allows me to hold it, but that's the extent of his commitment. "At least they get buff shoulders out of the deal."

I squeeze his fingers to get his attention. "I've held hands with dead fish who participated more. What is up with you?"

He gives me a sidelong glance. "Just cut it out, okay? I'm sick of putting on a show."

He swoops Axel up in his arms and props him on his shoulders. The two of them take off down the path, yelling like they belong in one of the enclosures themselves.

*Putting on a show?* Is that what we're doing?

I do my best to ignore the knife buried in my heart. I thought we were getting to a better place, but apparently I'm an even bigger fool than I thought.

I catch up to them at the Highland cows, tiny little things with horns longer than Axel's arm. They're kind of cute, if you can overlook the fact that they could trample you with their hooves if they had a mind to.

As we step inside, I keep an eye out for any cow pies lurking in the tall grass. While it might complete the farm girl look I've adopted for the day, I can't imagine riding home with that stench would be pleasurable for anyone.

My careful observation saves me from stepping into a soft mound. It does not, however, save me from walking straight into the low-hanging branches of a tree whose entire purpose on earth appears to be gouging people with its massive thorns.

"Ow!" I say as a thistle scrapes my bare shoulder. I try to move away, but it has punctured the wide strap of my white tank. It's too close to my face for me to extract it myself.

Davies has already assessed the situation and is making his way into the cattle enclosure. Before he can reach me, Henry appears at my side. I yelp in surprise.

"You're determined to leave as much of yourself in this place as possible, aren't you?" He sizes up the embedded thorn.

"Just get this thing out of me. Where's Axel?"

He nods over to the other side of the enclosure. "Gonna try his hand at cattle wrestling."

I peer over his shoulder. A park guide is helping Axel twirl a rope as big as the kid's wrist. "This should be interesting."

"Hold still." Henry reaches for me.

"Ouch! What are you doing?"

He holds up the offending thorn, brows raised. "Saving you?"

A quick peek shows that, while the thorn is gone, between the giant hole and the blood, my top is also headed for the garbage.

"Shit." Henry is inspecting my shoulder. "She's bleeding," he says to someone behind me.

Davies hands him the first aid kit he apparently keeps on him. Henry pulls out an antiseptic wipe and begins cleaning the wound. I don't even register the sting. I'm too busy focusing on the feel of his hands on my skin, firm and gentle, holding me in place like he does in bed.

He's sticking the bandage on when Axel swings the rope. I grab Henry's arm. "Oh my god, look!"

He turns around as Axel maneuvers the rope in a poor circle and loops it over the cow's horn. The cow looks at him as though he's as interesting as dried mud and continues chomping grass.

I laugh and clap enthusiastically. "You did it!"

Axel looks back at me, a satisfied grin on his face. When I glance at Henry, his eyes are full of wonder. And while Axel's feat was pretty impressive for a three-year-old, he's not looking at his son.

He's looking at me.

We take a break to get lunch from the little café and sit at one of the round picnic tables clustered in front of the awning. The camera crews have disappeared for now, giving us temporary privacy.

Axel chows down his hot dog faster than I've ever seen a toddler do.

"If I was in doubt about his parentage before, consider me fully convinced." I nod pointedly at the boy's already empty food basket and then at Henry's, which isn't empty yet, but only because it started out containing four hot dogs, a mess of crisps, and an order of mozzarella sticks.

He picks up his single remaining hot dog. "We can't all eat like a princess." He looks at the salad on my plate. "Or like rabbits."

I slug his shoulder with my fist. "Try *queen*. And how else do you expect me to keep my figure?"

He uses the time it takes him to chew to peruse my body from head to toe, then moves his gaze back up. It drags along my skin like nails. "I hardly think *this* is responsible for *that*," he says, nodding first at my salad and then at me. "But if so, I have no complaints."

I know my face is glowing right now. The luminescence is a tangible feeling. I don't say anything, just stare back at him and envision a future where this is normal again.

Henry reaches out with a finger and swipes at my cheek. "Dressing," he says before popping it into his mouth, eyes still locked on mine.

What is happening?

There was no dressing there. I'm sure of that. When I was Axel's age, my mother taught me to use a napkin after every bite, which I have done ever since. A queen should never be seen with spaghetti sauce on her chin.

Elizabeth has yet to teach her son the same thing. He is smeared with mustard from cheek to cheek. There's even a smudge on his nose.

"Buddy, I think you're wearing more of that hot dog than you're eating," I say. Wetting my napkin with water, I lean across the table to wipe his face.

He giggles and squirms away from me. "It's cold!"

"I'm sorry, but it's either this or a cow tongue. Your pick."

He holds still after that, and I'm reaching for the bit on his nose when something warm touches my lower back. I instinctively know it's Henry's hand.

My top has ridden up, so it's not only on my back, but on my bare skin. It's like being touched by the sun. I'm terrified to sit back down, afraid that he'll remove it and I'll never get to experience this toe-tingling pleasure again.

When I've wiped Axel's nose approximately forty times and it's become evident he won't tolerate any more, I force myself back down. Much to my surprise and delight, Henry's hand not only stays planted on my back, but my top slides over it, leaving it covered and me a shaky mess. This might be the most sensual experience I've ever had, judging from the way my thighs are quaking right now.

He skims his thumb over my bare skin, as if he knows the struggle I'm undergoing but has faith that I can get through this. My appetite gone, I push my salad away and immediately regret it. With both of them already done eating, I was the only one still keeping us here.

Henry drags his hand out from beneath my shirt, running the backs of his fingers over my hip bone as he does so. I nearly convulse. If there weren't a dozen cameramen lurking somewhere, as well as half a dozen PPOs shoveling down hot dogs and one curious three-year-old boy nearby, I would be looking for the nearest bathroom and begging Henry to do anything he wants to me.

The rest of the animals pass in a blur. The only things I'm cognizant of are the excuses Henry finds for touching me. Placing his hand on my elbow to steer me away from some dangerous-looking peacock droppings. Using it to brush the hair from my eyes as I hold a baby chick out for Axel to pet. Resting it on the center of my back in the lemur enclosure as he leans over to whisper "These things freak me the fuck out."

To anyone on the outside, we look like a blissful family of three, exploring the zoo and making sweet memories. And the truth is, for a second, I allow myself that fantasy. It doesn't even matter that Axel isn't my son, because today I can imagine a time and place where I do have a child with Henry and we are this picture-perfect family in the park. Yesterday, it would have been impossible.

But I think I've just won back my husband.

# 28

# "Adore You" - Harry Styles

UNFORTUNATELY, ALL GOOD THINGS must come to an end, and when we finish up at the children's farm, I find I'm actually disappointed. Axel is completely wiped out, his little head bobbing on Henry's shoulder as he carries him to the car.

The day was even more magical than I hoped. I never thought I'd find myself falling for someone who still wears training pants to bed and doesn't stand taller than my waist, but here we are.

When we drop Axel off at Elizabeth's house, I try not to count the minutes Henry is inside with the door shut. Not after the way he responded to me.

When he finally returns to the car, my heart unravels from the tight ball it has knotted itself into. His eyes meet mine in the dim light, and I recognize the hunger in them. He settles beside me in the back seat, his thigh brushing against mine and causing a thrill to race up my leg, directly to the space between my thighs.

The silence ticks by, heightening the tension between us. I'm still trying to think of a way to break the awkwardness when he says, "You were amazing today."

I glance at him in surprise. "Was it the way I fed my jacket to the goats? Or became a human target for that chimp throwing apples?"

He drapes his arm behind me on the seat, his thumb brushing against my bare shoulder. "Actually, I was referring to the way you nearly jumped out of your skin when that donkey bumped your ass."

"I thought something was coming after the rest of my clothes." I jab him in the ribs, then move my finger up to what I know is a ticklish spot for him.

Henry jerks away from me and grabs my hand before I can torture him further, twisting it so that I'm nearly in his lap. Then with his other hand, he tickles my own exposed side. I bury my face in his chest and squirm to get away. When he finally relents, I'm breathless and still laughing.

As our laughter fades, we both become aware of what just happened. We haven't done something like this in a year or more. I'm still trapped against him by an arm that feels more like a cable. I relish the moment and inhale his scent deeply.

"Stop sniffing my stomach," he says. "Weirdo."

I give his abs another exaggerated sniff, wiggling my face back and forth. I want to bite him. He inhales sharply and tugs me until I'm upright again, but he doesn't let go. Instead, he slides his hand up my neck and into my hair, then pulls me toward him. The hunger in his eyes has intensified, and my mouth goes dry.

He kisses me slowly and tentatively at first, as if he's unsure he's ready to commit. But when I swipe my tongue across his bottom lip, he groans and welds his mouth to mine.

I reach hungry fists to his chest and bunch up handfuls of his shirt. His hand slides over my hip and yanks me harder toward him. I hover on the verge of climbing into his lap. He tilts my head back and peppers my throat with kisses.

When he reaches the space between my clavicles, I teeter on the brink of combustion.

"I wanted to fuck you so hard when you made him smile," he says against my skin.

I jerk my head back in surprise. "Wha—"

Henry cuts me off with his mouth, chasing every thought from my mind with his tongue. It's a decadent feeling, and I'm drowning. He tightens his fingers at the back of my head so I can't move.

"Axel," he says, as breathless as I am. "Watching you with him." His mouth sinks to mine again, as though he can't go more than a few seconds without another dose. When he comes up for air, he says, "I wanted to take you against that wall."

Sweet adrenaline shoots through my veins like I've just had a hit of cocaine. "Move back in with me," I say against his lips.

He leans back, too far to retain contact. "C . . ." His eyes are sad, pulling down at the corners.

My heart drops to the floor. "Why not? You just said—"

"I said I wanted to fuck you, yes."

The rest of his sentence hangs between us, unspoken but not unheard. *But that doesn't mean I want to be with you.*

"So that's it, then?" I untangle myself from him and shift back in my seat. "We're going to have this magical day, and you're just going to leave again at the end of it?"

His eyes flutter shut. "Is that why you invited us? As some kind of power play to get me to move back into the palace?"

"No." I shake my head. "Of course not. I *miss* you. Maybe that's hard for you to comprehend, but my body and heart are still very much under the impression that they belong to you." My voice breaks at the end.

"They *do* belong to me," he growls, hauling me against himself. His mouth finds mine like a greedy zombie looking for its next victim. Gone is the delicacy from earlier. In its place is a fierce hunger that threatens to consume every part of me. I welcome it with open arms.

His hand slides up my shirt and cups my breast. I cry out when he rubs his thumb over my nipple, but he swallows the sound. He pulls my bra down just enough to release my breast, then rolls the nipple between his finger and thumb. I exclaim again and feel him smile against my mouth.

A new kind of desperation overtakes him, and he pushes my top up. Breaking off the kiss, he turns his attention to the peaks of my eager chest. I moan as he takes one into his mouth, sucking and pulling and licking and tasting me into oblivion.

"Henry!" I gasp after one particularly hard nip.

He chuckles and offers an apology by way of gentle kisses.

"What are we doing?" I say dreamily. I would sell my soul for this to never end, but it doesn't stop me from feeling confused.

He lifts his head and meets my gaze. "I miss you."

"Then come home."

He flicks his thumb back over my nipple a few more times, then readjusts my bra and top. A deep sigh passes his lips. "It's not that easy."

"What isn't easy about it? You live there. We're *married*. You certainly don't act like someone who doesn't want to share my bed."

"Just because I can't keep my hands off you doesn't mean—" He leans forward and rests his head in his hands. "You lied to me, C. I can't just pretend that never happened."

It feels like a lit torch is stuck in my lungs. "You lied too."

For a minute he doesn't say anything or move. Then he looks back at me over his shoulder. "You're right. I did."

I rest a tentative palm on his back. "Can't we work through this together?"

He moves a hand to my knee, rubbing his thumb back and forth. "I'm still upset."

"Fine. Be upset," I say. "But do it at home so we can at least have hot makeup sex." I slide my other hand up his thigh and toward his crotch.

He hisses through his teeth when I reach his impressive erection, snatching up my wrist. "God, Celia. That's not fighting fair."

I giggle and press a kiss to his cheek. "You liked it. Admit it."

"Define *like*," he says, sitting up and pulling me across his lap in one motion. "If you mean that I want to take you in the back of this limo, then yes. I *liked* it."

I don't even have time to catch my breath before his mouth is on mine again, taking everything I'll give him. When he reaches for the zipper on my pants, I push his hand away and come up for air.

"We're almost home. Say you'll stay, and we can do this for the rest of the night."

His eyes move between mine. "No more secrets."

I nod. "No more secrets."

It's a miracle I can walk today after the night I had. You would think after a few years of marriage, a person's husband would stop surprising them, but that is not the case, at least not for yours truly. Not that I'm complaining, although Maisie did give me a weird look when I hobbled over to the window to let in a breeze after Henry texted me.

> **Henry:** How do you feel about office sex? I've just had my desk polished.

The image of dragging him down on top of me with the tie he was wearing when he left this morning is enough to make me pant.

A knock on the door startles me, and I can only hope my face isn't as red as it feels. Preston steps inside and approaches my desk. "We need to talk. Do you have a minute?"

"Sure." I remain seated. If he's hoping for a continuation of what happened the last time he was in here, he's about to be sorely disappointed.

"You asked me to tie up any loose ends at the hospital."

I nod as my stomach churns. I miss the days of no one knowing my name or caring what I did yesterday. "Did everyone sign the NDA?"

He sets a file on my desk, presumably full of the medical staff's nondisclosure contracts. "Everyone signed."

"I sense a *but* coming."

He sighs and pushes his hair from his forehead. "These things have a way of leaking to the press anyway. The hospital's a big place, and with the Princess Royal being taken by ambulance . . . I just think it's best if we prepare for a media circus."

Preston's job is to maintain our reputation. There will be no way of "maintaining" anything once Bea's miscarriage becomes public knowledge. That will be a lit match to the royal family's image.

"What are you suggesting?" I ask, folding my hands in front of me.

"We need to prepare a statement to address the issue once it arises."

"I'd rather we not let it arise." Bea is in too fragile a state to let the entire country feast on her pain like jackals on a carcass.

Preston shakes his head. "I don't see a way to avoid it."

I slap my palm onto the stack of NDAs. "You just had everyone sign this."

"Celia, we're talking about more than thirty people." He braces his arms on the desk. "And that's if we can trust the staff to keep their mouths shut."

"There has to be a way."

"I have yet to find one."

I stand up, and even though Preston towers over me, he shifts his weight backward. "You are paid to take care of things like this. Think of something!"

He runs his tongue over his bottom lip. "My father might know some people who could—"

"Please do not finish that sentence. No one is setting fire to the news stations." I've had enough of Preston's shady acquaintances. I stare down at my desk like the answers might be waiting there. Then I remember something Maisie said weeks ago. "What about a distraction?"

"I'm sorry?" He raises his brows in confusion.

"A distraction. Something to keep them busy until they forget. We can slip in the news that Beatrice was in the hospital for a gallbladder attack while we provide them with a juicier story."

"Go on." He narrows his eyes.

"We've got the perfect scandal to draw them in already." I'm warming to this idea every second. "I'll make a press statement about how amazing it is to have this new 'family.'"

"And this new family consists of . . . ?"

"Me, Henry, and Axel."

Preston nods, the cogs in that brilliant head of his already turning, forming ideas and plans. "Okay. That could work. How soon can you give the statement?"

I issue a press statement the next day. Just as we hoped, the media is thoroughly distracted by my open-armed embrace of Axel into our family. If I had known how well they would react to this kind of response from me, I might have done it sooner.

It's not fake, either. Henry and I take Axel on a nonpublicized outing to a local ice cream shop. Of course, you can't be the queen of Wesbourne and not have people capture you on camera, but we didn't do it for publicity. We did it because, despite the odds, this is starting to feel a little like a family.

# 29

# "The Lucky One" - Taylor Swift

I MAY HAVE BEEN overambitious in what I agreed to when I was brainstorming ways to get the press's attention on us and off of Bea. I blame the sex hormones. With Henry back home and neither of us under the illusion that we are trying for a baby, it's like our honeymoon all over again.

He's been keeping me fully distracted with the incredible things he can do with his hands, which somehow leads to me losing all common sense and arranging a private meeting with Elizabeth Gable. Regret plagues me as I wait for her to appear in the Audience Room.

I'm wearing a green suit and four-inch heels. When I put it on this morning, it made me feel powerful and confident, but the second Elizabeth walks into the room, I know it was the wrong choice.

She's even more stunning than I remember and has chosen the perfect outfit for the occasion, as always. As far as I know, she doesn't have a stylist and hairdresser to aid her in such choices, and she still manages to look like Blake Lively.

She's wearing a floral dress that hits a few inches above her knees, the flirty hemline floating through the air as she walks. She's thrown a soft pink cardigan on top. The whole thing screams "romantic stroll through the farmer's market, and also open to stealing husbands that aren't nailed down!"

At least Henry won't be joining us this time.

She crosses her legs on the sofa opposite me and softly bounces her foot. I wonder if it's a nervous tic.

"I wanted to speak to you about Axel," I begin.

Her foot stops moving. "Is everything okay?"

*Other than you taking a wrecking ball to my life?* "Absolutely. He's a great kid."

She beams, and I suppose she does deserve some credit for shaping him this way. "Thank you. He's my entire world."

I brush my hands across the fabric of my trousers. "Given the circumstances, we would like to ensure that he has a bright future. Opportunities, you know."

Her eyes narrow like a cat's. "Are you implying he doesn't already have those things?" It's the first time I've heard anything other than pure maple syrup in her tone.

"Of course not," I say. "We just want to do what we can to assist."

"Will Henry be joining us?" Elizabeth looks around the room as if he might pop out from behind the Chinese silk screen.

I resist the smirk that is begging to lift the side of my mouth. "He wanted to be here, but unfortunately, he had some important things to sort out." In reality, he doesn't even know I'm meeting with her. I'm not planning to keep it a secret; I just haven't had a chance to tell him yet. Every time we're together, our mouths tend to be busy with other things. "I thought it would give us the chance to talk, woman to woman."

If she's intimidated by this, she doesn't show it. Instead, she crosses her hands over her knee and smiles. "Great idea."

"How do you feel about boarding school?" I say. "Eton is the classic choice, of course, but—"

"I don't think so."

I smooth out the list of schools in my lap. "Well, there are plenty of other options. Henry went to—"

She shakes her head. "Axel belongs with me."

"Of course he does. Preparatory school is still years away, but now is the time to make these kinds of plans. Waitlists tend to fill up, after all."

"Forgive me, Your Majesty, but I don't want my son shipped off to another country for years. He's all I have."

I blink at her. Most people would be thrilled to have their child's funding to the most elite schools in the world covered. "What do you plan to do instead?"

"He can go to school right here in Wesbourne. I went to Hawthorne Prep myself, and while it's not Eton, I don't have any gaps in my education."

"S-sure," I stammer. "But he's the son of the prince consort. There are certain expectations—"

"I don't care about any of that." She tilts her chin upward. Her voice is firm.

I search her face, trying to solve the puzzle of what she's after. "Then what do you care about?"

"My son."

"Of course," I say. "But why did you come barging into our lives like this if you didn't expect things to change?"

"I told you before, I don't need or want your money. I only want Axel to have a father."

I notice she doesn't say *his* father. "Couldn't you marry someone and give him a normal family? It won't be easy to grow up in the public eye."

A light laugh bubbles out of her. "I don't know if you've seen the available men out there these days, but trust me when I tell you, it's not a pretty sight."

There's something more here, but I can't put my finger on it. "But why Henry? You've disrupted the entire nation over this, with no foreseeable benefit to your son."

"Family is everything," she says softly.

I think of my own family, and how wrecked we became the minute my dad was diagnosed with the brain tumor that stole him from us. "Yeah, it is."

Something else occurs to me. "You should know that the Sutherland family is . . ." I wrestle for the right words. "Well, they aren't the healthiest family in the world, at least not emotionally."

Elizabeth laughs again. "Find me the one that is."

"I don't mean in the way that all families have their quirks and struggles," I say. "I mean in some pretty serious ways. You should be aware of that before you expose your son to things that could potentially mess up the rest of his life."

This is something I've been working through. Bringing a child into the world only for them to be hurt isn't right. But at the same time, I have to trust that Henry is a different person than his father. He's far from perfect, but he has traits William could only ever dream about.

"I gave this a lot of thought before I sent that letter." Her foot bounces again. "I know that the situation is far from ideal, but I think the benefits outweigh all of that."

*For who?* I want to ask. But these thoughts of William have reminded me of something else, something that's been niggling at the back of my mind for days. Something I've been too distracted to pay much heed to until now.

"Why did you visit William in prison?" I blurt out.

Her foot stops midbounce, and she slowly lowers it to the floor. "How do you know about that?" Her eyes drop to the floral print of her dress.

"I don't think that's the issue here."

"Did you follow me?"

I bark out a laugh. "As if I don't have better things to do than trail you around the country." I cross my own legs and drape my wrists over them. It's about time I was back in charge of this conversation. "So what was it? You thought you'd inform him that he has a grandson?"

She keeps her gaze on her lap as a pink tinge colors her face. "No."

"What then? Were you asking him for advice on raising boys? Because trust me, he is the last person you want to ask."

"Of course not." The words come out in a whisper.

"Then tell me why someone like you"—I give her outfit a meaningful look—"would visit a federal prison to chat with a convicted felon."

Elizabeth is twisting her hands together, and for a minute, I don't think she's going to answer me. But she lifts her gaze to mine and says in a quavering voice, "Because I had to."

"You *had* to?" I say. "Did he summon you or something?"

She diverts her gaze, her jaw twitching as she struggles to hold back tears. "I doubt he even remembered me."

"Remembered you? Were the two of you acquainted?"

She gives her head a tiny shake. "Not exactly."

"Then how did you expect him to remember you?"

She loses her grip on her emotions, and a single sob slips out. "You don't understand. I needed closure. Or I thought I did. But he was so nasty about it all—" She runs a finger under each eye to push out the tears caught there. "I thought I was ready to handle it, but after seeing him, I realized I wasn't."

My forehead creases. "I'm not following. Closure from what?"

It takes a long time for her to look up at me, and when she does, her eyes are wet. "He raped me."

Every line on my face melts away, and my mouth falls open. "He *what?*"

"It was years ago," she says. "Before you became queen. I came to the palace for one of Henry's parties."

I've heard about these parties, although I never received an invitation to one myself. Infamous for their raucous debauchery, all manner of drugs, high-end alcohol on tap, women in nothing but their underwear, shared and swapped partners, games of truth or dare that always got out of hand. I don't know how many of the rumors are true, but for my own sanity, I'd rather not find out.

"I left to find the restroom," she continues, taking a deep breath. "I got turned around in one of the hallways. He ran into me, and I was so speechless to be face-to-face with the king that when he told me to follow him, I did it without thinking."

A skeletal hand grips my heart and squeezes tightly. I wish I'd never asked about her visit to William, because I don't want to hear the rest of this story.

"He took me into a dark room, and it wasn't until he locked the door that I got scared. I was drunk and a little high, but hearing that lock click into place sobered me up pretty quickly. I told him no, but he didn't listen, just forced me onto the sofa, and—" She squeezes her eyes shut as if trying to erase the memory.

"I'm sorry," she says after a long exhale. "My therapist thought I was ready to face my demons, but clearly I wasn't."

I blink several times. "Your therapist encouraged you to see your rapist?"

Her eyes flicker to me, then back down to her lap, where she fiddles with the lace hem of her dress. "She didn't know that's what I was planning to do. We were trying to find closure. I was the one who thought it might help."

"I am so sorry." I reach across and place my hand on top of hers. "No one should have to endure something like that." *Not even you.*

Her throat bobs as she swallows several times in a row. "There's more," she says softly. Her breath catches. "William is Axel's father."

The room shifts around me, and I brace my palms against the sofa to keep from shifting with it. I heard what she said, but I can't make sense of it. She's clearly waiting for me to speak, but I don't have a clue how to respond.

"I know this must come as a shock," she says.

"A shock?" I let out a cackle. It sounds awful, but it feels cathartic. "Please tell me you're joking." My mind whirls. After everything that's happened, she's admitting it's all been a lie?

"I wouldn't joke about something like this," she says.

"How can you possibly know he's Axel's father?"

Her face flushes an even deeper pink. "I wasn't seeing anyone at the time."

"You just said you were at one of Henry's parties. I've heard enough stories—"

"It wasn't anyone there, trust me. Those parties had a worse reputation than they deserved."

I shake my head, hoping it will rearrange the pieces of this whole conversation into an order that makes some semblance of sense. "No. This can't be right. We did DNA testing. It said Henry is the father."

"All I know is that Henry and I had sex several months before that. The timing wouldn't have been right."

My brain trips over her blatant announcement that she slept with my husband. That is not something I want to dwell on. "Maybe you got the timing wrong?" I don't know why I'm fighting her on this when she's giving me exactly what I've been wanting all along: proof that she's lying.

"I didn't," she says.

"Then why did the DNA spit out a 97 percent chance of paternity?"

She takes a deep breath and smooths her dress over her legs. "I did a lot of research on this to make sure it would work. These companies only test small amounts of data due to time and cost constraints. A child receives one copy of their genes from each parent. Because Henry and William share much of the same DNA as father and son, Axel received a lot of the same DNA from William that Henry did, making Henry's test positive. If it had been tested alongside William's DNA, it would have been obvious who the real father was."

I let this sink in for a few moments. "Then why did you concoct this ridiculous story? If you're not after money, what is it you want? Why go to these lengths?"

"I didn't lie about that part. I want Axel to have a father. I made some bad decisions in the past, but becoming a mother changed me. I want to be someone he can look up to and be proud of." She wipes away her tears, leaving a tiny streak of mascara beneath each eye.

"Surely there are plenty of men who would be thrilled to be a part of yours and Axel's life. Why not one of them? Why Henry?"

She turns pink. "Because he's . . . Henry." The dreamy softness in her voice causes my stomach to turn over as the realization smacks me between the eyes.

"Oh my god. You're in love with him," I say.

Her expression grows panicked. "I would never do anything, I promise."

I don't know if I believe her, but it doesn't matter, because I believe Henry, and he has assured me over and over of his faithfulness. "Why are you telling me this? I could ruin your entire plan. All I need to do is tell him the truth."

She stares at me with an intense gaze that is a little unnerving. Beneath that soft, feminine exterior, this woman has a backbone of steel. "I'm trusting that you love your husband too much to do that."

# 30

# "Waiting for Love" - Avicii

S LEEP IS NOT COMING easily tonight. While Henry is out like a light bulb with a blown fuse beside me, I'm kept awake by the dilemma of what to do with Elizabeth's confession. Before leaving, she begged me not to tell Henry.

Maybe it makes me a cold-hearted bitch, but I don't give a damn what Elizabeth Gable wants. She marched into our lives, blew them up with her nuclear bomb of an announcement, and now that I know she lied about the whole thing, has the audacity to ask me to keep it a secret?

If I choose not to say anything, it won't be for her sake.

It will be for his.

I look over at Henry's dreaming form, the newly formed lines on his face softened with sleep. He's happier than I've seen him in a long time. If this is what being a father does to him, I wish I had been more willing to consider a baby before now. It's not as if I'm opposed to the idea. It just felt too inconvenient and too terrifying.

If I tell him the truth—that Axel is in fact his brother and not his son—he'll be devastated. He's become so attached to him. He'll also break into prison and kill his father, and that could get messy.

But if I don't say anything and he finds out later, he'll be angry that I kept this from him, especially since we agreed not to keep any more secrets.

The easy thing to do would be to tell him, to announce from the rooftops that the royal family isn't as scandalous as everyone has been led to believe. This news would go a long way toward keeping our image with the public.

But it would destroy Henry.

I stroke his thick hair, twining it between my fingers. I can't do that to him. I can't ruin everything he thinks he has. Elizabeth is right—if I truly love him, I will keep this from him.

So I fall asleep with the resolution to be the best possible stepmother I can be to a child who isn't even my husband's.

While on my way to cut the ribbon for a new bypass, I get a message from Henry. *Parents' meeting at Axel's school tonight.*

Dread settles over me like a blanket. Is this what it's going to be like from now on, the four of us traipsing to all kinds of events for the next fifteen years? Soccer matches and award banquets and spelling contests.

I type out *He's THREE* but delete it instead of sending it. I write back *Okay!* with a smiley face that conveys the exact opposite of how I feel. It's a good thing we're texting, because Henry would see right through me otherwise.

"Do you still want me to stay late tonight?" Maisie asks from the seat beside me.

I glance up to see if she is reading over my shoulder, but she's engrossed in her own phone. "Actually, it looks like I'll be attending a parents' meeting tonight."

We were planning to draft my quarterly newsletter, which goes out in a few weeks to the two million subscribers on my email list.

A look of relief washes over her face. "So I don't need to stay? Beck has been pestering me about trying this new place down on Twenty-Third."

"Yeah, go. Sounds like I'll be stuck looking at blobs of modeling clay that are supposed to be dragons and listening to a teacher drone on about what a gifted child Axel is."

Maisie shoots me a grimace that says "sorry about that, but I'm glad it's you and not me," even though she rubs her stomach as if she's thinking "I can't wait until it's me. "

I leave my office earlier than usual, intent on showing Henry that I can be the kind of woman who raises a family. I may not know exactly what to do yet, but I'm willing to try.

He's already changing when I get to our suite, and I take a few moments to appreciate the sculpted muscles in his back as he bends over to pull his socks on.

"Hey," he says when he catches me staring. He yanks me against him and gifts me with a long kiss. Just when I think it's going to develop into more, he breaks it off with a reluctant grin. "Don't want to be late, but maybe afterwards."

"What does one wear to these things anyway?" I stare at the row of colorful jackets that are my usual go-to when I need a boost of confidence.

"I'm just going casual," he says over his shoulder.

No suit, then. I close the closet doors and move to the next one, pulling out a dress with a small geometric pattern and tiny buttons down the front. It looks like something Elizabeth might wear. I hold it up. "Do you think this would be okay?"

Henry turns around, and for a second, he looks confused. Then his face falls into what can only be described as pity. "C, I'm so sorry. I didn't realize—" He drops the shoe he's holding and walks over to me. "There are only two spots per kid."

I frown at him, but then it hits me what he's saying. Two spots for the parents. And since both of Axel's parents will already be there, I'm only a third wheel. Unnecessary.

I ignore the giant lump of emotion that has suddenly formed in my throat and nod. "Oh, okay. I assumed we were both going, but that makes sense." I turn to hang the dress back in the closet.

His hand slides up my arm. "I'm so sorry," he whispers.

"It's fine. Honestly." I force a smile onto my face as I turn back to him. "I'll be fine. Relieved actually. This will give me a chance to catch up on some reading. I haven't read a book in forever. Besides, I'm super tired." I'm rambling, so I snap my jaw shut.

His eyes travel over my face as if trying to determine whether I'm telling the truth or not. Finally, he presses a kiss to my temple and murmurs, "Hopefully not too tired."

My chuckle sounds false, and I pray he doesn't notice. "Never."

He finishes getting ready, and ten minutes later, he's gone and I'm left here with nothing but an empty suite and the knowledge that I could have prevented all of this if I had just told him Elizabeth's secret. Regret swirls through me like an ocean eddy.

The media responded with hesitant acceptance to our announcement that we're making Axel part of our family. It feels like they're waiting for the punchline. Some reporters have gone so far as to paint me as the poor, betrayed wife. Much as I shared that sentiment a few weeks ago, having the people feel sorry for their queen is not good for any country's morale. But aside from revealing that Elizabeth has been lying this entire time and completely destroying Henry's dreams, what else can I do?

I call Bea to invite her to join me for a movie night. She's fully recovered, but I know she's still grieving the baby. A distraction will be good for both of us. While I wait for her to arrive, I text Henry to ask how it's going. I can only imagine how bored he must be right now, gazing at so many crayon drawings his eyes are starting to glaze over. Several minutes later, he still hasn't opened my message.

Bea arrives with a giant tub of popcorn and a thermos of hot chocolate. I let her pick the movie, and she queues *This Means War*. I've seen it before, but it's been years. I could use a good laugh.

We do laugh, so hard I spit hot chocolate back into my cup on multiple occasions. At least until Tom Hardy and his son take over the screen. All I can think about is Henry and Axel. I already know how this one ends, too. Tom doesn't get the new girl. He gets back together with the mother of his son.

I look at my phone again, but there are no new notifications.

"You need to stop checking that thing," Bea says, eyes still on the TV.

I push it under my leg. "I don't know what you're talking about."

"Right." She shoves another large handful of popcorn into her mouth. "You've been looking at it every thirty seconds."

"He still hasn't texted me back." It's been over an hour.

"Maybe he's busy. It happens occasionally, you know," she says, even though when she's the one waiting on a text from a man, she goes on a rampage until she finally hears from him.

"He's with her," I say.

She turns to me then, brows pulled together. "Who?"

"Elizabeth," I say. "They're at some thing at Axel's school."

"So they're in public."

"I think so?" I don't know a thing about parents' meetings. For all I know, this could be a private meeting between both parents, orchestrated by Elizabeth herself to get Henry alone. She did confess to being in love with him, after all. And we've already established that she has no trouble lying, so there's no way I'm going to believe her when she says she won't act on her feelings.

"Celia."

I glance at Bea's face before dropping my eyes back to my lap. I sneak another peek at my screen. Nothing.

"You have to get out of your head," she says, placing a hand on my leg.

"How long does it take to text back 'all good'?"

She sighs. "He probably hasn't checked his phone."

"Who doesn't check their phone in an hour?"

Bea raises a brow and stuffs another handful of popcorn in her mouth.

"Okay, fine. Who besides me doesn't check their phone for that long? Definitely not Henry."

"Maybe they have a no-phones policy. Or maybe he's just trying to be present. Either way, you shouldn't be worrying about it. You should be ogling Chris Pine with me."

She's right, of course, so I turn my attention back to the movie and the eye-feast that is two attractive men rolling through broken glass over the girl they both want. But it does little to keep my thoughts there.

What are Henry and Elizabeth doing right now? Did they stop for a bite to eat afterward, is he tucking Axel into bed, are they sharing a nightcap and a heart-to-heart at Elizabeth's pristine kitchen table, which probably looks like something directly from the set of one of those home renovation shows?

I wonder how beautiful she looks tonight, and if he feels a flicker of attraction for her. Of course he does. There isn't a heterosexual man who wouldn't. She's gorgeous and sexy. I wonder if she'll go to press a kiss to his cheek that will "accidentally" turn into something more.

The final credits roll on the movie, and there's still no response from Henry. If there was an accident, I would have been notified immediately, which leads me to the only other plausible conclusion. They are out together, doing god knows what.

I may not know much about parents' meetings, but I know they don't take this long. My veins flood with adrenaline, and I rub my hands up and down my thighs, trying to convince my body to relax.

Bea traps one of my hands against my leg. "Relax. He'll be back soon, and you'll see that you were worried for nothing."

My eyes stay focused on my lap. "What if he's cheating on me?"

She sets down the popcorn tub and grabs my face. "Look at me. Do you really think Henry would do that?"

I consider this for a second before shaking my head. "No."

"Then trust him." She drops her hands. "And if he does, I'll be first in line to help you dispose of his favorite body part."

I can't stop the small smile that lifts the corner of my mouth. "Thanks for the offer. I'm sorry for suspecting that you and he—" I break off as all my blood rushes to my face.

She rolls her eyes. "You should apologize to him for that, not me. Personally, I'd have done it if he'd been interested."

I gasp and smack her arm. "Beatrice!"

She grins and pops another bite into her mouth. "Just kidding. I lost my chance a long time ago."

I shake my head, still unsure whether she's serious or not. "I'm also sorry for the way I pressured you before. About . . . you know." I gesture to her empty belly.

Her brows pinch together in pain. "I don't blame you for it. You were just trying to protect me, to protect all of us."

"That doesn't mean I should have tried to make decisions for you."

Her eyes skim over me, and she gives me a sad smile. "Something good did come out of all of this, you know. I realized that it's time for me to grow up. I was a mother for a few short weeks, and that experience changed me. It made me realize I want a family of my own, someone who loves me even when I'm acting like a bitch, and a baby I can raise to be a good person."

My little sister has out-matured me. She has been through things no less trying than my own experiences, and she's allowed them to shape her into the person she is today.

"I'm so proud of you, Bea." I squeeze her hand.

I hope she finds that person at the right time. I hope he treats her the way she deserves. I hope he doesn't come with a love child packed away in the closet, ready to destroy everything. And I hope he doesn't stay out with the mother of that child the way my husband has for the past three hours.

Where in the bloody hell is he?

# 31

# "Skinny Love" - Birdy

AFTER BEA LEAVES, I become dangerous in the suite alone. I try calling Henry, but when the call cuts off after only two rings, I know he's hung up on me. I don't want to think about why you might hang up on your wife when she calls while you're out with another woman.

Eventually I decide to head to my office to work on the correspondence Maisie left on my desk. Maybe by focusing on other people's problems will help me forget my own.

The corridors are dimly lit by wall sconces. Most of the staff have already gone home for the day. We employ only a small group to attend to the bare necessities at night: personal protection officers, exterior security guards, and a few household staff in case of medical emergencies or the need for a late-night snack.

Walking the hallways now isn't as weird as it maybe should be. I've spent many evenings in my office, trying to stay ahead of everything calling my name. And what good has any of that done me? I'm currently waist-deep in a mess I can't find a way out of. I'll be lucky if it doesn't pull us all under and drown us before the year is up.

There's a noise ahead, and I instantly tense. I'm not being escorted, because Davies's shift ends right after dinner. It's probably only a few remaining staff members, but just to be safe, I try to stay as quiet as possible until I know who's there.

Small alcoves dot the main corridors. Most contain benches where one can have a quick and private rest before entering a state room filled with guests. One of these is up ahead, and I can just make out the two shadowy figures inside.

If they're staff members, I don't want to embarrass them. I'm considering turning back when Bea's voice floats down the hall. It's quiet but unmistakable.

"I'm so tired of waiting."

A man's voice murmurs something in response, but it's too low to make out. I stand frozen, a complete statue, as they continue whispering. Is this Bea's mysterious lover, the one she refused to name?

Curiosity mixed with irritation at my own lover makes me snap. I march straight ahead, loudly enough that they hear me coming.

Bea gives a little gasp, but it's too late to hide. She turns to face me, her cheeks as crimson as the rug beneath our feet. Behind her, Davies gives a stiff bow.

"Your Majesty," he says quietly.

My eyes skim over them, looking as guilty as the day is long. Bea withers beneath my gaze, but Davies stands tall as ever, his chin jutted out like he's daring me to find fault with either of them.

"What is going on here?" I ask.

"Celia, please—" Bea starts, but I hold up my hand.

"Are you two *seeing* each other?"

Bea drops her eyes to the floor, and Davies clears his throat. "That's correct, ma'am."

I appreciate his honesty, even if it's only the result of getting caught. "For how long?"

"Six months," Bea whispers.

Six months? Six whole *months*? My brain tries to process this information, but it keeps tripping over the fact that my sister and my personal bodyguard have been together for half a year and I never even suspected.

I lift shaky hands to my temples. This night is turning into a nightmare. Leveling a glare on Davies, I hiss, "You slept with my little sister?"

Bea crosses her arms. "I am twenty-two. That's old enough to make my own decisions."

An incredulous laugh slips past my lips. "Did you know he has a fourteen-year-old son, Bea? Surely I don't need to do the math for—"

"Of course I knew that." She steps forward, leaving Davies behind in the shadows. "We love each other."

I shake my head and look down the corridor. If Henry was here, he would help me handle this situation. "Bea, you fall in love with every person you date."

Her lower lip trembles. "That's not fair."

Davies steps out of the alcove. "I love Beatrice, ma'am. And I'm willing to do anything to protect her reputation."

I swing my gaze to him. "Was getting her pregnant part of that plan?"

"Celia!" Bea cries.

"Not very responsible of you," I say to Davies. "Especially since you already know the effects children can have on a marriage." He's been divorced for over a decade. He once told me his ex couldn't handle being both a wife and a mother.

His face remains impassive. "I'm willing to do the right thing."

"Even if it costs you your job?" I can only imagine the chaos that will ensue when this latest scandal hits the papers.

Bea comes close enough to rest her hand on my folded arms. "Celia, please. I wouldn't do this if it didn't feel right. He treats me better than anyone I've ever been with before."

"He got you *pregnant*," I snap.

"Accidents happen." Her eyes are wet with unshed tears. "I know this will cause a big scene, so I'm willing to wait until the time is right, but we are going to be together."

I study her face. I've rarely seen her this serious about anything, with the exception of keeping her baby.

If I try hard enough, I can wreck this relationship. One word and I can have Davies shipped to the Arctic, where he'll never set eyes on Beatrice again. But what has controlling ever gotten me in the past? A temporary reprieve and a lifetime of dealing with angry people. No one likes being controlled, and the minute you tell someone they can't do something, the desire increases tenfold.

"Okay." I hold up my hands. "I don't know that it will work, but I'm willing to look the other way while you figure it out."

"Thank you, Celia. You're the best sister ever." Relief floods Bea's voice. I remain stiff as she throws her arms around my neck.

When my gaze meets Davies's over Bea's shoulder, he bows his head. "We appreciate that, ma'am. This will not affect my work."

"See to it that it doesn't, or you'll be looking for another job," I say.

Bea releases me, then steps back until she's flush against Davies's chest. It might take a vat of acid to erase the mental image of my sister with my PPO.

I take a deep breath and shake my head. "I'll leave you"—I wave my hands in a circular gesture I immediately regret—"to it." Taking several steps down the hallway, I stop and turn back. "And Davies, if you plan to get her pregnant again, at least marry her first."

# 32

# "Turning Tables" - Adele

M Y OFFICE PROVIDES THE exact distraction I need if I'm to have any hope of ever getting through this night. A five-inch stack of mail sits in my inbox. I'm three letters in when Preston sticks his head inside.

My surprise must show, because he offers a wry smile. "I was working late and saw your light. Got a second?"

When I nod, he comes in and shuts the door behind him. I have a sudden flashback to what happened the last time we were alone like this.

"Do you mind leaving that open?" My voice comes out sharper than I intend. "Please," I add, to show that I'm not upset. At least not at him.

Beatrice? Maybe. Davies? Most certainly. Henry? Don't even get me started.

Preston halts in front of my desk. When he makes no move to open the door, I raise my brows and give it a significant look. His nostrils flare, but he cracks it a few centimeters. Instead of approaching me again, he walks to the window, where there's nothing to see but his own reflection staring back at him in the dark glass.

"Is everything okay?" I ask, leaning back in my chair.

His laugh is chilling. "I thought so. But maybe I'm just a fool you thought you could take advantage of."

"Excuse me?"

"Don't pretend you don't know." He thrusts his hands into his pockets.

I pinch the bridge of my nose, ready for this day to be over, then check my phone. There's still nothing from Henry. "I have no idea what you're talking about."

He spins around. "Of course you don't. Innocent until proven guilty, right?"

"Preston, I swear to god—" I'm not sure how to end that sentence. I swear to god I'm about to collapse from exhaustion? Scream until my lungs are raw? Throw in the towel on saving the monarchy?

His eyes are wild. Was he drinking before coming here? "We had something." He gestures to the space between us.

"We did?" I'm sure my face looks as skeptical as my voice sounds.

He turns a brighter shade of red. "Are you actually going to deny it?" He shakes his head and turns toward the window again. "Unbelievable."

"Would you please fill me in on what exactly you're accusing me of? Because I'm still in the dark over here."

He keeps his back to me. "You led me on."

I bolt upright in my chair. A million thoughts fly through my mind right now, none of them good. "I did *what*?"

"You made me think you wanted more."

I know it's not what he means, but I can't resist. The whole thing is too preposterous. "I do want more." Preston jerks his head around. "I want more peace for the world, more happiness. I want the income divide to be smaller. I want—"

"More with *me*," he growls.

For the first time, a shiver of apprehension slides down my spine. "I do not remember *ever* giving you that impression."

He places his hands on his narrow hips. I doubt he realizes how unattractive he becomes when he's mad. Kind of like Don Knotts, with his lower lip protruding and the vein in his forehead pulsing.

"You kissed me," he says.

Revulsion fills my mouth at the memory of that kiss, if it can even be called that. It felt more like paralysis, the way a deer stays in the road as headlights approach. "Actually," I say. "*You* kissed *me*."

"And you kissed me back!"

I definitely didn't, but I'm too tired to argue the point right now. If there was a way to crawl into bed and sleep for one hundred years, I'd be the first in line. "Look, Preston, I—"

"Don't try placating me like I'm some child."

"Then stop acting like one."

He rears back as if I've slapped him.

"I'm a married woman, for god's sake," I say. "And I'm not interested in starting an affair with you or anyone else."

He looks aghast. "I comforted you *twice* after he hurt you."

I squeeze my eyes shut. "I know. That was wrong on my part. I should've sent you away. I wasn't thinking clearly either time."

He approaches me, excitement rolling off him in waves. "But that's just my point. He messes with your head and leaves you feeling like you're not enough. How many times has he driven you to tears in the past month alone?"

I press my fingertips to my throbbing temples. "That's irrelevant."

"Of course it's relevant."

"This isn't going anywhere, Preston, whether he hurts me or not. I'm sorry if I did anything that made you think otherwise."

"I care about you," he says, leaning over my desk. "I can't stand by and watch him treat you like this over and over."

I furrow my brow as I look up at him. "Just how do you think Henry is hurting me?"

"You're here, aren't you? You always come here when you're trying to escape."

"I couldn't sleep," I mutter. "The only thing I'm escaping is insomnia."

"Right." His voice turns cool. "So where is he, then? Back in bed while you figure this out on your own?" He lifts a crystal paperweight and shifts it between his hands.

I let out a deep sigh. "That's none of your business."

"You made it my business when you let me hold you."

I don't remember any particular holding, but it's a trivial point. "You were a great friend, and I appreciate you being there for me—"

"He doesn't deserve you," he spits out.

My lips part in surprise. "That's for me to decide."

"Except you'll keep running back to the bloody bastard every time because—what? He's good in bed? He's charming and attractive? What does he have that I don't?"

"He's my husband!" I stand up so fast my chair teeters on its legs.

"So you're staying with him to avoid scandal." Preston places the paperweight back onto the desk with a small crash.

"I'm staying with him because I love him." It comes out through my teeth. "Is that good enough for you?"

"He doesn't make you happy!" he roars.

The breath whooshes from my lungs, and the room goes quiet. Shaking my head slowly to clear the fog doesn't help. "Go." I point to the door. "Get your things and don't come back."

"You can't fire me," he says, humor and disbelief both vying for top spot in his tone.

I lift my eyes to his. "Really? I just did."

"You're going to need me to clean up this entire mess after he's done wrecking your whole family."

"This may come as a shock, but you're not the only one qualified to handle the press." I sit down and turn back to my correspondence, unwilling to give him another second of my time or mental bandwidth.

"You cannot be serious."

I pull out another letter and unfold it. "Do I appear to be joking? Did you think I would keep someone on staff who speaks to me the way you just did?" I look up at him. "I am your queen, which you seem to have forgotten."

"I never forgot." Preston smirks and walks backward to the door. "Why do you think I wanted you in the first place?"

Once he leaves, I close my eyes and rest my head in my hands. He thinks Henry doesn't make me happy? I let my mind wander, thinking back over the past year. If I haven't been happy, it wasn't because of Henry. I'm the one who lied to him and kept that stupid birth control secret. If anyone's to blame for the downfall in our marriage, it's me.

I finish reading the letter in my hands and slide it back into its envelope. As I'm reaching for another one, the door opens again, and my heart sinks. I'll have to call night security to escort him out.

"I can't do this again, Preston," I say.

There's no reply.

I look up, but it's not Preston standing in the doorway.

# 33

# "Let It Go" - James Bay

HENRY LOOKS LIKE HE'S struggling to hold it together. I do a quick scan to make sure he doesn't have any injuries. He looks perfectly normal, still wearing his shirt and pants from earlier, although they're a little rumpled now.

His face is lined with anger. What he's angry about is a mystery, though, since I'm the one who has been waiting on him for the past . . . I check my phone. Four hours.

"Where have you been?" I say, getting to my feet. "You ignored my calls."

He comes inside and shuts the door. "You knew?"

"Knew what?"

"Just answer the question, Celia." He remains on the other side of the room, arms folded over his chest.

"I don't know what you're talking about!" It's like my conversation with Preston all over again.

"Elizabeth! I'm talking about Elizabeth."

My mind spins. Is she sick, maybe with cancer or something? She looked perfectly healthy the last time I saw her.

Then it hits me.

Henry registers the change on my face. "C." There's a warning in his tone. "Tell me you didn't know."

"Why don't you tell me what you think I know," I say.

He takes a few long steps toward me. "Did you know that Axel isn't mine?"

"I—" It's all I can get out. My throat feels as though it's closing up.

"Libby said she told you. Tell me she's wrong so I can take you across your desk right now."

My brain is instantly sidetracked by that thought, causing a flush to climb my neck and face. As much as I want to dwell on what he's proposed, I drag my mind back to the issue at hand. "I can't."

His eyes narrow. "You can't deny it?"

I slowly shake my head. It hurts to look at him right now. I thought I was doing the right thing by not telling him. Opening my desk drawer, I reach for the aspirin bottle at the back. I shake several of them into my palm and swallow them dry.

Henry lets out an angry snort and begins pacing. "You knew that Axel wasn't my son and you let me believe it anyway?"

I hope no one can hear him in the hallway. "I thought it was what you would want."

"What I wanted was for us to have no more secrets."

I squeeze my eyes shut to keep the tears from falling. "I'm sorry," I whisper.

"Did you know my father *raped* her?" His voice is so loud, I'm pretty sure it can be heard from Maisie's office across the corridor.

"Yes." Dropping my head, I stare at the envelopes on my desk, the pastel colors blurring.

"I guess your fears about me being the father of your children weren't unfounded after all."

I suck in a deep breath and look up at him. "That's not true," I say. "You are not your father. I never should have doubted you."

Henry gives me a sardonic grin. "I think we both know you dodged a bullet though, right?"

I start to shake my head, but he turns and walks across the room again. "I understand that you were trying to protect me," he says.

"Yes." I want to shout it, there is so much relief coursing through my veins right now. "I thought you would prefer it this way. So that you can be Axel's father in all the ways that matter."

"Which I fully intend to do. But that doesn't change what you did."

The bottom of my stomach drops out, leaving a horrible chasm behind. "Elizabeth asked me not to tell you."

"And I asked you not to keep secrets from me." He turns to look at me.

"It was an impossible choice," I say.

"No." He shakes his head. "Not impossible. Because I'm your husband. You should always choose me."

"I thought I was!"

"You kept this from me. How could you possibly think I would be okay with that?"

I wipe the moisture on my cheek away with the back of my hand. "If I had told you what she said, you would have said I was just trying to sabotage the whole thing."

"And why do you think that is?" There is so much sorrow in his voice, it cracks my heart in two.

"I'm so sorry, Henry." A sob works its way up my throat. "You have no idea how sorry. It won't happen again, I promise."

The corners of his mouth lift in what could be a smile but is way too sad. "I know it won't," he says. "Because I'm leaving."

The room tilts, and I place my palms on my desk to keep from spinning with it. "Please don't," I whisper. Not again.

This can't be happening again.

His face crumples as he fights to hold back his emotions. "C, I wanted this to work so badly. But I can't be with someone who has such a strong need to control everything."

I want to tell him that that *was* me releasing control. That if I wanted control, I would have sold Elizabeth's story to the press and basked in our scandal-free name. I wouldn't have spared Bea the public scrutiny by distracting them with something that only made my own image look worse.

But I don't say anything.

"My father controlled me for years. I can't saddle myself with that again."

Henry's right. Of course he's right. I have attempted to control his actions for our entire marriage, not to mention those of the other members of our family. But I'm done with that.

I nod, and the action makes more tears brim over and slide down my face. Several of them drop from my chin and splatter onto the envelopes on the desk. A splash of pink, ivory, and yellow.

Adelaide warned me weeks ago that only the weak think controlling others constitutes real power.

"Okay," I manage to get out. "I understand."

I don't know if it's the answer he's expecting. His actions are the opposite of what I'm expecting. He approaches the desk, and my body immediately responds the way it does any time he's near—every nerve in my body tingles with anticipation.

Warm hands slide around my neck and lift my head. I look up at him through my tears. His eyes are wet with moisture, too. He uses his thumbs to brush the drops from my cheeks, then he leans down to presses his lips to mine.

The kiss is soft and sweet, and I want to enjoy it, I really do, but I can only taste the bittersweet flavors of a future ending before it ever began. This isn't *I forgive you* or *I'm sorry* or *Come to bed with me*.

This is goodbye.

And my heart shatters into a million little pieces.

I want to cling to him, to beg him not to go, to forgive me, to understand, to please give us another shot. But I've already lost him by doing that very thing. It's time to allow people to make their own choices, regardless of the consequences.

And so I accept his kiss and seal it away in my memory. The spearmint taste of his mouth. The way he cradles my face in his hands. The softness of those lips. The smooth glide of his tongue.

And when he lets go of me and takes a step backward, I stay where I am. I don't race around the desk to stop him. I don't call after him. I don't say anything at all. I stay here and do the hardest thing I've ever done.

I watch him leave.

# 34

# "The Scientist" - Coldplay

I'M NOT SURE HOW I got to sleep last night. I lay in bed for hours playing Henry's words over and over in my head, looking for a way I could have prevented this. I thought I was doing what he wanted by staying out of it.

The problem is, there wasn't a right choice. They were both wrong, and I chose the one I thought would hurt him the least.

The sun is shining through the window and hitting the gold coverlet just right, throwing sparkling flecks all around the room. I must have slept past my alarm, which hasn't happened in years.

My face is swollen, and my eyes are puffy. I wet a washcloth with cold water and hold it over them. It does little to reduce the signs of a night spent crying. I step into the shower, and the warmth relieves the tension in my shoulders. Unfortunately, there's nothing that can relieve the ache in my heart.

Daphne does not comment on my appearance when I tell her I'm ready for my hair and makeup. Instead, she prattles on about the weather and her one-year-old daughter. I smile when she pulls out her phone to show me videos of little Arabella grinning and splashing in a mud puddle.

As soon as Daphne leaves, Maisie knocks and enters my suite. The look on her face forces all the tension right back into my shoulders.

"What's wrong?" I ask.

She hands me her tablet without a word.

The article is brief but succinct. They published it first thing this morning, while I was still sleeping and unaware of the chaos being unleashed.

### Queen Covers Up DNA Scandal

*In the past few weeks, the public has been shocked to discover that our very own Prince Henry has a love child. Earlier this year, Elizabeth Gable came forward, claiming to have had a child with the prince consort and asking him to be a part of their son's life.*

*Reactions from the palace were mixed. At first, Ms. Gable's claims were ignored. But when her story was published online, the outrage was immediate. In this modern society, we don't expect perfection from our monarchs and leaders. We do, however, expect them to take responsibility for their actions.*

*And what could be more irresponsible than ignoring your own child? That's what we all thought, and apparently the pressure got to be too much for the royal family. They issued a press statement soon after, saying they were "willing to discuss the issue and have already started to do so."*

*What I wouldn't have given to be a fly on the wall at these "discussions." Unfortunately for most of us, we've been kept in the dark most of this time. After issuing her statement, Queen Celia went back to life as usual, without a ruffle in that flawless expression of hers.*

*But all is not well in fairy tale land. Many of us saw the footage of our queen and her prince consort on an outing at the Bay River Children's Farm. The surprising new element was little Axel Gable with them. The three of them looked like a charming family, but only if you didn't look too closely. Anyone familiar with the usual dynamic chemistry between*

*Queen Celia and Prince Henry would have picked up on the obvious tension between them. While not much for PDA under the best of circumstances, the ice queen was in full regalia that day, seemingly unaffected by the warm temperatures.*

*And who could blame her? Not many of us would welcome the love child of our significant other popping up after three years. Sources inside the palace have also confirmed that things have been rocky for our royal couple since their marriage two years ago.*

*Unfortunately for Queen Celia, that's only the beginning of the story. A source, who has chosen to remain anonymous, revealed that not only did the queen know that Prince Henry is not, in fact, Axel Gable's birth father, but she also hid this knowledge from the public and even her own husband.*

*Speculations as to why she might have done so run the gamut. Was she trying to garner attention from the media? Was she trying to gain sympathy as the poor wife, left on the sidelines while her husband started a family with another woman? Or maybe she was trying to finally produce an heir for the throne. It's no secret that people have been anxiously awaiting an announcement that our royal couple is expecting their first child, but the palace has been silent on the matter.*

*Regardless of her reasons, the fact that Queen Celia hid this information begs the question, what else has she been hiding? While her intentions may have been good, it's obvious what the right thing to do would have been, especially when you take into consideration who Axel Gable's real father is.*

*Our source confirmed that the boy was fathered by none other than the former king, William Sutherland. He is currently serving a twenty-five-year sentence at Staggart Prison for leading the nation's largest drug ring, which was responsible for the escalating rise of insidion, the most coveted drug by our country's youth.*

*As if this wasn't bad enough, we also have solid evidence proving that Ms. Gable was raped by Mr. Sutherland, yet another thing our queen chose to cover up. While there's no question Wesbourne is better off in the hands of Queen Celia than King William, one can't help but wonder, how much better off?*

I hand the device back to Maisie, glad I haven't eaten breakfast yet. "Was it really necessary to show me that?"

She blinks at me. "How much of it is true?"

"Let me think." I pretend to consider this. "All of it."

"*All* of it?"

"Yes, Maisie. All of it. Except they left out the part where Henry left me last night." I sink into the nearest chair, no longer trusting that my legs to hold me up.

"What? *Again*?"

Sighing, I lean my head back. "Why are you here, Maisie?"

"I wanted to show you the article and tell you that Preston hasn't come in yet. Normally he handles these things, but when he didn't show up, I wasn't sure what to do. Do you know when he'll be in?"

I squeeze the bridge of my nose. "He won't."

"Okay," she says. "Should we wait until tomorrow to handle it, or—"

"He won't be here tomorrow either, because I fired him. I suspect he is their anonymous source." He must have been listening outside the door last night. Considering the volume of Henry's voice, it wouldn't have been difficult to eavesdrop.

"Ah."

She's still waiting on an answer about what to do, so I sit up. "Forget about the press for now. We'll need to hire a new press secretary, but honestly, Maisie, I can't think about that right now. Cancel the dinner tonight, please. Tell everyone I'm not feeling well." I can't face a room full of people and explain to them why my husband isn't there. Not when I don't even understand it myself.

Maisie assures me she'll handle it and leaves the room. The second she's gone, I wish I hadn't sent her away so quickly. The apartment feels too quiet in her absence.

I call Adelaide. She arrives an hour later, arms laden with a dozen or more shopping bags. When I open the door, she gives me a single appraising look, then heads for the kitchen.

"What is all of that?" I call after her.

"Provisions." She's in the process of setting the groceries down when I walk in. I help her put everything onto the marble countertop.

We rarely use the kitchen in our apartment. There's no need when you have a world-class chef preparing every meal for you, but sometimes it's nice to have some semblance of a normal home life.

I slide onto one of the bar stools as Adelaide washes her hands at the sink. "Are you going to tell me why you brought"—I pull out a knobby thing from one of the bags and hold it up—"a tree root?"

She takes it from me and sets it down. "That's ginger. It's going into the soup."

"All of this is to make soup?" Raising a brow, I glance at the crowded counter. "I just invited you here to talk."

"I talk better when my hands are busy. Hand me a cutting board, would you?"

Moving to a cabinet on the other side of the kitchen, I grab one. "You realize it's supposed to be ninety degrees today."

She cuts me a sharp glance. "Soup is good for healing hearts."

I set the board down and start pulling onions from a bag. "Whose heart needs healing?"

"I saw the news."

Of course she did. "It's no worse than any of the other stuff they've published."

"It is if it's true." She begins peeling vegetables.

I watch her. Even if I knew how to help, my hands aren't cooperating right now. I thought I'd hit rock bottom weeks ago when Elizabeth Gable showed up. Guess there are always new depths to plummet to.

"Well?" Adelaide's sharp tone startles me out of my thoughts, and an onion drops from my hand and rolls across the floor.

I bend to retrieve it. "Well what?"

"Don't play dumb with me, poppet." She chops with speed and precision, her knife hardly moving as it dices. "Is the boy Henry's or not?"

"Not," I whisper, sagging against the counter.

She keeps cutting, only stopping after the slices of three onions are heaped into neat little piles on the board. When she's done, she wipes her hands on her apron and turns to face me. "And you knew?"

"I found out a few days ago."

A tiny furrow appears on her brow as she scans the kitchen. "Cooking pot?"

I direct her to the collection of professional-grade cookware, most of it never touched. Even if Henry and I wanted to attempt *The Donna Reed Show: Royal Edition*, I can't make anything more complicated than coffee.

Adelaide chooses the largest one and begins to drag it out of the cupboard. When I offer to help get it down for her, she glares at me until I retreat. She sets it onto the stove with a bang. "And what did Henry say? Did he know, or were they right about you covering it up?"

I gnaw my bottom lip. I can usually handle Adelaide's judgment, but my nerves are so frayed right now that I don't want to be at the receiving end of her ridicule.

My face must give me away, because she frowns. She returns to the cutting board and begins mincing several cloves of garlic. "I take it he was upset?"

It takes me several seconds to find my voice. Everything that happened last night is starting to sink in. "He left me," I say quietly. "For good this time."

The knife clatters as she sets it down and grabs me, pulling me into a hug that smells like garlic and lavender. "Oh, poppet," she murmurs into my hair.

She holds me tightly against her frail frame as my body heaves. Everything I've been bottling up for the past two years pours out. She alternates between rubbing my back and stroking my hair.

When my sobs subside into sniffles, she grabs my shoulders. "I need to put the onions in the pot. Wait right here." She dumps them in and gives them a stir.

By the time she's done, I've found a few tissues and blotted my eyes as best as I can. "I'm fine." I perch back onto the bar stool I vacated. "It's just fresh."

Adelaide's eyes are sharp and penetrating. "I warned you this would happen."

"I know."

"What are you going to do?"

I shrug and let out a heavy sigh. "Nothing. There's nothing I can do. He's made his choice."

She stops fiddling with the soup and looks at me. "That may be the wisest thing I've ever heard you say."

"I do not feel wise right now. More like a fool."

"A fool keeps doing the same things and wondering why he doesn't get different results." She gestures toward me with the tip of her knife. "You, my dear, are growing and maturing."

"Maybe, but it's too late now. I've lost him." It takes everything in me to keep my voice steady.

"I wouldn't be so sure." She rinses a bunch of carrots. The dirt and grime from the field flow down the drain. "If there were ever two people meant to be together, it's the two of you."

"He says I'm too controlling."

"Are you?"

I look at her without lifting my head. "You and I both know the answer to that."

She shakes the water from the vegetables, and several drops land on my arms. "The best thing you can do for your relationship is to let the other person be. You can't force them to become someone they're not. You can't make them do things they don't want to. You can only make those decisions for yourself."

I touch the droplets on my arm. They cling to my fingertip but don't shatter.

"But I think you've already realized that, haven't you?" she says.

"I'm trying."

"Then don't give up hope, poppet. They say if you love someone, set them free." She peels a long, thin curl off a carrot and drops it into the sink. "If they come back, they're yours; if they don't, they never were."

After Adelaide leaves—her giant pot of soup stowed away in the fridge—I pull up videos of babies babbling on YouTube. Their chubby cheeks and high-pitched squeals make me smile. It's like a bandage wrapping around my heart. Not healing it, but holding the pieces together until they can be mended.

One baby in particular makes me laugh out loud. He's sitting in a high chair, and every time someone off-camera blows a raspberry, he convulses into hysterical giggles. It might be the cutest thing I've ever seen. I rewatch the video at least two dozen times.

Suddenly, something flutters in my stomach. At first I ignore it, but as I hit replay, it happens again. I wipe my cheeks—they're happy tears this time. I recognize the feeling. *Longing.*

I want this in my life. I want the joy of a child, the laughter, the way they can brighten any room they're in without doing a single thing except being themselves. I want that closeness, the knowledge that this person belongs to me, that no matter what, it's my job to love them unconditionally.

I spend the rest of the day in the apartment, watching silly videos and allowing them to be a balm for my soul. I browse baby name sites and consider whether I want a boy or girl, then realize I don't care at all, not even a little bit. I'll take either one—or both.

When my alarm for my birth control goes off at ten o'clock, I can't believe the entire day has passed and I've done nothing productive. Even more surprising is my lack of guilt over it. I grab the pink compact from my bag and take it to the bathroom, punching each of the tiny pills out of the foil and into the toilet. When it's empty, I flush them down. Joy swirls in my chest as they spiral in the water and disappear forever.

This is what Henry wanted all along. For me to let go, to relax, to start a family with him. To stop trying to control other people's expectations and actions. To allow myself to live fully and truly. And he was right. It feels incredible.

The only problem?

I'm too late.

# 35

# "Burn" - Ellie Goulding

THERE'S A QUOTE BY Charles Dickens: "The broken heart. You think you will die, but you just keep living, day after terrible day." It's been seven days since Henry left. An entire week.

Adelaide said if they come back, they're yours. But what's the time frame on something like that? Is there some kind of deadline? Are they officially marked "never yours" once a hundred days pass without their return? Two hundred? Five years?

Everyone knows that the first few days are crucial in a missing person's case. After that, clues start to dry up and hope starts to disintegrate. You tell yourself to get used to what may be your new normal.

The days are starting to pass in a blur, each bleeding right into the next like watercolors on a page. I get up and go to my office or whatever event is scheduled. I do my best to smile for any cameras that might be there, but I don't worry about whether they're getting the shots that will help my image the most.

I just don't care anymore.

After I've made it through the day, I either face a full table of dignitaries and other select guests or I face dinner alone. I haven't yet decided which is worse. I force myself to eat because I know it's important, not because I have an appetite.

I take a shower to clear my head and wash the day off before going to bed and starting the whole day over again.

Which is what I'm doing now when the bathroom door opens. A strangled shriek flies out of my mouth, and I move to cover myself. Through the fogged glass of the shower stall, I can make out a figure moving through the space. Innately I know who it is, but my muscles are locked into place.

Henry steps over my pile of discarded clothes until he's past the glass partition. I'm not sure if I would rather launch myself at him or pummel his chest with my fists.

He doesn't smile, doesn't say anything, just keeps his eyes locked on mine as he slowly undoes the buttons of his shirt. The seconds grow long, expanding and stretching between us. My chest heaves with every breath I take. Water sluices off me, but I don't move out from under the spray.

When he's finished, he shrugs the shirt off and lets it drop. I let my gaze fall from his just long enough to skirt over his bare chest, those gorgeous tattoos, and that rock-hard set of abs.

When his fingers reach for his belt, my eyes dart back to his face. He's still expressionless, and I'm dying to know what he's thinking, what he's doing here, but my lips are glued together.

I jerk as his buckle hits the tile floor. His hands move to his zipper, and nothing could stop me from watching this. He slides his pants off, letting them puddle around his ankles, revealing muscled thighs that make mine suddenly weak.

He strips off the boxer briefs he's wearing and tosses them aside. A tiny gasp slips past my lips as he steps into the shower.

I don't dare move for fear this apparition will disappear. Is this what happens when you're left alone with grief? You start seeing things? I'm dying to know how real it will feel if he tries to kiss me.

I don't have to wait long. He grabs my wrist and jerks me toward him. It feels more real than normal life, his touch searing through my wet skin. I land against his chest with a thump, and he lets out a halting exhale.

Using his body, he presses me against the cool shower wall. I suck in a jagged breath as he sandwiches me between himself and the tile, two hard and unrelenting surfaces.

He still hasn't breathed a word. I'm glad, because I'm not sure what he would say, and I don't want anything shattering this right now.

Grasping my jaw and tilting my face up, he presses his mouth against mine, saying things no words could express. My body floods with heat, the kind that leaves you breathless, anxiously anticipating the next dose.

His teeth skate over my lower lip, and I groan as his tongue pushes inside, which only makes him more aggressive. Digging his fingers into my hair, he uses the leverage to move me where he wants me. His hand closes around my throat, slowly sliding up and down my slick skin. Then he gathers my strands into his fist and yanks my head backward. He swallows my gasp and deepens the kiss, pressing into me even harder now that he has full control of both of us.

This whole time I've had my hands resting on his hips, but now I slide them around to palm his ass. He pulls back and swoops them up between his fingers, pinning them against the wall above my head. Then he wraps my wet hair in his fist again and leans in close.

His mouth hovers right above mine, warm breath brushing me as he exhales. I try to meet his lips, but he keeps a tight hold on my makeshift ponytail, preventing me from moving more than a centimeter.

"Hi," he breathes into my mouth.

The sudden urge to sob rises in my chest. "Hi," I say back, swallowing it down.

Then he kisses me again. Only this time, it has none of the decadence from a few seconds ago. This kiss is the desperate lunge for a lifesaver. Reaching for the last drop of antidote. Clinging to the edge of the cliff. Crawling the last foot to the doorstep of safety.

I struggle to release my hands from his grasp—I want to *touch* him—but he holds them firmly, like they're nothing more than twigs. He swallows my groan of frustration and growls in response.

His body is hard and slick, the statue of David in the rain. Without breaking the kiss, he releases my jaw and slides his hand down to cup my breast. I cry out as he rolls my nipple between his thumb and finger, the sensation so powerful I nearly sink to my knees.

He keeps me upright, his body still pushing me against the wall. I ache to touch him, to slide my body down his, to take him in my mouth. He doesn't allow any of it. The only thing I can do is feel.

And feel I do. The rollercoaster of emotion is so strong, I want to cry until there's nothing left. I've been wrung out and hung in the sun to dry. As if he can sense my desperation, he releases my hands and slides his mouth down. Down my neck, down my chest, down my stomach, settling on the crease between my thighs as he crouches in front of me.

I silently beg him to meet my gaze. He finally looks up, the words he hasn't spoken clear in his eyes.

This is *sorry*.

I splinter into tiny little fragments as he tastes me. My body takes over and arches into him. He responds by cupping my ass and angling me toward him. He puts me back together as he licks and sucks me into white-hot pleasure.

I bury my fingers in his wet hair, urging him on with gentle tugs and small thrusts of my hips. When I know I won't last much longer, I tug him harder and say, "More."

He trails hot kisses up my stomach as he rises, lingering to make sure each one brands me. Grabbing my thighs, he lifts me until he's positioned at my entrance. Right before he slides me down onto him, he stops and leans his head against my shoulder.

"Shit. I don't have a condom, babe."

I shake my head. "I don't want one."

"You sure?"

I moan and tilt my head up, eager for him to be inside me. "Yes," I manage to get out.

With a sudden thrust, he enters me, filling me to the brim. Using his shoulders for leverage, I push up so I can feel him sliding in again, making him swear as he meets my thrusts with his own.

Our shower-slicked bodies glide together, eager for the release we both crave. With my legs snaked around his waist and him seated deeply inside me, he lifts me up so slowly and so far I'm afraid he's going to slip out, but right as I reach his tip, he brings me back down with sudden force. I cry out, and he does it again, his eyes never leaving mine.

"I was a shit," he says, yanking me down once more.

I press my forehead against his and shake my head, not sure if it's shower water or tears blinding me.

He lifts me again, then thrusts upward as he brings me down. "I promised I'd never leave you again." He buries his face against my neck. "I broke that promise."

Now I know it's tears running down my face. I curl myself over him, wanting to take him even further inside me, but he's already as deep as he can go. "I wasn't exactly easy to live with."

"That's no excuse." He drives himself in again. "From this moment on, I'm in, one thousand percent."

I tighten my grip on him. I appreciate what he's saying, but my body wishes he would save the talking for later.

"You believe me?" he asks.

I nod against his shoulder.

That is all the answer he requires to finish the job he set out to do. With the next hard ram of his body against mine, I fall apart, crying out as waves of pleasure whisk me away to heaven. He follows right behind me, a deep, low growl tearing out of him and into my neck.

We stay like that until it passes, then he slowly extradites himself and lowers me to my feet. I'm surprised when they manage to hold me up.

"I meant everything I said." He cups my face tenderly.

"I know," I tell him.

"You deserve so much better than that." His voice is husky with emotion.

I lay a finger across his full lips. "I'm done trying to control you. Bea. The media. Our children."

He blinks. "Children?"

I can only nod, not trusting my feeble voice right now.

"I love you," he says against my finger. "Forever and always."

"Forever and always."

# 36

# "Euphoria" - Loreen

### *Three Months Later*

T HE DAY IS UNSEASONABLY warm for September. I adjust the belt of my floral-print dress and hope I don't sweat through it, then wink at Axel on the seat across from us. He's kicking his short legs, probably imagining the ice cream cone we promised him if he came along.

After the initial uproar following Preston's press leak, the public accepted the fact that we're not any more perfect than they are. When we issued a statement concerning our choice to keep Axel a part of our lives, the response was overwhelming.

Henry is acting as a sort of surrogate father to him, filling the shoes that William never could—for Henry or Axel. And while they may be brothers, they can certainly pass for father and son. My fears were completely unfounded, because Henry is a wonderful dad. He would rather cut off his own arms and legs than hurt Axel.

Elizabeth and I tolerate each other. I can't say that she wouldn't love to steal my husband, but I'm no longer worried about it. Henry drives those thoughts away every night. Sometimes during the day, too.

His eyes catch on mine and darken. I flush as that familiar tingling starts between my thighs. He grins as if he knows exactly what he's just done.

The car stops, and I scan the crowd waiting for us outside. They're behind steel barricades, waving small Wesbourne flags, holding posters and banners, and grinning in anticipation.

It's incredible, this feeling of bringing so much joy to people. Just my presence is enough to make them take the day off work, to stand in the heat or the rain. To be the highlight of their week, or in some cases, their year—there's nothing like it.

Henry helps me out of the car, and I reach back inside for Axel. The crowd goes wild, their applause thundering. We smile and wave dutifully. Axel sticks his thumb in his mouth and clutches my hand with his free one.

Rosalind, Beatrice, and Olivia are exiting their own car. Bea and Davies are still seeing each other, but they've chosen to keep it a secret for now. I don't know if their relationship will last, but I trust Davies with my life. There's no one better on the planet to protect my sister than him.

I study her for a few more seconds. She's finally regained her color, and a genuine smile is stretched across her face. In some ways, having Axel around has helped draw her from her cocoon of grief. Now he spots her and bolts toward her, and she opens her arms wide for him.

Olivia smiles at the two of them. The woman is unflappable. I was a mess when I thought my husband had had a child without me. She found out her husband *raped* a woman while they were married, and there she stands like the goddess she is.

My mother tugs on the back of Bea's dress, urging her to stand up straight. I hide my grin. Why should I worry about putting my best foot forward when I have my mum to do it for all of us?

I let my eyes wander over the crowds again, hoping my plan will work.

A hand gently squeezes my elbow. "You okay?" Henry asks, his breath warm against my neck. Goosebumps scurry across my skin in spite of the warm day.

I nod and turn my smile on him. "Perfect."

He grins back. "I know. That thing you did last night—"

I pinch what little skin I can grab on his stomach.

"Ow," he says, still smiling like a bloody prat.

Davies approaches my right shoulder. "You're all set, ma'am."

"Thank you," I tell him before turning back to Henry. "Ready?"

We make our way to the people directly ahead of us. Their cheers grow even louder. Henry and I split up, each going in a different direction to shake hands with as many of them as possible. We're planning to sacrifice several hundred engagements over the course of the next year between our two schedules, but if it means that we can do more of them together, it'll be worth it.

Time passes quickly. Davies remains nearby, encouraging me to continue walking and ready to step in if necessary. Fortunately, it never is. We don't discuss that night in the corridor three months ago. I think we both prefer to pretend it never happened.

I want this day to be perfect. I've spent weeks planning for it, and I just want to get as close to the vision in my head as possible. We have ten more minutes of greetings before it's time to go to the rendezvous spot, where the six of us will meet up and wave our final goodbyes.

When we're several yards away from the end of the line, Davies approaches. "Ready for this, ma'am?" His voice carries that cool professionalism I've come to rely on.

"I think I might be sick from nerves," I say under my breath. "Does that count?"

He smiles. "Say the word, and I'll put a stop to it."

"I'm not sure even you are powerful enough for that," I tease him. I smile at the group of teens pressed against the barricade, glad they're not too cool to come see their queen.

After the final greetings, my gaze darts over the crowd. If they don't play their role soon, my plan will fall apart.

Suddenly, a voice shouts through the hubbub. "Congratulations, Your Majesty!"

Relief floods my veins. Everything is going as planned after all. A quick glance at the rest of my family confirms they have no clue what's going on.

Henry steps closer and slips an arm around my waist. "What are they congratulating us for?"

"Being happy, I guess," I murmur, reaching up to press a kiss to his lips. The din from the crowd grows louder.

A gasp sounds from beside us, one I recognize as my sister's. I break off the kiss as Olivia squeals. My mother hisses at Bea, "What's going on?"

Henry and I leave our bubble to face the crowds. It takes a split second for my eyes to find them: a cluster of people holding up colorfully designed signs that say *You're Having A Baby!!* Henry is smiling at Axel and ruffling his hair, completely oblivious to all of it.

"Oh my god," Rosalind says when she finally notices the posters.

Olivia walks over to us and folds me into her arms. "I'm so happy for you."

Henry meets my eyes over her shoulder, and his frown all but shouts *What the fuck is she talking about?*

I can't stop the grin spreading over my face. He scans the people surrounding us, and I watch as recognition hits him. His mouth goes slack, and he swivels his gaze back to me. Olivia steps out of my embrace and wipes tears from the corners of her eyes.

"Is this real?" he says breathlessly.

"Is what real?" I grin like a drunk who just won a free pitcher of beer.

He yanks me against him. "You know what."

I bury my face in his suit jacket and inhale amber, whiskey, and pine. The fabric rubs against my cheek as I nod. "You're going to be a dad. For real this time."

He crushes me in his arms and bows his head over mine, emotion trembling through his body. My own heart is a powder keg, ready to explode at the slightest provocation.

"How long have you known?" His voice is muffled by my hair.

"Two months."

His arms tighten even further. "And you didn't tell me before now?"

"I wanted to make sure everything was fine after Bea . . ."

At the mention of my sister, I pull away just enough to spot her. She's smiling, but there's a tightness to the lines. This won't be easy, but I hope we can work through it. Given enough time, she will find her own happily ever after. Maybe with Davies, maybe not.

"I can't believe you did all of this." Henry drags his gaze over the spectators, who are going nuts over our announcement. "Actually, on second thought, yes I can."

I meet his lips again, my arms still snug around his waist. "Sometimes a little control is a good thing."

**Need more Henry & Celia?** Download a sweet bonus chapter about the birth of their first child at https://jessicajude.com/crowns-we-save -bonus

Thank you for reading *Crowns We Save*! If you enjoyed this book, it would mean the world to me if you left a review, even if it's short. Reviews are like tips for authors, and every one helps!

**What's next?** If you're in a reading slump after that or just want more of the same, you might want to try the Hand of Revenge series, starting with Ace of Betrayal!

xoxo Jess

P.S. Want to discuss my books, dissect Easter eggs, and spiral with other like-minded readers? Join my exclusive reader groups on Facebook and Discord. We'd love to see you there! You can also join my email list at jessicajude.com/newsletter to receive updates and exclusive bonus content!

# Also by Jessica Jude

**Thrones We Steal Trilogy**
*Thrones We Steal*
*Castles We Storm*
*Crowns We Save*

**Hand of Revenge Series**
*Ace of Betrayal*
*Queen of Vengeance*
*King of Obsession*
*Joker's Endgame*

A group of wealthy friends plays poker to determine the victims of their weekly revenge plots. What they don't bargain on? Falling in love with the people who could destroy them.

## Embers of Us Series
*Flare* (coming 9.15.26 – pre-order now!)

# About the Author

JESSICA JUDE LOVES NOTHING better than sending her characters on an emotional roller coaster of love, angst, and drama, but in reality her life is very ordinary, drama-free, and probably boring to anyone watching. (Which would be weird. And creepy.)

She married her high school sweetheart at nineteen. Being an author is a dream she's had since she was six years old and wrote her first book, which was ten pages long, about a girl named Mary getting lost in the woods. (It was never published, but good news: Mary was eventually rescued.)

When she's not writing, Jess is reading, reading about writing, or eating ice cream. In another life, she would live in England in a sprawling manor house with hidden passages and secret stairways, but for now, she's content with her old brick farmhouse in the Midwestern United States.

Still a fan? Here are some ways you can ~~stalk~~ stay connected!

https://jessicajude.com/newsletter

Instagram @JessicaJudeBooks

Threads @JessicaJudeBooks

TikTok @JessicaJudeBooks